RECALLING AMNESIA

A novel by

SID GARDNER

RECALLING AMNESIA

This is a work of fiction. All of the characters, names, incidents, organizations, and dialogue in this novel are either the products of the author's imagination or are used fictitiously.

iUniverse books may be ordered through booksellers or by contacting:

iUniverse
1663 Liberty Drive
Bloomington, IN 47403
www.iuniverse.com
1-800-Authors (1-800-288-4677)

ISBN: 978-1-4917-7096-2 (sc)
ISBN: 978-1-4917-7097-9 (e)

Print information available on the last page.

iUniverse rev. date: 07/07/2015

We were startled by the beauty of the country and surprised by its size.
Ward Just, *To What End*

The fringes of their deserts were strewn with broken faiths.
T.E. Lawrence, *The Seven Pillars of Wisdom*

But you gotta know the territory.
Meredith Wilson, *The Music Man*

PART ONE

Southeast Asia 1967-68

Once upon a time, in a very wet, very green country in Southeast Asia, a young man walked down the stairs from a plane at an airport surrounded by military vehicles. He was dressed in Army fatigues, and was part of a similarly dressed group of young soldiers entering the country for the first time.

The group spilled off the plane quickly, looking around with the curiosity and caution of young men finding themselves in a totally unfamiliar place. Commands were barked, and the troops fell into formation and then marched to a line of green buses parked near the terminal.

Boarding the buses, the young man and the other new arrivals then rode for an hour until they arrived at a military command building in the middle of a vast, sprawling city of palaces and slums, steaming in a humid, tropical summer along a fetid river.

The young man's name was Will Putnam. He was 25 years old, and he looked even younger. He had been drafted six months before, and was on his way to a unit somewhere in Saigon, the capital city of South Vietnam.

He was hopeful, anxious, and ambitious. He was more than a little scared, being in a war zone where thousands of Americans had already been killed. And he was defiant, having gotten there through the most painful episode of his young life.

After in-processing, Putnam boarded another troop bus, this time off to the BEQ—the bachelor enlisted quarters, which turned out to be a rundown hotel on the edge of Cholon, the Chinese section of the city. The trip through the city was full of smells and sounds far beyond Putnam's experience, and he kept craning his neck to look around at the street scenes rolling by outside the windows of the bus. Bars, vegetable markets, electronic repair shops, people washing themselves and their clothes and their children in the street, white-gloved police at most of the busier intersections directing traffic. And women, wearing wide conical hats, white blouses and black silk trousers that swung invitingly around their slim bodies.

The bus arrived at the BEQ and the soldiers filed out of the bus into a five story "hotel," with yellow, fading paint that made it stand out from the surrounding buildings. Two round concrete outposts guarded each corner of the building, facing the street. As he walked past the enclosed posts and the MPs standing within them, Putnam was thankful he'd passed up the attractions of military police duty as he'd moved through the Army's mysterious process of deciding where 19 and 20-year olds without careers were going to have their first jobs.

Carrying his duffel bag and a small soft-sided briefcase past an impatient staff seargeant who handed each man his room assignment, Putnam walked up the stairs to the third floor. He found Room 3-K and walked in.

Two sizable Seabees were unpacking their sea bags, and introduced themselves to Putnam. The tall, hefty one with blond hair was in the bottom bunk under what Putnam realized was his top bunk by forfeit. After the Seabee nodded and introduced himself as "Dave from Goleta," he began setting up a very large tape deck on the dresser next to his bed. Putnam assumed the equipment was going to supply most of his auditory stimulus for the next several months.

The second Seabee was also blond, shorter, stocky, and less ebullient than Dave from Goleta. He announced himself as "Bruce from Des Moines" as he shook Putnam's hand and then went back to unpacking his bag, spreading out his clothes and other equipment on the single bed that took up the rest of the room.

Will Putnam had grown up in Vista, California, a then-small suburban town in northern San Diego County. He played Little League baseball, rode his bike up and down the hills on the eastern side of town, and lived in a three bedroom house with his three sisters and one brother. He was the youngest, and was incessantly told by his siblings that he "got away with murder" compared with how they were disciplined.

His father was a high school teacher and football coach, and his mother mostly stayed at home, serving as organist for the local Methodist church and occasionally teaching piano to private students. The family routines included ample sports, rooting for the LA Rams, unvarying attendance at church, wearing hand-me-down clothes from their cousins, eating day-old bread because it was cheaper, and listening to their mother's music. The family values included unquestioning mainstream Methodism, hard work, and education. Especially education.

Will Putnam was a good student, good enough to get into a small college in Los Angeles where he majored in international relations. He vaguely thought he would be a journalist or go into the Foreign Service, without a very clear idea of what either career really involved. He ended up getting a scholarship to attend graduate school at Cornell in northern New York State.

Part of his decision to go to Cornell was about geographic genealogy. An oft-repeated bit of family lore was that his great-grandfather had been Billy the Kid's lawyer in New Mexico. That set of relatives came from upstate New York. Another set of relatives clustered around eastern Connecticut, and Will spent time in Storrs and the surrounding towns after meeting a girl from the University of Connecticut at a dance in Ithaca.

After the bland weather of Southern California, Will was fascinated by experiencing real seasons for the first time. Fall colors, snow and ice, spring's early flowers—he relished it all. As he became familiar with Connecticut, he enjoyed its small towns even more. Village greens, woody countrysides, small lakes and ponds unexpectedly popping up as he drove across the state—all new parts of his transplanted life. He bought a used car, an Opel, from a local dealer, and put thousands of miles on it moving across New York State, New England, and occasional forays into Canada.

Will Putnam was an inveterate introvert. Whenever he took any form of personality test, he scored on the high end of any measures of introversion. He was less shy than cautious, willing to get through personal relationships by letting others make the moves. He spoke out in classes when he knew the subject, confident that he wouldn't embarrass himself. But his standard MO was quietly observing the flow of conversation, making sure that his eventual contribution to class or social occasions was on target. Growing up, his sisters teased him because he was quiet, and he came back at them, accusing them of wanting to live in the spotlights.

In college and then graduate school, he had experimented with girls, sex, and alcohol, finding that he liked them in roughly that order. It took a fairly assertive girl to draw him out, and luckily for him, assertive girls were an abundant feature of college life in the middle 60's.

So Will came to the end of graduate school, having done well enough that he was likely to have numerous opportunities. He carefully reviewed his options. Take the Foreign Service test? Return to California and find a spot in state or local government? Go on for a Ph.D.? Travel in Europe?

He decided to go back home, drawn by a job in Sacramento and a girl he hoped was still around and available. The job was all he hoped for, but the girl was unavailable. So Will turned to more work and more available girls, and both met his needs for a time.

Unfortunately for Will, there was a war on, and there was a draft as well. The war and the draft both found him, through a combination of strange circumstances, and he soon found himself in Southeast Asia.

The first morning after arriving in Saigon, Will boarded a shuttle bus, noting the bars on its windows, and after a half hour ride was discharged with the other newcomers in front of a three-story building facing the river in what he assumed was the downtown area. Barges, fishing boats, sampans, and two U.S. Navy ships lined up along the docks. Navy crews were busy unloading containers from the ships and loading them into large trucks.

Following a sign that said 'New Personnel Processing,' Will entered a long room lined with folding chairs, with several desks in front where five sergeants were quickly interviewing soldiers and a few sailors. Will assumed they were getting their orders for their first assignments.

After twenty minutes of watching, his name was called and he quickly walked to the front of the room. The sergeant who had called his name motioned to the chair beside his desk.

The sergeant was holding a folder on which Putnam saw his name in large letters. The sergeant said, "So, Putnam, you're 11Bravo. Basic infantry. Turned down OCS." He squinted at the folder for a moment. "You used to write speeches and work with the press?"

"Yes, sergeant."

"Well, we're going to send you over to the embassy. You're not going out to the boonies, private, not just yet. The press office needs some help, and you may be just what they're looking for."

"All right, sergeant. How soon do I start?"

"Sergeant Lasswell is waiting for you up at the JUSPAO building. That's the Joint US Public Affairs Office—part of the embassy. It's three blocks up Tu Do Street—the street that starts across from the docks. Three blocks up and across the plaza. Try not to get lost. Lasswell will be on the second floor in the office marked 'Enlisted.' Good luck, Putnam." And he turned and picked up another folder, calling out another name as Will walked back out the door.

The walk to JUSPAO was Will's first exposure to the city on foot, and as he left the Processing building he was immediately assaulted by the smells of the river, the sight of the French colonial buildings facing the docks, and the cries of the street vendors who spotted him and his fatigues as he came down the steps of the building.

Amid the rapid rising and falling tones of Vietnamese, he heard more familiar pitches. "Hey GI, got smokes?" "Hey GI, want girl, beautiful girl?" And more quietly, "GI—you want good hash—best hash from Laos? Only fifty pi."

He waved them off, and set off down the street that had a sign saying *Rue Catinat* and underneath, *Tu Do*. Nearest the docks, he walked past restaurants, bars, what appeared to be clothing stores, and fruit stands that lined both sides of the street. Every few feet or so someone was squatting on their heels on the sidewalk next to a basket of fruit or some other item Will couldn't identify.

He paused in amazement at an open storefront with ducks and chickens hanging in the front, fish piled up on ice with their heads removed. He then discovered the heads floating in a plastic barrel next to the door. A very strong odor came from the barrel. He leaned over, sniffing it, and then pulled back quickly.

A tall civilian stopped and spoke to him, chuckling. "Breathe deep, son. You're never going to smell anything like that again in your life, and you'd better get used to it here. It's *nuoc mam*—fermented fish heads they make into a sauce they put on everything."

He put out his hand. "George Diver, soldier. What's your name?"

"Will Putnam, sir. I'm looking for the JUSPAO building. They told me it was up this street."

"It sure is. Come on—I'm headed that way. You just come in country?"

By now Will had heard enough of the drawl to guess Diver was from somewhere South. As they walked, he answered Diver. "Yes, sir, just got in yesterday."

"Will, I haven't been knighted yet and they'd never let me be an officer, so drop the sir. Just George—George from Texas, so far south in Texas we can see Mexico better than we can see Texas. Where you from, Will?"

"I'm from Southern California. Got drafted six months ago and decided to see it through." He stopped, aware that telling the longer version of the story was impossible and inappropriate during a casual walk down the street to his new job.

Diver talked nearly every step of the way to the JUSPAO building. He told Will that he was a civilian employee for USAID, the foreign assistance agency of the U.S. government, and was serving as the provincial representative from USAID to a province far up the Saigon River near the Cambodian border. He had been there for seven months, and had gone to work for USAID after serving with the Peace Corps in Bolivia. He invited Will to come visit the province, explaining how to access military flights when Will got time off.

As they arrived at the building, Will saw that it was an older office building that had obviously been converted to U.S. government agency use. It was painted dirty brown on the outside, was five stories high, and had the now–familiar concrete guard post in front of both entrances to the building.

Will thanked Diver, who headed off to the main embassy building two blocks away. As Will watched him walk away, he thought how lucky he had been to run into Diver—not only because he had gotten a fine guide on the route to JUSPAO, but also because Diver's brief review of what was happening in the provinces had immediately whetted Will's appetite to get out of the city into the rural parts of the country.

Will stopped at the top of Tu Do Street. He knew he had just walked down a street unlike any he had ever seen in his life. His senses were overloaded with new smells and sights and sounds, and he said to himself *it ain't Kansas anymore. It ain't Sacramento either.*

Later, Will realized that was the day he began building his in-country network. Diver was the first of a group of people willing to give him some time and some advice, both of which became major assets in his attempt to understand what he was doing in Southeast Asia, and what it meant to the rest of his life.

After a few weeks, Will had mastered the tasks he had been given and was getting hungry for more. He had learned to take the weekly translations of the local press, which were censored but still revealed important divisions among the many Vietnamese political and military factions. He began to be able to read some of the subtext allowed by the censors and to see what was getting through the censors as a measure of the conflicts among the elite.

He had read somewhere that T.E. Lawrence had a similar role in Cairo, summarizing the Arab press, when he was in the British Army in World War I before his exploits in the desert. *Me and Lawrence of Arabia*, he thought. *Putnam of Indochina.*

And then his imagination met up with his ambition, and he began to fantasize about staying in country for many years, conquering the language, seeping into the culture, traveling into the furthest back reaches of the country. He would become neither the quiet nor the ugly American—he would be the *effective American*, known far and wide for his deep understanding of Vietnamese culture and society.

"Putnam, go downstairs and pick up the shipment of mimeo ink—we're out."

Reality intruded. He put his fantasies aside and trudged off to the elevator.

The first time a 105 shell dropped into Saigon, Will was simply scared shitless. He saw a flash a few blocks away and then heard the concussion. It was about 7 pm and he had gone up on the roof of the BEQ to have a brief cigar. Will liked small cigars, having been introduced to Schimmelpennicks by an agency head he had gotten to know in his legislative work in California. The agency head smoked the long ones—thin, dense, and dark. Will acquired the taste, and when he found that they were on sale in the lobby of the Continental, he was in heaven.

But the thought that the rebels were able to fire artillery at will at the capital city of Vietnam was anything but heaven. The logical thought that occurred to him next was *why wouldn't they target this building, full of soldiers and sailors?*

The next day, when he gingerly asked his supervising sergeant about it, the sergeant laughed and said "It's a war zone, Putnam. Of course they're shooting at you. They wheel their artillery up out of their underground hideouts, fire off a shell, and thirty seconds later they're underground again. They aren't aiming at anything—they're just trying to keep us off balance. So stay in balance, private. It happens almost every night."

So Will tried to think of random artillery shells as normal. It wasn't easy.

Getting used to the weather was also a challenge. The monsoon that hit the city most afternoons for a few very wet hours was unexpected, and again reminded Will how far he was from "normal" Southern California weather. He had worked at the State Department in Washington during the summer between undergraduate and graduate school.

One August afternoon that summer he walked out into a thunderstorm that was unlike any weather he had ever experienced. Thunder, lightning, torrents of rain pouring down. But the city went on, cabs and buses kept driving, and umbrellas blossomed everywhere for an hour or so until the storm blew through the area.

A week later, he and the others in his intern class, including a future US Senator and a future prize-winning historian, walked down two blocks from the State Department to hear a speech delivered on the mall in front of the Lincoln Memorial. The speech was about an American dream, delivered by Dr. Martin Luther King, and Will and his fellow interns would remember being there for the rest of their lives. Will knew he had been part of a slice of history that day. Four years later, half a world away, he realized that he was now part of another, very different slice.

Will noticed that every day around 4 pm, the rhythm of the JUSPAO office picked up, and after a week or so he asked the captain in the next office why everyone started scurrying around late in the afternoon.

"It's the five o'clock briefing—the press guys call it the five o'clock follies. But you'd better not use that phrase in this office."

"Can I attend?"

"Sure. It's after hours. Just stand in the back and stay out of people's way."

The captain had been friendly, though a bit distant. A full colonel supervised the officers in the JUSPAO units, but Will had never met him.

Will's education in media cross-fires began the next afternoon. As he lined up on the wall in the back of the large auditorium, he saw a table and a podium on the stage at the front of the room. Seats for a hundred or so were rapidly filling up, and he noticed reporters from what appeared to be a wide variety of international and U.S dailies and weeklies. There were no TV cameras, but he had passed a media room before he got to the auditorium that was set up with multiple cameras and lighting.

The briefer, whose name Will had not caught but who was a lieutenant colonel in the Army, strode to the podium and began arranging his notes.

Will remembered reading while still in the U.S. about a briefer who began his session with the press—Will assumed in this very room—by stating how proud he was that Marine casualties had exceeded those of the Army for the first time. Will assumed that briefer was no longer assigned to this duty.

This briefer began with some statistics on the war, summarizing what had happened the day before. Enemy killed in action, "light casualties" on the US side, some casualties for the South Vietnamese army, called the ARVN—the Army of the Republic of Vietnam.. Bombing continued on "enemy sanctuaries" along the Cambodian border.

He finished and asked for questions. Instead of hands going up, about twenty reporters started yelling at the same time. Calmly, the briefer pointed to one, whom Will recognized as the very large, very famous correspondent of the New York Times.

"Jack, you said US casualties in Eye Corps were light. What's that mean?"

Will had learned that the four regions of the country were divided into Corps areas, and the northernmost, I Corps, was always pronounced "Eye Corps."

"We're still assembling those figures from the several units involved. We'll have that for you tomorrow, probably." Then he quickly called on another reporter.

"Jack, President Kieu has said he will be talking with the Ambassador and General Thorpe about civilian casualties in I Corps. What do you have on that?"

"I don't have any information on that. You might want to ask the Embassy."

Later, Will learned from reporters that the supposed handoff to the embassy was an often-used dodge. There was a lowly press aide at the Embassy, but the control over information from both the civilian and military side all ran through JUSPAO and its head, Harry Zimball, and the official lid usually stayed on. That wasn't to say leaking wasn't a widely practiced art form, which Will would soon learn.

As he watched the press session, Will saw quickly that it was a bizarre contest, with rules and patterns that Will could only guess at in his first exposure. He'd seen a lot of media contact in California, but this was different in ways he didn't really understand yet.

As Will turned to leave, he caught the eye of a reporter from the *LA Times* sitting next to another from the *Sacramento Bee*. Both had covered Will's boss in the legislature, and had met with Will many times. He waved, and saw the surprised look on the face of the guy from the *Bee* that meant he would probably try to contact Will.

And then Will realized that he would have to decide how visible he wanted to be. The events of his getting drafted had become very public for a while, and Will's posting would be a juicy follow-up story if he allowed it. He began to weigh that visibility against the impression it would make—and then admitted to himself that he was already trying to calculate the political effects of his presence in Vietnam.

After Will had asked Sergeant Lasswell for additional assignments, and had shown that he could whip out the weekly summary in a few days, he was called into the colonel's office.

The colonel was abrupt. "You have an appointment with Z tomorrow. He wants to talk to you about doing some work for him. See what he wants and let me know."

The director of JUSPAO was named Harry Zimball. But everyone, copying the James Bond films that had begun to emerge, just called him Z. Irreverently, a few of the reporters referred to him as "fat Z." A stocky, rumpled and short man, Zimball had moved through a career in media and public relations after working as a beat reporter in Chicago. He had some political connection with the White House that no one really understood, but he was obviously trusted to explain the war to an increasingly skeptical press.

Will sat down in the chair in front of Zimball's desk.

"Private, they tell me you used to write speeches." Zimball was eying Will with a steady gaze, tapping a pen on the desk in front of him.

"Yes sir. In Sacramento and around California politics a bit."

"Well, the Ambassador is giving a talk to the American Chamber of Commerce here, and wants a speech about our economic development efforts. Here's a folder of some background stuff. Knock out a draft—should be about ten minutes or so. The Ambassador never likes to go on too long. Bring me something by the end of the week."

"Yes sir."

Will left the office, finished an hour of work on the press summary, and set to work on the speech. He was mildly excited, both because he had succeeded in getting something new to do and because he knew he could get something back to Z the next day if he hustled.

The next afternoon he dropped off the draft to Z's secretary. He heard nothing for the next week and nearly forgot about the assignment.

The clerk from the front office opposite the elevator on the second floor came running into Will's office, yelling "Putnam, Putnam—the Ambassador is on the phone. He wants to talk to you."

As he picked up the phone, Will noted with amusement that the clerk had managed to inform everyone within a few hundred feet what was happening. A few enlisted and one captain stuck their heads into Will's office to satisfy their curiosity about why the Ambassador would call a private.

Will said "Private Putnam here," and then heard a courtly, New England accent: "Just wanted to thank you for that fine speech you wrote for me, Putnam. I appreciate it. Used it and look forward to more in the future."

"You're welcome, sir. Glad you liked it. And I'd be glad to help out if I can."

"Count on it." And then abruptly, the connection clicked off.

As Will hung up the phone, the captain blurted out "'Glad to help you out?' You'd be glad to help the Ambassador out?! Damn straight you would, private."

The enlisteds' faces were a mixture of awe and envy, which one finally expressed by saying "Nice going, Putnam. Put in a good word for us, will you?"

"For sure."

Will's sense of triumph didn't last long, however. The war reached out and jammed its realities in his face, realities far from the embassy hallways.

That afternoon, he read the list of KIA in the daily Stars and Stripes, a daily ritual he forced himself to undergo. For the first time, one of his buddies from basic was on the list. Dale Shirley was a smart kid from Oklahoma. They were all kids to Will, who was four years older than most of them, and got the nickname "Uncle Will" two days into basic. Shirley and Will were the first two platoon leaders to be picked for their company, Will, he supposed, because of his education, and Shirley because he was just a natural leader. Tall, ready smile on his face, soft Oklahoma drawl,

Shirley was the first real friend Will had made in basic. The paper said nothing about his death other than the date. Will thought *Three months. He only got through three months.*

Years later, Dale Shirley was always the first name that Will looked for on the Wall.

The next day Will got the call he'd been expecting from his friend at the *Bee*, Buzz Weinstein, who asked Will to join him for a drink at the Continental. Will knew how persistent Weinstein could be, and actually enjoyed his company most of the time they had been in contact in Sacramento. So he agreed.

Buzz had gotten one of the front tables on the veranda of the Continental hotel, facing the plaza. It was the prime place to see and be seen, and Will was a little anxious about that, selecting a chair where his back would be to the street. Then the thought flickered that any motorbike rider could easily flip a grenade onto the veranda and he would never know what hit him. Attacks on American personnel were infrequent in the center of the city, but they happened. Will assumed that the insurgents knew that killing a reporter would be much more harmful to the cause than the benefits of knocking off a lowly enlisted man.

Weinstein lifted his glass of beer, toasting Will, and saying "Will, Will, who knew that all those headlines would bring us together again?"

With his first words, Buzz Weinstein had forced Will back into the most chaotic chapter of his brief political life.

When he returned to California from graduate school, Will had lined up a very junior staff assistant position to a very junior state senator from Southern California, Bill Bagson. At first he was assigned the constituent letters, helping residents in the senator's home district deal with state agencies and answering their queries about the senator's positions. He did those tasks well enough to graduate to writing occasional speeches for the senator, and then to researching his positions on bills before the legislature.

The senator was younger than most, in his mid-thirties, and as Will's role expanded somewhat, the senator sought him out for discussions about legislative issues, and then, more personal issues. The senator, like Will, was a great admirer of William Brammer's extraordinary book about politics in the Texas legislature, *The Gay Place*. The senator once called it "the best American political fiction since Robert Penn Warren's *All the King's Men*." Will had come across the book in graduate school, and having read little political fiction at that point in his life beyond *Advice and Consent*, Will was inclined to agree.

It was early in 1966, and Will knew the draft would beckon now that he was out of graduate school. So he enrolled, with some advice from the senator, in a National Guard unit based in Sacramento. Several other legislative staff members his age were in the unit, and he faithfully attended drills and the two-week summer camp at Fort Ord that was required.

Then the congressman who had been the incumbent for twenty-four years in the senator's district announced that he was retiring. The senator immediately announced that he would be running, and soon after, a state representative from the district also announced he was running. The state rep was a very conservative, very anti-communist politician who was known to have substantial funding from the John Birch Society and other right-wing groups. Will's senator was better known, but fund-raising had not been one of his strong points. It looked as though the primary would be intense.

Soon Will was on the campaign trail, and was missing his Guard drills. He assumed, with the innocence of youth, that he would be able to make them up or justify his absences based on state legislative duties.

He was wrong.

The state rep went for the jugular. His first press release raised the issue of the senator's lack of military experience "in a time of national emergency when we are at war." His second was far worse. "The senator should look at his own staff which includes some bona fide draft dodgers. Why should other Southern California boys be fighting and dying while the senator's staff are going off once a month to march in circles at Fort Ord?" And then for good measure, he added, "I see no reason why these pampered, elite Ivy Leaguers should get a deferral when thousands of other young men are doing their duty."

As the only member of the staff who had attended an Ivy League university, Will was shell-shocked by the personal attack. He immediately offered to resign, which Bagson laughed off, saying "If someone resigned every time an asshole behaved like an asshole, no one would ever work in politics or government." He pointed out that Will didn't get a deferral, that he was doing what hundreds of thousands of young men were doing at that time, and that the state rep probably had polls showing he was going to lose and was going negative because of it.

"We're going to win, Will, and you're going to Washington with me."

But instead, Will ended up going to El Paso.

The final chapter was capped off by the actions of an unknown person who had carefully compiled all the state rep's press releases, the resulting newspaper stories, and a copy of the roster of his Guard unit showing his absences from drills. The package arrived at Will's draft board, and three days later the Board met and Will's draft notice was sent. His orders were to report to Ft. Bliss in El Paso for basic training.

Two years later, the federal Selective Service Board issued regulations that made clear that draft boards were not allowed to automatically draft Guard members who were delinquent in their drills but still in good standing. But it was too late for Will.

At a final dinner with Bagson, Will explained his decision. Bagson had told Will he would pull whatever strings he could to get Will re-enrolled in the Guard, whatever the effects on his campaign. But Will refused.

"Why, Will, for God's sake? Get back in the Guard, do your six months after the campaign is over, and get on with your life. Come with me to DC—we're going to raise hell and have fun doing it."

Will shook his head. "I need to do this. They called me a coward, and this is the only way I can answer them. My father was in the Army Air Force in WWII, and that's part of it, too." He paused, wondering if he should reveal the other half of his reasoning. "Look, Senator, I admire what you've done and how you do it. Someday I might want to run myself. And this is the only way to get rid of what some other bastard might try to do to me if I stay out."

Bagson continued to argue his case, but Will was immovable. It was the first time he had ever had to make a life decision on his own, and it felt right. He was in control of the decisions again, after feeling for a few days that he had lost control of his life. He thought he understood the risk, and he wanted to take it.

Basic training and advanced infantry training: monotonous, momentarily terrifying, an education in the fantasies of high school graduates and dropouts, sadistic and life-saving drill instructors, running and crawling, sand and dirt, deserts and mountains. There were very few enlisted college graduates, which led to Will's getting offers to go Officers' Candidate School, which then led to curiosity from the others when he turned it down.

And every day, Will became more aware that nearly all of these young men would end up in Vietnam.

Buzz Weinstein went on. "You haven't done that badly for an enlisted guy. Nice job in the embassy. Beautiful women here in Saigon," as he motioned toward the sidewalk where the usual parade of bicycling young women and men were riding by. "How do you like it?"

"It's a long way from Sacramento, Buzz," Will answered. "I'm still trying to figure out what's going on here—the war, the countryside, the culture. A lot to try to figure out all at once." Then, wanting to shift the focus, he asked, "What do you make of it? You've been covering the war for a year now. What do you think?"

Weinstein frowned. "I think it's a godawful mess, and I don't trust a word I hear from those flacks you work for in the embassy. Body counts every day, but you've probably noticed that nothing stops the VC from dropping a 105 shell in from the suburbs every night or so. And these clowns in the South Vietnamese government—what a bunch of jokers. Each one more corrupt than the ones that went before."

Then he got a sly look on his face, and asked Will, "So what do you hear inside—do you see the cable traffic? What's the inside story on how we're doing?"

Will had gotten deep enough into California politics to know when he was being set up for a leak, deliberate or accidental. "No, they keep us flunkies away from the serious stuff. You saw that I went to the press briefing a few days ago. Interesting."

"The five o'clock follies? Are you serious? That's the biggest joke of all. Z or one of his flunkies stands up there and tells us how great things are going, and refers all the questions they get to someone who won't answer any of them."

As they talked, Will watched the restaurant fill up with reporters, American officers and civilians, and their Vietnamese counterparts. He recognized a few TV reporters who appeared to have their own tables set off in a quieter part of the restaurant.

They talked some more, Buzz prodding Will and Will dodging his questions. Neither of them got as much out of the encounter as they had hoped, and Will resolved to be more careful with his press contacts.

Walking around Saigon became another part of Will's education. There were many signs of America that were not-quite-America: misspelled "massage parlers," "shoe shins," "cigarets." There were many more signs in Chinese characters or the Latinized Vietnamese language. As the bus moved through the streets of the city each morning from the BEQ to JUSPAO, the vaguely familiar yielded to the completely foreign. The smells were the hardest to get used to, and he found that breathing through his mouth helped. But after a few months, he noticed that he didn't notice them anymore.

Will's phone rang, and he picked it up and heard a woman's voice say, "This is a football friend from Cornell. Can you meet me for lunch at the coffee shop in the Hilton?"

"Uh, yeah."

"OK, see you then."

Will had figured out who was calling, but he had no idea why. He had spent time with a woman at Cornell who happened to be a fanatic New York Giants fan, and they had attended games when they could get away to go to the City—to Yankee Stadium, in those days. But what she was doing in Vietnam was a mystery.

He spotted Yvonne Cohen in the back of the coffee shop as soon as he walked in. She was tall, brunette, slim, and with an angular face that was a bit too long to be classic but was graced with a lovely mouth that he knew from experience could both smile and beguile. The net effect was a stunning woman whose personality doubled the effect.

He hugged her, feeling parts of her he had once known quite well, and they sat down.

"What the hell are you doing here, Yvonne?"

"I'm staffing Congressman Bronstein from New York. You remember I interned for him after we graduated? I'm on his staff now. He's here on an info tour." She paused. "I wanted to talk with you to see if you could help us."

Will's warning signals were all going off. "Wait, isn't he leading the anti-war coalition in the House?"

"Yes. Of course. Do you think I'd be working for a hawk, Will?" She was irritated, but he knew her well enough to know she was trying to keep from exploding, which she was quick to do, in his experience with her politics. They had disagreed about as often as they had agreed. Bronstein was a good fit with what Will remembered of her views on the war, which were negative and absolute.

"OK, I know where you're coming from, Yvonne. But I'm just a tiny cog here, in this mammoth machine. And I just got here a few months ago. Not sure I could be much help."

"Will, the Congressman wants to meet some Buddhists. And he wants to visit the orphanages. Do you know how to get in touch with them? We have some names from people in the antiwar groups, but when we called them, they were mostly people from ten years ago. Their contacts aren't current."

As it happened, from his review of the weekly papers, Will had learned something about the leadership of the Buddhist groups. "I can help with the Buddhists. And I can give you the names of some of the bigger orphanages in the city."

"We need you to come with us. We need someone from the embassy to introduce the congressman to these people."

Will was trying to control himself, without much success. "Are you bloody serious? I can't be seen with an antiwar congressman—I work for the embassy."

"What are they going to do, Will, demote you?"

"No, they have this very effective thing they call a court-martial. Not to mention curfew and the fact that some of these places aren't in safe parts of the city. Come on, Yvonne, this is crazy." Then he stopped, another thought catching up to his rapid attempt to read her.

"Yvonne, how did you know I was here?"

"Oh, come on, Will. You're famous back among the Cornell gang. You're the guy who got drafted because of a political campaign."

"Great."

"Will, I remember a lot of what you used to say about foreign policy in class. You were never a real dove, you didn't buy the domino bullshit, but you thought we might be able to protect people from the North and give them a chance to live better. That's what this is about. Bronstein wants to see if the out-groups and the people in the villages are doing any better, or if this is hopeless because the Kieu gang will never share power with anyone and they don't care about the villages anyway."

They talked for an hour, and then Will left to go back to JUSPAO. He told her he would think about it and meet her at the coffee shop the next day. He admired her, intellectually at least, for not pressuring him by making plans to meet with him that night in her hotel. But he'd still hoped for the invitation.

It was dark, and Will's anxiety was notching up a few ticks every minute. Curfew was an hour away, and their taxi driver had lost his way. At least that was what Will and Yvonne hoped, as opposed to his having decided he would claim a prize by delivering a US congressman to the VC.

"Le Loi Street, it's right here," Will yelled, but the driver just kept shaking his head and peering out the dirt-smeared windshield.

They turned around a corner, and Yvonne said "Look, there's a plaque on that big building. Maybe that's the Buddhist place."

And it was. They had stumbled into the headquarters of the biggest of the Buddhist opposition groups.

When Will called, he had asked if they would need a translator, but had been assured they had several English-speaking monks who could translate. The claim was accurate—they did speak English. But their ability to translate was far short of what Will would have hoped for, and the translator's frequent phrase "I don't understand" was very frustrating.

Bronstein, happily, was the opposite of the stereotype of an impatient, self-impressed congressman. He was patient with the young translator, as he kept asking the same two questions over and over in different ways: *Do you think your groups can ever agree to become part of the government? Will the Kieu administration allow your groups to be part of the government?*

Despite the tangled translation, the message back from the Buddhists was clear. They saw no way the current power structure would recognize the sizable segment of the rural population that was more or less Buddhist.

As the conversation and translation wound on, Will watched the two main leaders of the Buddhist group. They were both wearing orange robes, with shaved heads and an ascetic demeanor. But one gave in to a bright smile from time to time, while the other frowned throughout the interview. *Good cop and bad cop*, Will thought, irreverently.

The room they were meeting in was cold, with no detectable heat. Faded wall paintings took up the two largest walls, with little furniture. They were all sitting on a rug in the center of the room; the rest of the floor was scuffed wooden boards, looking as though they hadn't been swept in a long time.

After an hour so of the back and forth translation, Bronstein bowed to the two monks and rose slowly, thanking them for their time. Will and Yvonne moved toward the door, hoping that the retainer they had given the cab driver was enough to hold him. And it was, or at least someone who worked with him. The cab was right outside the door—sitting in the full glare of the headlights of a jeep with two MPs in it.

A lengthy conversation followed, with the congressman identifying himself and gambling that he would be able to vouch for Will and Yvonne without Will having to show his ID. Will was glad he had worn civilian clothes, and marveled quietly at Bronstein's ability to calmly explain that they were on a fact-finding mission and these were two of his staff. The MPs weren't happy about their being out after curfew, but once they saw Bronstein's credentials and that he was registered at the Hilton, they told him to head back there. Then they drove away.

"Whew," said Will, as they rode through the dark streets toward the hotel. "Thanks, Congressman. That was a little too close."

"Least we can do, Will, for the help you've given us. We really appreciate it."

They got to the hotel and sat down in the lobby. After a brief review of the night, the congressman rose and headed to the elevator.

Yvonne leaned into Will and murmured, "You did good, Will. Nice work. It's just what we needed." She waited until the congressman had gone up in the elevator, and then turned back to Will. "Guess what? Will gets laid tonight."

And he did.

The thrill of a hotel room and a willing woman, in a setting as exotic as any Will had ever experienced, resulted in a night with far more frolicking than sleep. Washington had done nothing to curb Yvonne's appetites, which Will recalled and then confirmed as sizable. She was that rare woman who was neither needy nor greedy, but who just loved sex and understood it as giving and getting in roughly equal balance.

By morning, Will was glad for a fast coffee and the recollection that he had an extra shirt in his office closet as insurance against a hoped-for night out. Yvonne had reminded him that the next phase of their fact-finding was to visit an orphanage, and Will promised to work on that immediately.

Later that afternoon, Yvonne and Bronstein met Will in the Continental Hotel lobby. He had arranged for a visit to the orphanage he had heard about from the USAID reps in the Embassy. They arrived in a cab just as the children were finishing dinner. About fifty children were carefully putting their dinner plates and utensils into a set of boxes next to the kitchen, where older children were busily washing dishes.

Will watched the children carefully, trying to understand what the orphanage did and why the children were there. His brother had worked with special education classes in a local school district in California, and Will could tell that some of the children were disabled, both physically and mentally.

One girl was blind, and was being led around by another child. Will estimated their ages at six or seven, though it was difficult to guess ages with the small stature of the children. The girl held her hand lightly on the back of the other child, walking confidently through the rapidly moving groups of children. As Will watched her, he could see that she was smiling, talking continuously to the child who was leading her.

The director of the orphanage was delighted to have the congressman visiting, and after a tour of the buildings, she gathered them around a table in her office. She was Japanese, working for the orphanage under a contract with UNICEF, the United Nations Children's Fund.

"How can we help you, Congressman?"

"I'd be interested in how these children came to live here, Ms. Aoki. How did they lose their parents?"

She lowered her head and then quickly looked back at him. "Most of them came here from rural villages. A few are from the city, and lost their parents due to illness. But most came here from villages that were evacuated after bombing or when the village was declared part of a free-fire zone. Often that happens after the Viet Cong come into the village and your troops and the South Vietnamese attack the village to drive the VC out. Civilians often get caught in the crossfire, and these children are some of those whose parents were killed."

She described the events in a matter-of-fact tone, almost as if it were routine.

"Do you have any idea how many children there are like this throughout the country?"

"Not really. A team from UNICEF was here last year and estimated that it could be as many as 250,000. But your government disputed that number, and it is not official."

"I know you are funded by UNICEF. Are there other funders?"

"Yes, USAID contributes some of our funding. And we occasionally get donations of food from USAID as well."

Yvonne asked, "What's the trend? Has the flow of children increased or decreased during the last year?"

Ms. Aoki answered, "I'm afraid it has increased. We have had to turn away some children in the last three months. A few have been able to live with relatives, and others may have found temporary shelters. But some just end up on the streets, begging—or worse—if they are older."

Bronstein quietly thanked her and told her that he would do what he could to see if additional US aid might be possible. She thanked him and saw them to the front gate.

Will asked Ms. Aoki as they stood at the front gate, "Tell me about the little girl who's blind."

"She was injured in a bombing in her village. They brought her here a year or so ago, and she has done very well. As you can see, she gets around and the other children help her. These children look out for each other, because most of them have no family."

As they waited for a taxi, Bronstein said to Yvonne and Will, "Another kind of body count, I guess. But not one we're keeping track of, it would seem."

The remark made a deep impression on Will and he spoke up. "Actually, sir, you could ask State, if the UNICEF counts are not accurate, what our own best estimates would be. The USAID people have been doing some informal surveys in the villages and among the refugees in the larger camps. They have some numbers that might be helpful."

"Thanks, Will. I think you just gave me the guts of my next subcommittee hearing. I'll let you know if anything comes of it."

Yvonne lightly punched Will on the shoulder. "Good work, soldier boy." And then winked at him.

As Will walked back to JUSPAO to catch a cab to the BEQ, he thought *First time I really crossed the line. Used something from inside with outsiders. Felt weird. Felt good, too.*

Another political visit left Will more disturbed. He had gotten a call from a political operative he had known in Sacramento, a research director for a firm that worked for candidates all over California. The contact, Nick Cervantes, was working for a presidential candidate in the 1968 election that was beginning to heat up. His candidate, a Midwestern Governor, was challenging Richard Nixon and the others who were lining up to take on the Democratic field, now that President Johnson had announced he would not seek re-election.

"Will, I'd like you to be part of a group we're putting together to brief the Governor. You've been around California politics for a while and now you're over here. Seems to me you might have some insights into our policy."

So Will joined a group at dinner a week later and met the Governor. The Governor was far more likable than many candidates Will had encountered in the past, seeming to be someone who was comfortable with himself and with others. The format was an informal roundtable, and Will had a chance to tell the Governor about some of the news reports he had summarized, using the phrase "worsening trends" and mentioning the damage to the civilian population he had become aware of in his brief travels in Saigon.

The Governor was reflective at the end of the briefing, and began talking about his earlier trip to South Vietnam. He had committed one or two gaffes on that trip, and he was still tender about it. "You know, the media just cut me and cut me after I made a few bloopers. None of what I had to say about the war got through—all they wanted to talk about was a few sentences I said in a speech after I got back. They cut me and cut me."

As Will rode back to the BEQ in a taxi, he thought about politics at the level he had seen briefly that night. The Governor had been savaged, just as Will had been savaged at a far lower level. He wondered to himself, *Maybe it's not the great adventure after all.*

One afternoon, Buzz Weinstein called Will and said, "Will, I want to introduce you to some friends of mine. Let's have dinner tonight."

Will agreed, wondering what Buzz was up to.

When he arrived at the Continental, he saw Buzz seated at a table with two attractive women. When they got up to greet Will, he saw that one was tall and one was not. The taller one was blonde and bosomy. The other one was also blonde, but petite, with short, curly hair, and a lovely face. As they spoke, he heard their distinctive British accents.

After Buzz had described Will's role in the embassy, overstating considerably what Will did and how important it was, he told Will that the women were working for an American construction firm. He had met them while doing a story on the firm's work in Saigon.

Will made conversation by asking them how they had fared during the Tet attacks.

The petite one, whose name was Belle, said, "We were a little worried about the VC coming after us if they had broken through the barriers around our offices. It was a bit frightful, really."

Making an uncharacteristic joke, Will patted the holstered .45 he had been assigned to carry since the Tet attacks, and said, "I would consider it an honor to protect your sacred Anglo-Saxon purity, and I assure you I would never let them take you alive."

The bosomy one gasped, and said, "Now I think I'm more frightened of you than the VC!"

Will was still having trouble understanding how two delectable women had turned up in Saigon. So he asked them, "How did you get here?"

Belle answered lightly, saying "We were dealing cards in a casino in Beirut and someone offered us jobs out here. The pay is outrageous, and we thought we'd give it a look."

"But—in a war zone? Why would you come to a war zone, with 105s dropping in every night?"

Belle stared at him for a moment, and then laughed. "Darling, we're British. We lived through the Blitz in London. This is *nothing.*"

For the rest of the evening, Will talked with Belle. She was animated, joyful, and playful, her voice conjuring up a mixture of the BBC broadcasts he listened to from time to time and an interview with Marianne Faithful he'd seen on television while living in Sacramento. He'd heard somewhere that most Americans secretly believed that Brits spoke English as it should be, and felt inferior when they heard it. He believed it.

She told him, with a charming giggle, "They give us all ranks, you know. I'm a major. Can you believe it? So I could take you to dinner at the officer's club. Would you like that?" she asked, smiling the brightest smile he'd seen in a long time.

"I'd love that," he answered, "Not sure the officers would, though."

"Poo on them. You'd be my guest."

"Sure, that would be great."

A week later, Will called Buzz and asked if he had heard from the two women. Buzz told him, with considerable disappointment, that they had been transferred to the firm's Manila offices.

And then he began to spend time with Thuy Thieu. She was a translator in the Embassy press section, and he had met her because she did the first drafts of the local press coverage. After she had quietly handed him the first two weeks of press coverage and walked away, the next time she brought the translations, he stopped her said "Would you like some feedback on this? It's very good, but maybe I could give you some suggestions."

She looked startled at first, blinking her eyes several times and then ventured a small smile, covering her mouth with her tiny hand.

"Yes, I would like that very much if you could show me how to make it better." Her English was excellent, accented with near-musical French overtones. Speaking three languages, he realized, meant that she was more internationally competent than he was so far, at least in linguistic terms.

So they began meeting for lunch downstairs in the cafeteria, and later, once he'd gotten his stomach around local food, out in local restaurants where she clearly felt much freer to talk. He'd showed her how to write the core of the story or editorial in briefer sentences, and he could see that her work immediately moved in the directions he'd suggested.

Later, as they ate in a local restaurant, she'd told him that she had been propositioned several times by other enlisteds and officers, but had told them she was engaged.

She said, smiling slightly, "But I am not engaged, Will. Before I worked here, my professor told me that all the Americans wanted from Vietnamese women was the sex thing, and so I was frightened to work here. But my family needed the money and," she gestured to the bar where three girls her age were rapidly pouring drinks in near-bikini outfits, "it's better than what they do."

She was in her late twenties, looking much younger, as many of them did. At work she wore the diaphanous white clothing, long flowing pants and a tight top that most of the young girls and women wore, with a colored overblouse.

When she came over to the apartment he had rented with several other enlisted men for purposes of drinking and assignations, she changed into slacks and a sweater in the cooler months or shorts and a loose blouse in the heat.

In bed, she wore nothing, and her lithe body became a marvel of exquisite, pale energy that taught him far more about the wonders of women than he had learned in the furtive couplings of his college years. She was more skilled in love-making than Will, and far more at ease, and he spent more energy than he wanted in refraining from asking her where she had learned all that she knew. He reveled in her, but he wondered about her.

He had bought her a few paperback versions of some of the better works of American and English literature. He was deeply moved one night when she slowly slid atop him and, looking into his face from a few inches away and touching him intimately, whispered "Only connect."

Then it became her catch phrase for making love. *Only connect.*

But Will was driven by other urges beyond those of his body. He wanted to understand Vietnam, to master a new subject as he had mastered most of his classes in college. And so he coaxed Thuy into becoming his new professor, his mentor in things Vietnamese. From food, they graduated to the geography of the capital, and Thuy showed him the safer parts of the city: the National Opera House, the waterfront, the legislature, the Chinese sections of the city. They walked through neighborhoods where the police presence was strong enough to make it relatively safe— although Will had been told in mimeographed instructions not to leave the downtown area under any circumstances. Thuy borrowed a motorbike, and they used it to travel from neighborhood to neighborhood, with her slim arms wrapped around his chest as they zipped along the crowded streets.

She took him to noodle shops, after making sure that he knew that he had to wear civilian clothes. She taught him the names of the foods, laughing at his mispronunciation of the words.

"You like music so much, Will. Our language has tones—so *sing it*, don't say it in your one-tone drone."

His movement through the city was aided by the standing orders for embassy staff, even enlisted, to wear civilian clothes most of the time. He still stood out as a round-eye, but he knew his appearance was less provocative than if he had been dressed in fatigues.

Once he had been riding with Thuy through an unfamiliar section of the city and he happened to notice a young man on the sidewalk scowling at him and pointing his index finger and thumb at him in the universal sign for a gun. When the man flexed his finger as if to shoot Will, he winced and quickly looked away.

One day in late January, as work ended, Will picked up the chatter among the officers in his unit. They were headed for a big party of the senior embassy staff that was being held at the tennis club where many social events were held. Will assumed a party like that was security-conscious, and that probably meant that everyone expected that the Tet New Year celebrations would be quiet. He had heard the Vietnamese staff talking with excitement about the Tet parties that would begin that night and run for the next three days.

He caught a bus back to the BEQ and read until he fell asleep.

Explosions and small arms fire woke Will. The sounds were much closer than he was used to, and then he heard one of the Seabees yelling into the hall. "There's big attacks all over the city; get loaded up, take your weapons, bus is taking us all out of here to the airport or downtown, wherever you're supposed to go in an emergency. This is *real*, man! *Move!*"

They raced downstairs, the explosions continuing, and piled into the bus. Two guards with M-16s and extra clips sat on the front steps of the bus once they got loaded, and the bus raced through the deserted streets. By then it was about 3 am. The bus quickly dropped Will and five other soldiers off at JUSPAO and then tore off down Le Loi Street. As they raced into the building, they could still hear small arms fire—both the brrrr of M-16s on full automatic and the slower-cycling AK-47, chattering louder than the M-16.

Will reported to Sergeant Lasswell, who told him to go down to the lobby and check in with the Marine guard there. He got to the lobby and found three other enlisted men there—two guys he knew slightly and a Marine guard, Sergeant Christopher, who had been sent over from the Main Embassy. The Marine stationed them around the lobby, putting Will behind the receptionist's desk in the front of the room. Will couldn't help but notice that his "protection" was a flimsy, stained plywood section of the receptionist's desk.

Christopher quickly explained the basics of fields of fire to Will and the other two and showed them how to watch for rebels using the sides of the buildings for cover.

"They'll use grenades if they get close enough. They've already attacked the Main Embassy, but haven't gotten inside yet. Our job is to keep them far enough away to make it impossible to lob a grenade through the front window. Unless they're Sandy Koufax."

Will, a lifelong Dodger fan, appreciated the reference. But his mind was racing, realizing that this was as close as he had come—so far—to the Real War.

His brain seemed to be running on a dozen parallel tracks.

If they couldn't get into the Main Embassy, maybe this is the secondary target.

What's our backup plan if a lot of them rush the building?

I hope I don't screw up.

I wonder where Thuy is.

Where's the rest of our ammunition?

I hope I don't screw up.

The occasional sounds of small arms fire close by added to the tension.

"Probably just the white mice shooting at stray dogs," said Christopher. Remembering that the local police, who wore white uniforms, were called the white mice, Will wondered if that was true, or just the sergeant's way of calming them down.

The night passed slowly. The small arms fire continued, then stopped for an hour or so. Then they heard explosions again, but farther away from the earlier ones they'd heard.

The four men were quiet most of the time. Christopher sat in a big desk chair he'd hauled out of one of the offices, an M-16 across his lap and a shotgun on the floor beside him. Will stayed crouched behind the receptionist's desk, with a clear view of the front door and a slice of the street beyond. After a while he sat down on the floor, back to the wall, keeping his eye on the door.

The other two, who were on the far side of the lobby behind an overturned desk, were mail clerks Will had met once or twice in the cafeteria—Roswell from Minnesota and a skinny guy from Elk Grove in northern California whose name Will couldn't remember.

Christopher had a walkie-talkie that was wired into the main command post at the airport, but Will couldn't hear most of the back and forth. He caught snatches of the reports: "ten charlies confirmed down at the race track," "sapper squad still firing at the palace," "Charlie unit of six headed south on Le Loi."

As they began their watch, Will worried about staying awake. But the combination of adrenalin, the occasional firing, and the steady gaze of the Marine sergeant made sleep irrelevant.

As the sun began to rise, the sergeant was murmuring on the walkie-talkie. He clicked off and stood up, telling the three of them, "It's quieting down. No units spotted around here in the last few hours. We'll get relieved in an hour or so. Roswell, go see if anyone's cooking anything in the cafeteria."

Roswell came back in a few minutes with a thermos of coffee and four plastic cups. "Nothing but coffee so far, sergeant."

Will couldn't remember coffee ever tasting so good. It was February 1st, and Will remembered with some amazement that in a few days, he would turn 26.

He was safe. Ever after, he tried to sort out the proportions of relief and guilt he felt about how far he was from the real action.

Later that morning, Will went with a detail over to the Main Embassy, which had been attacked by what turned out to be a sapper unit of the NVA. They had knocked a hole in the embassy's outer wall, but had been killed before they could penetrate the building itself. By the time Will got there, they had dragged away the bodies of the NVA unit who had gotten inside the outer wall before they were cut down by helicopters and M-60 fire from the windows and roof of the main building.

Will walked over to the wall and picked up a piece of the front facing of the building that had been blasted into the street. It was marble on one side, jagged stone on the other. Will looked up at the huge, six-story marble-faced building, and then down at the rock. Will thought *The most powerful nation in history—and they blew open a hole in the front wall of our embassy.*

The first wave of Tet 1968 was over. The fighting would continue for several weeks around the country, with continuing losses and the attackers driven out of every city they had attacked.

But late in February, Walter Cronkite used the word "stalemate" for the first time, and the case against the war back in the US gained credibility and strength. As Will read the papers over the next few weeks—both

Vietnamese and American—he could see that Tet was a military loss for the VC and the North Vietnamese, but a political win.

Three days after Tet, Will was called into the colonel's office. The colonel functioned more or less as Zimball's chief of staff, running the office and responsible for the military contingent, while Zimball supervised the civilians.

"Zimball wants us to work on some stories for the USIA monthly, stories on how well the recovery from Tet is going. They're hoping that then the regular press guys will pick them up and do their own stories. Right now all anyone is reading is how terrible it is. So you and some guy who's coming in from State next week are going to go out to some bases and a couple of cities and find the good news of Tet."

"Sir? The good news of Tet?"

"You know what I mean. The good news about brave villagers and charismatic Vietnamese troop commanders working together to repair the damage after the NLF have all been killed or chased out of the villages and cities."

"Oh. That news."

Sensing Putnam's tone of skepticism, the colonel added, "Get it right, Putnam. Find what looks positive and write about it."

"Yes, sir."

"I'll get you your itinerary tomorrow. Pack for a week. Maybe more."

So Will set off on what he came to refer to, privately, as the Great Tet Comeback Tour. Interviews were scheduled with commanding officers at US and Vietnamese bases around the capital, in the Delta, and up in the Highlands. Flying around in army helicopters, treated as much more than an enlisted nobody—realizing when he saw the incredulous looks on the faces of some of his greeters that they had been told "Staff from the embassy" would be coming, not a lowly enlisted guy.

The drill quickly became familiar.

"How is recovery coming?" *We're doing great, we've rebuilt most of what was destroyed in the Tet attacks.*

"How is the morale of the people?" *It's great, they really hate the NLF even more now because of the disruption they caused at Tet.*

"How well did the ARVN fight?" *They were very effective in repelling the NLF forces, even though they took big losses in the first wave.*

He took it down and he wrote it up and he sent it back to JUSPAO. And he wondered when someone would tell him the truth.

Then he came to the Delta, the furthest locations for the Tet attacks, where the attacking forces were clearly more often local insurgents than regular forces from the North. And after the briefing he was given at IV Corps headquarters, he noticed two officers standing in the back of the briefing room. They were paying close attention to the briefing, but they were watching Will even more closely.

As the group broke up, Will waited at the front of the room. As he had expected, the two officers slowly approached him, waiting until most of the higher-ranking officers had cleared out of the room. The taller of the two introduced himself as Rick Zepeda, and Will noticed his Ranger insignia along with a Purple Heart. The other officer was a Navy lieutenant who called himself Swifty and wouldn't give a last name, explaining that he was undercover and wasn't able to give his name. His insignia were covered and Will assumed he was from the swift gunboat teams that operated at night along the river.

Zepeda said "We wanted to talk to you because Buzz Weinstein was down here a few weeks ago and mentioned that you might be one of the few people in the embassy who hadn't bought the party line."

"The party line?"

"The line that Tet was just a little bump in the road instead of a bloody disaster for us."

The Navy officer said "Look, we know you're going to write what they want you to. But we wanted to give you a different picture so that you may be able to push it up the line when someone really wants to know what's going on."

Will answered, "OK, I think I get it. So what's the real story?"

Zepeda looked at "Swifty" and nodded. He began talking in a low tone, looking around occasionally to see if they were being observed. "It was a disaster. The VC poured out of the rivers and paddies at us, far more than we'd ever seen before. We mowed them down and they kept coming, it was like what you read about in Korea, human wave stuff. And the South

Vietnamese Army was terrified. They only had a few units that stood and fought and they were cut to pieces until we got air cover for them."

By that time Will had heard every argument for and against the case they were making. "OK, but tell me—are you saying that there won't be another wave coming, if you killed so many of the VC when they surfaced?"

"No. We're saying they still have thousands of irregulars down here and more coming down the Trail from the north to make it impossible to ever withdraw from this area. And that's what we need you to understand the most—this will either turn into a pure occupation in which our troops and boats are the occupying power, or we will back away and the VC and the North will take over. There is no middle ground left, Putnam. What Tet really showed was that the South can't hold its ground. Our guys beat them back, but once we're gone, the North owns this place."

"If that's true, then why has every briefing I've gotten for the last two weeks said we're coming back strong from Tet and doing better than ever?"

"Because they're trying to convince themselves that it's true. Or they just can't break with the cover story and tell the truth."

Will and the two officers talked for another two hours, and by the end, Will was mostly convinced that they were not only truth-tellers, but gifted strategists who should be advising the senior command.

But when he got back and tried to insert some of this perspective in his articles, it was at first edited out and then, when he continued, he was called in and instructed to "drop this defeatist bullshit, wherever you picked it up."

As Will landed in the base in the Central Highlands, he noticed a lot more activity than he had seen at the other bases. Sandbags were being piled around the perimeter, artillery was being wheeled into position, and new helicopters seemed to be clustered around the far end of the airfield as ordinance was being loaded into them.

"Something happening?" he asked the public affairs liaison lieutenant who escorted him into the command post.

"We've gotten word about some kind of second wave attack by troops from the North, coming in off the trail. We've picked up some massing of their regular troops in Cambodia that looks like it's headed this way.

May just be a fake, or may be real. We have recon patrols out, but no word back yet."

Will went ahead with his interviews of senior base officials, but he could see that they were nervous about claiming that Tet and post-Tet had stabilized things, compared to the other places he'd been. When he asked about ARVN troops, the eye rolls were much more visible than at the other bases. "We don't count on them much. We have some Hmong irregulars out with our patrols, and they're a big help, but there aren't enough of them."

As he wrapped up the interviews, the liaison lieutenant said with some embarrassment, "Putnam, your chopper back has been diverted, so looks like you'll get to take advantage of our fine hospitality tonight. Hopefully no light show will come with it."

Will bunked down in the enlisted hooch which was a heavily sandbagged area of the base. He got about two hours of uneasy sleep and was then prodded awake by a Spec 5 who said "Report to the northern wall—that way!"

When Will got there a fast-talking sergeant told him, "Specialist, I'm putting you over on that perimeter with our fire crew. You'll have the same M-16 they all have. Load up with plenty of clips in the carry bags we have in the corner. Could be a long night."

It was.

The mortars came in on the dot at 0230. The first salvos landed outside the perimeter, but the range quickly adjusted and the rounds began hitting inside the base. The staff sergeant in charge of Will's area of the perimeter seemed calm, walking hunched over from post to post along the outer wall of sandbags. "They usually try to come in after 15 to 30 minutes of shelling.

"We've got our artillery ready to go once they start tripping the sensors, and—"

Just then the 105s, 155s, and mortars behind the fire team began going off with a deafening roar. Will had heard nothing like it since basic, and he started gulping air to try to equalize the pressure from the air concussions they were getting from the outgoing barrage. For all the noise and pressure, it was reassuring to hear the outgoing as it combined with and eventually drowned out the incoming.

The initial probes came just as the flares went off, casting an eerie light across the entire north and western sides of the base. Through the view hole Will could see massed troops in black and grey uniforms, and as they began running toward the walls of the base, the M-16 and M-60 fire broke out across the wall, and Will fired his first shots at something other than a cardboard target.

The millennia-old equation of *fire and take cover* was in full view, as soldiers rose out of their crouch behind the sandbag wall, fired off rounds, and quickly ducked and moved from where they had been. Will remembered his drill sergeant from basic saying "The better the shot you have at them, the better the shot they have at you. So shoot and *move.*"

The problem with that theory was that moving meant you were on top of the guy who had been posted a yard or two away from you. And when Will tried to move into that guy's space, that guy was just as often moving into Will's space—which meant that neither of them was any less exposed than he had been a few seconds before. The problem seemed to get solved by firing rounds and then ducking or firing through a small view hole, which of course meant you couldn't see anything, but you got rounds off and were relatively safe.

Relatively, that is. Will saw two or three soldiers on his line spin around or slump to the ground with wounds or worse. Medics rushed up and dragged some of them away, while others lay where they had fallen until a second detail came out and hustled them away on stretchers.

The firefight seemed as if it had been going on for hours, but as Will realized the sound had died down with a lull in the action, he saw it was only 0400. Behind him to the east the beginnings of sunlight were barely visible, but in front it was still dark.

But sensors must have been tripped because the firing began again and the flare guns started popping. The howitzers were now firing "Killer Junior" shells that detonated in the air above the attacking VC and NVA troops, slicing anyone in range into shreds. Will could hear their screams, which were very different from the cries of men shot by shouldered weapons.

The artillery from outside the base had stopped, either because the guns had been located and silenced or because the ammunition carried from the North had run out. But light weapons AK-47 fire continued, though less intense.

Then with a sudden whoosh as a camouflaged plane ripped by, napalm was dropped so close to the walls that Will could feel the heat rush. The aim must have been amazingly precise, however, as all but a few shots disappeared completely from outside the perimeter.

Will and the soldiers on either side of him stayed down, and ten minutes later heard a welcome "All clear."

As they slowly rose, they could see dozens of bodies—and parts of bodies, strewn across the slight hill sloping up to their walls. Smoke was still rising from those that had been napalmed.

The staff sergeant, whose name Will finally heard as Frick, muttered to Will as he stood by his post. "Tet was worse. But why are these fuckers still coming back after we tore them apart at Tet?"

And all Will could think of was Zepeda saying "Once we're gone, the North owns this place."

It was as close as Will had come to the real war, and it proved to be as close as he would ever come. He left the Highlands with a very different feeling about the real front lines of the war. After the firefight, he never forgot what he had felt in those few hours, seeing at close range what it meant for hundreds of thousands of young American who went through that almost daily in some parts of the country.

Tet was real, but his own risks had turned out to be minimal. But behind the barricades, he saw what competent officers and noncoms were worth, and how randomly their best efforts proved to be useless for some of them. He never again heard a discussion about deploying troops without thinking about the terrible blend of bravery and loss he had seen. And his anger grew as he realized how many of the civilians in those discussions had no idea what it really meant when they considered sending troops in harm's way.

As Tet faded from view and Will returned to Saigon, he resumed his daily routine. A new feature had been added to it, increasing the surreal nature of his experience.

He had grown up in a home where he had taken music—good music—for granted. It was church music, most of it, but his mother also played records of later classical music: Gershwin, Franck, piano music of Ravel and Debussy.

But mostly, the music he knew best was organ music from his mother's playing in church. Bach preludes, the Messiah arias set to organ accompaniment and the hymns from the Methodist Hymnal. For more than fifteen years, until he left for college, he sat in church next to his father, his brother, and his sisters with his mother presiding at the organ in front of them. When he was young, he rarely listened to sermons or anything else the minister said, since it was so obvious that his mother was in charge. She decided when people would stand up, sit down, and when they would sing.

At home, before church, there was a program of music that came on from Salt Lake City that his mother listened to faithfully. Many years later, he sat with his sister in the auditorium watching one of the broadcasts being recorded, filled with the memories of the announcers' stately cadences and the soaring music sung by a massive choir.

Then, at college, he learned that the world was divided into people who listened to classical music and those who didn't. Most of his classmates tolerated the required musical segments of their "History of Civilization" courses, while he recognized familiar melodies and harmonies in the assigned material.

Once in Vietnam, Will soon discovered that there was a USIA center three blocks away from his office at JUSPAO. He could walk over there at noon, check out one of the many tapes that seemed totally unused, put on decent headphones, and spend an hour listening to excellent music. He explored composers he hadn't known before, Poulenc, Elgar, Fauré, and others, thankful to his fellow taxpayers' support for the USIA library, while adding further to his vague sense of guilt about his insulation from the reality of the war.

In near-total contrast, however, was the music played by the Seabees in their room at the BEQ. The Seabees kept Will current with the music back home. Somehow his roommates had gotten hold of tapes with all the latest hit songs, and the room was filled with the bizarre sounds of the Beatles, the Doors, the Jefferson Airplane, the Supremes—all of the tones of the summer of love, all nearly the exact opposite of the summer of 1967 in Southeast Asia.

The Doors were the Seabees' favorite, played over and over at ear-shattering volume. "Strange Days" was the one song that became, for the rest of his life, music from the war zone for Will, music from the strange days he and a half million other Americans were living.

Through Weinstein, Will gradually met several of the other reporters, who mixed their interest in his political background with their curiosity about his status as an embassy insider. Will had been careful from the first to answer vaguely and downplay his role—which wasn't difficult—whenever someone asked him for anything that sounded like inside information. But he still routinely got probing questions from the reporters he had gotten to know.

"So Will, what's happening over there in the embassy?"

"Will, any hot stories we should be working on?"

"Tell me what you really do over there, Will, old buddy."

He became fairly skilled at diverting their curiosity and ignoring their prompts, though there were a few that were more subtle, and with those he had to watch himself. They would ask about his work with the Vietnamese papers, and express interest in the shifts in public and press opinion that he was tracking. They would discuss these, but then change the subject, and after a while, Will realized that they were cultivating him as a longer-term prospect, rather than trying to milk him for what he knew that might be immediately useful.

A few times, in conversations with reporters, he caught himself out on the edge of revealing information that he knew would fuel a controversial story.

Will had mentioned a USAID report on civilian casualties when Congressman Bronstein had been in town, and he had decided to look into the status of the report to see if it had been issued. He made inquiries of the press liaison to USAID, and was told, with some irritation on the part of the woman who was handling that role, that the report was "highly confidential" and unlikely to be released until it had gone through "DC clearance." Will assumed this meant people in State were reviewing it, concerned that it might counter the Army's claims that civilian casualties were kept to a minimum.

March was a full month, both in Vietnam and in the US. Within weeks, McNamara had resigned, Johnson had stepped down, and the commanders were turning over as well. And then Will began to hear some of the informal reports about what had happened at a place called My Lai.

One of the reporters worked for a left-wing magazine that Will had read while he was working in politics in California. The reporter, Harry Dodson, was a quiet, intense man in his late forties. Will had read his articles in Sacramento and knew that he was unrelenting in digging out the details of a story. He had broken two stories about payola scandals in the state legislature that had led to the conviction of one state assemblyman and the defeat of another.

One afternoon Will had taken a break and was having coffee with Dodson. After a casual conversation about the war, the reporter said, "I know you can't talk about this, Will, but there's a story going around about something that happened at a place called My Lai. Just tell me, if you can, if you've heard anything about this.

Carefully, Will answered, "I heard some talk about it, yes. But that's all."

Dodson said, "This could be the worst thing that our troops have been caught doing here. Some of the helicopter pilots who evacuated civilians reported it to their higher command, and the coverup is off and running." He was silent, watching the traffic in the plaza. Then he said, quietly but with great heat, "We heard that children were killed, and that some of those killings were totally avoidable. The deliberate killing of children in war is a war crime. This is going to be huge when it breaks."

Will was silent, both because he was not sure of the details and because he wanted no part of the sourcing on Dodson's story. But he was glad he had been marginally helpful to Bronstein when he was in Vietnam, and wondered if Yvonne was going to get involved in digging out the story.

Then he asked Dodson "Have you followed the USAID review of civilian casualties? Seems to be stuck in State somewhere."

Dodson gave him a sharp look. "I heard they were still working on it. Not ready for publication. But if it's in State already, the report is done."

Will knew that was a question, and he knew he was on the edge. "That's what I understood."

Dodson was quiet, then changed the subject. A year later, when the My Lai reporting was everywhere, Dodson was the only reporter to link it to the report in State—which remained buried. Will wondered if he had anything to do with that link, but by that time Dodson had returned to the U.S. and was covering State directly, so he could have gotten the lead from some other source. The State part of the story was not the lead, but it confirmed the breadth of the coverup efforts, and Dodson's publication continued running a series of reports titled "Other My Lais?"

There was one reporter, however, whom Will spent more time with than any other. Lee Bernard was a reporter from the *Boston Globe* whom Will had met early in his time at JUSPAO. Bernard was the only one who seemed to realize how valuable it could be to watch the trends in the Vietnamese press, as Will did regularly. He often asked Will about the shifts in public and press opinion that he was monitoring, and did a few stories based on leads Will had given him, always sourcing them to the actual stories or editorials in the local papers.

Will was having dinner with Bernard one evening, and asked him what he thought about the embassy's relations with the press. "What does it look like from your side?" he asked Bernard.

Bernard said "Early in my career with the *Globe*, a veteran reporter took me aside and told me what he called 'the rule of four responses.' His idea was that there were four things that could happen when you are interviewing someone: they could tell you they didn't know the answer, they could make clear that they knew but wouldn't tell you, they could lie to you, or they could more or less tell you the truth. His point was that all four of them were stories worth writing—the evasions and the lies were just as much of a story as the truth."

He paused and watched the waiter bring their meal, then resumed. "It seems to me that Z and the rest of them know more about what is going wrong than they feel they can tell us, and so they either evade or shade the truth. Sometimes we have enough sources to know when that's happening, and that then creates a base of skepticism that we use as a filter even when they may be telling us the truth. It's not a very healthy relationship right now.

"Some of them will go off the record in criticizing the local government, and hope we'll print the criticism as a way of putting pressure on Kieu and the rest of them. We don't mind being used that way if there's a real story behind the criticism—and there often is. When the local troops aren't fighting or a provincial commander has made a deal with the VC or is stealing stuff—that's a story. But the bottom line is that the US is stuck with these guys unless the Ambassador and the military are able to stand up to them in public. Right now, I don't see that happening. Meanwhile, our troops are doing 95% of the fighting so they get the blame when somebody drops a bomb in the wrong place or sets fire to the wrong village. So we write the story about our destroying the village when the real story is where the hell were the local troops when that village was being used as a base for the VC? The real story is what didn't happen, but most of the time we write about what did happen—and it's almost always about US troops and not the AWOL South Vietnamese troops." He laughed. "Hard to write a headline that says 'What Didn't Happen Today.'"

Will was mostly quiet and listened, knowing that Bernard had learned more about the real war than he had. He knew he was getting a postgraduate course in media relations and wondered how he was going to reconcile what he was doing in the embassy with what he was learning about the real war.

George Diver had suggested Will look up a friend of his who was working for an American company that did some kind of mapping work for the embassy. The friend, Ernie Scott, was also from California, and so Will gave him a call and arranged to meet him for lunch.

Scott was a burly, tall man in his mid-thirties with a high forehead and a ready smile. He greeted Will and they traded California geography and *where have you lived* stories. Then Ernie leaned forward and asked "How much did George tell you about my work?"

"Not much—he just said you work for a company that does mapping."

"That's right, We do aerial surveys for the embassy, trying to find out where the vegetation and the hills provide cover for the troops from the North that are infiltrating down." He was quiet, watching Will. "I've read some of the press summaries you do. Pretty useful overview of where the locals are, even with the censorship they get."

"Thanks." Then Will began adding things up. If Scott had access to his internal press summaries, he was more than a contractor. Embassy documents were kept inside the official agencies fairly tightly. Will wondered if Scott was CIA, but he had learned enough to know that wasn't a question you asked.

"How would you summarize what you've read about public opinion so far?" Scott asked lightly, but Will still felt he was getting some kind of test. He decided to play it straight for the time being.

"My sense, just from the newspapers we get, is that the press can't really say what they feel about us being here or about their own government. There's a lot of indirect criticism, though. They'll say things like traffic has gotten worse or talk about security concerns in some province. But it's rarely direct. And when it is, it looks to me as though the government has pushed them to say it. I have no idea how widely the papers are read, but I know some of them are totally sponsored and funded by the government."

"What about the Buddhists?" Scott was pressing now.

"There are one or two papers that seem tied into the Buddhists, and they're more likely to talk about the need for negotiations. But most of the others have been very critical of the demonstrations. They'll talk about the need for national unity, which seems like some kind of code word for no open dissent."

"Do they talk about the performance of their own army or the militias?

"Never. There have been a few incidents of South Vietnamese army collapses that got to be a big deal in the five o'clock fo…uh, briefings, and I watched for those stories in the local press, but there was nothing."

Scott was silent, turning partly away from Will to look at the diners in the restaurant. "Will, you're very observant. You'll find often that what isn't in the paper—theirs or ours—is often the most important thing that happens. Watching for what isn't there can be as important as tracking what is visible."

Then he laughed. "I don't mean for this to sound like a seminar, but you've picked up some good stuff and I wanted to make sure you knew how important it was to watch for those kinds of things in the future."

Will said, "Thanks," as he heard the echo of what Lee Bernard had said about what didn't happen sometimes being the most important thing that happened. His mind raced to figure out why Scott was spending the time with him. *Maybe my job really does matter*, he thought.

Will was aware of the "spook side of the war," as George Diver had once called it, but the invisibility of the intelligence function made it hard for him to understand it. Before his session with Scott, he had met people who described their role as "assigned to the embassy," but who artfully changed the subject if you pressed them for details on what they actually did. The spooks ranged from the real snake-eaters who worked deep into the jungle and along the borders on the infiltration routes, to the green-eye shade auditor types who counted secret numbers over and over until they made sense—or seemed to. As fascinating as some of their exploits were when retold second-hand, Will never felt he had a grasp on how much they mattered. But everyone he talked to agreed that their numbers were increasing, so someone with budget authority obviously believed that they mattered a lot.

Will had put in for a trip to the provincial capital where George Diver was stationed, and to his surprise, it was approved. Diver had sent a request for Will to come review progress in pacification efforts in his province, and Will assumed that had helped get the signoff.

After riding a bus from the embassy out to the airport, Will was routed to a supply flight that loaded up with food and some farming equipment, and they took off. It was Will's first leisurely view of Vietnam from the air, since he had been on helicopters during his post-Tet tour. He was amazed at how quickly outside the city the landscape became green field after green field. It was fall, and the rice crop had just been harvested, so the fields were emptier than they would be a few months later during planting season.

After the dust and concrete of the city, Will was enthralled by the shades of green unfolding beneath him. The green of the rice paddies was different from the green of the palms, which was different in turn from the green of the rubber trees he saw in neatly aligned plantations. He remembered the greens of the pines and the green grasses of the savannah regions of the country that he had seen when he traveled to the central part of the country. He wondered idly *So why don't they call this place Greenland?*

The flight followed the Mekong River for most of the route, with its bends and turns clearly in view. As he looked out the window of the plane, he could see Navy gunboats zipping along the river, dodging in and out of the flow of smaller motorized fishing boats and sampans.

He dozed off and awoke to a strong thump. He was one of only four passengers, and the pilot came out and apologized for the landing. "They take us down fast—we took a few rounds from the rebels last week so we move quickly now. Knocked a hole or two in the wing but nothing vital." Will wondered what the game plan was if something "vital" got hit while they were still in flight, but didn't ask.

George Diver was waiting in the small hangar that served as the airport. He came over and gave Will a massive handshake, patting him on the back and picking up his softside case.

"Will, old pal, glad you could make it. We've killed the fatted calf and we're going to show you the town."

And he did, using his jeep to give Will a tour of the province office George shared with his Vietnamese counterpart, the "downtown" area of the city, and the Vietnamese militia base just outside of town.

They settled in at a riverside restaurant/bar with a magnificent view of the river, which was a quarter of a mile across at that point. Several of the local militia were in the restaurant, but Will and Diver had the upstairs patio with the river view to themselves.

The river was extraordinary, broad, dirty brown, with sampans and a few fishing boats in view. Will had read the history of the river in the USIA library, learning that it flowed all the way from the Tibetan highlands through China, Burma, Laos, Thailand, Cambodia, and Vietnam. The Mekong Delta began far up the river in Cambodia, and was the basis for the rice-growing culture of the southern provinces of Vietnam.

Diver began with an elaborate explanation of the local beer, known as "33" and rumored to be germ-free due to large components of formaldehyde included in the brewing process. He assured Will, with a broad smile, that "it's almost guaranteed to kill most of the rats that get into the brewing vats."

Will tried to mask his disgust but Diver got the stricken look he was hoping for, and laughed loudly and at length. "Just fooling with you, soldier. They haven't found any rats for at least a year now."

After more of the beer than Will intended to drink and some "appetizers" that Diver simply dismissed with a curt "don't ask" when Will asked what they were made of, Diver was joined by two officers from the local Special Forces base. Expansive as always, Diver introduced them as "Jackson from West Point and McWilliams from Houston. Two finer specimens of the U.S. Army you will never meet, Will."

Then he introduced Will as a "wheeler dealer California politician who knows everybody who is anybody in Sacramento. He decided he wanted to see what the war was all about."

With a smile, Jackson said, "So you got drafted.?"

"Yes, sir."

Diver said, "We're informal here, Will. Rank stops at the door when I'm buying the beer."

Diver and Jackson began idly talking about a raid on the province capital that had happened after Tet, and Will found himself trying to follow the conversation, realizing after a few minutes that they were talking about a skirmish that had taken place in the street out in front of the restaurant where they were drinking. Apparently the VC and NVA units had suffered major casualties, but the South Vietnamese militia had mostly checked out of the fighting and the raid was repulsed by Army helicopters brought in from the adjacent province, where there was a much larger Army base.

Jackson turned to Will, as the conversation wound down and said "How are you enjoying the tail duty, Will?" His tone was friendly, but with an edge.

Diver quickly said, "Go easy on the boy, Captain. As they say in the rodeos back home, 'he came a long way and he paid his own entry fee.'"

Will asked "Tail duty? What's that mean?"

"In the army, we talk about the teeth and the tail. The teeth is where they do the fighting and the tail is the backup."

Will had recently learned a new phrase, which he threw into the conversation. "So the tail is the remfs?"

"Right, rear echelon mother-fuckers. No disrespect intended to present company."

Will said, "No, I understand. It must be frustrating knowing there are six or seven of us to every one of you. Big army, I guess."

"Very big army. Lots of backup." Then, seeming bored, Jackson asked "George tells me you read all the Vietnamese papers for the embassy. What do they say about us—about the mission here?"

"They're censored, so none of it's direct. But there are occasional references to troops getting out of control in the cities, and civilian casualties."

McWilliams spoke up for the first time, "That'll happen when the enemy hides behind the civilians. and the civilians don't have the sense to get out of the way."

Jackson frowned and said, "Yeah, but every time we shoot up a village we recruit more VC. Body count looks great on paper back in Saigon, but it sure doesn't help us much out here when the bodies are mostly the civilians left behind when the men from the village are out laying ambushes."

Then he asked "Will, you ever read any Bernard Fall?"

Unsure whether it was a test or an honest question, and again grateful for the USIA library, Will said, "He wrote about the French and the history before we got here? The underlying causes of the insurgency? Yeah. Pretty powerful stuff."

Diver chimed in, "Nobody got closer to the truth about the French in Indochina than Fall. Nobody."

Jackson asked, "You work with our press? How do they see all this?"

McWilliams scoffed as he swigged his beer. "Bunch of defeatist wimps. No idea what's going on out here."

Will answered, "I wouldn't call them defeatist. But they sure don't believe what we're feeding them about body count and the brave Vietnamese army. They seem very skeptical about the Vietnamese leadership."

Jackson frowned. "They've got that part right. Those clowns couldn't govern a cockfight. Half of them have already cut their deals with the VC and the other half have already picked out their villas in the south of France when the North comes down to take over."

Will decided to press harder. "So how does it get better? Or does it?"

Again, McWilliams had a quick response. "When they let us go into the sanctuaries where these bastards are hiding out and bomb the shit out of them. They're holed up in big underground bases across the line in Cambodia, and we know where they are. We go over there when they let us, but we've never gone in with enough troops or air power to make a difference."

Jackson shook his head. "I doubt that. The amount of supplies coming down the trail from the North are more than enough to keep these guys fed with enough ammo to make our lives miserable. We'd cut it off for a few weeks and it would just start up again. The way I read the papers back home, these guys have a lot more time than we do. Tet was a disaster back home, even though we wiped them out when they came out of cover."

He looked at Will, and said, sadly, "I don't really know how it gets better, to tell you the truth. We're losing a lot of guys, and I'm not sure why any more. We're asking them to go out on patrols night after night, and I don't know what we're getting out of it."

He went on. "The ones I really feel sorry for are the Vietnamese kids. We taught some of them to play a half-assed form of football, and they loved it. After we got past the *gimme gum* stage, they began to talk to us and we got some of our translators to help us out. Most of those kids don't go to any kind of school. They go to work as soon as they can lift a jug of water. Out in the fields all day long, getting by all day on less than one of our kids would eat for a snack. It's pretty sad when you see how little they have to look forward to out here."

Diver looked up and saw another civilian entering the balcony section of the restaurant. "Hey, it's Hal Perloff, the scourge of USAID. Hal, come meet my friend Specialist 4 Putnam from California. He's out here soaking up all the local color he can get before he has to go back to Saigon and hide out in the embassy."

"Hey, George, guys." Perloff was a tall, somewhat hefty man in jeans and a sweatshirt. "Sorry about my outfit. We've been working on a well over in Dak To, and it got a little mucky."

Diver laughed and said, "Hal likes to work with the local folks. Hal, tell Will here how you got roped into this sorry work."

Hal stopped smiling and said "No one wants to hear that story, George, Makes me sound naïve and idealistic."

"Hell, Hall, we're all naïve and idealistic or we wouldn't be here. Tell the damn story."

So Perloff explained, to Will's surprise, how he had gone from the Peace Corps immediately after graduate school into USAID. "It seemed at the time like an extension of what I was doing in Guatemala. Community development, working with the locals, nation-building, all that good 60's stuff that came in with Kennedy. Who knew they would be shooting at us? So we went off to Pearl Harbor to learn Vietnamese and get ready to reshape history. Which turned out to be digging wells and dodging bullets."

Will noticed that as Perloff and Diver continued to discuss the war in their province, Jackson had gradually been drinking more and talking less. Then he straightened up in his chair and said, "Maybe we should have an Army Little Big Horn award."

Diver said "Huh? Explain."

"Yeah. Awarded annually to recognize decisions as bad as George Armstrong Custer's defeat in 1876 at the Little Big Horn. The inscription could be 'For military leadership in sending too few troops with too little support to too many places they didn't need to be.'"

McWilliams scoffed and said "Too many contenders to decide who wins."

As the USAID and military men continued trading stories, Will could tell that they worked closely together—at least in this province. Both sets of men had obvious admiration for the others, although they clearly came at their work from different angles. The conversation continued, and the beer and the river kept flowing freely.

Later that night, Will ended up as drunk as he'd ever been, aided only briefly by massive, rapid, and involuntary off-loading of most the beer he'd drunk.

Back in Saigon, Will returned to his newspaper summaries, feeling he had learned more on the trip to see Diver and his crew than he could ever learn in the embassy. Then he heard that the Vice President had been scheduled to visit the embassy and some of the military bases on a trip to Vietnam, and he checked to see when he was going to be briefing the press.

Vice President Stratton had been called the "Happy Warrior" during his unsuccessful campaign for the Presidency in 1960. He was a naturally ebullient politician, with the flat tones of the upper Midwest, a loyal defender of the President's war policies despite his earlier links to the liberal wing of the Democratic party. As Will listened to him tell about the "excellent visits I had with our troops and the Vietnamese troops," Will wondered where he had been taken.

Finally, the Vice President wound up his remarks, saying "I know you will agree with me when I say I have been proud to see how well we are doing on our great adventure here in Southeast Asia."

Our great adventure, Will thought as he walked back to his office. *That's one way of describing it, I guess.*

Will found himself enjoying the time with Thuy more and more. They met two or three times a week at the apartment he shared, having arranged it with an innocuous message he would leave for her at her JUSPAO desk. She usually brought food she had picked up at a nearby restaurant, and Will had adjusted his tastes to most kinds of Vietnamese food, with some major exceptions, especially meat dishes whose origins were obscure.

The apartment was small, sparsely furnished with second and third-hand furniture, but with a decent shower and bathtub. One of its prior occupants had left on the room's walls several pen and ink drawings of river scenes sketched with a few broad strokes, which Will studied carefully, trying to understand how the artist had been able to convey so much with so few lines. From time to time the noise of the city filtered up through the windows, but they were up three stories, and the din was usually muted.

Thuy insisted on spending some of their time together in what she called "cultural lessons" and practicing Will's Vietnamese, which was still mostly incomprehensible to anyone but her.

One night after a language lesson, Thuy was lying on her stomach on the bed, fresh from her bath, her head resting on her arms and her lovely rear and its perfect curves on innocent display.

Will said, "I wish to speak French rather than Vietnamese. Your *derrière* inspires me. *Derrière*—a fine word hearkening back to the French influence on your culture. *Vous avez un derrière classique. J'aime votre derrière, ma chère.*"

"Do you wish to kiss my *derrière*, Will?" she said, smiling.

Will started laughing so hard he almost fell out of bed.

"Why is that funny?"

"Because the phrase 'kiss my ass' is very rude in American slang. But in your case, your perfectly curvaceous, newly washed *derrière* is for me an object of great desire, rather than rude talk."

So they stopped talking for a while, allowing other sounds and movements to take over their inter-cultural communication.

After, Will asked her, "Tell me about your parents."

"They are simple people. My parents work in the rice fields outside our village during the growing seasons. My mother has an old sewing machine that she uses to make and repair clothes for some of the people in the village.

"My father insisted that my brother and I both go on past the elementary school that most of the children in the village attend. My mother used some of her sewing money to send us to what you call high school in Thanh Do. I had a teacher who thought my work was good enough to attend the Catholic university, and I was able to pass the English tests so I could take some of my classes in English. Others I took in French."

"Did you enjoy it?"

"Oh, yes. I could read as much as I wanted. The work was not difficult and I read many books from the library while I was there."

She seemed slightly embarrassed, and added, "I had a boyfriend while I was in university, but he was from a wealthy family and he wanted to be with many girls."

"I am not wealthy, Thuy, and I want only to be with you. I'm glad you studied so much English. My French is execrable," he deliberately used a word that was the same in English and French. "And you know how bad my Vietnamese is."

Then he asked, "Where is your brother?"

Her manner changed, and she spoke quietly, looking away from Will. "We do not see him very often. He works far from home most of the time."

"What does he do?"

She was quiet for a long time. Then, slowly, she said, "He is with the NLF. No one here at JUSPAO knows that or I would lose my job. You won't tell anyone, will you?"

Will wondered what level of infraction he would be guilty of if he said nothing. Then he realized that no one had ever told him, nor had he ever read anything, about any responsibility to scour the family backgrounds of embassy employees. In a country where loyalties were divided as deeply as they were in South Vietnam, Will assumed that few of the embassy's employees were 100% free of any entanglements with the North or the NLF.

So he lightly answered Thuy, "No, I don't see any reason to tell anyone."

"Thank you." She added, "We really haven't seen him for over a year, and I have no idea where he is now."

She smiled, wanting to change the subject. "Tell me about your parents."

"My father is a high school teacher. He was in the Army Air Force in World War II, and then was part of the occupation in Japan. My mother stayed home with my sisters and me, and now she teaches music. They are good parents, they were strict about our education, but they took us on camping trips and we traveled around California to visit our relatives."

"What is 'occupation?'"

"That's when our troops were in Japan after the war was over and we basically ran the government."

"Like you do here?"

Her tone was innocent, but Will saw a twinkle of teasing. He said, "No, not really the same. Here you have your own government." Then he despaired of explaining the exact differences, and it was his turn to change the subject.

"If you hadn't gone to work for the embassy, what would you have done after university?"

"I would probably have stayed and worked at the university. Maybe our government, if I could find someone who would sponsor me."

"Are women able to get promoted in those kinds of jobs or do they stay at low levels?"

"Oh yes, women have many important jobs." She went on to point out the powerful role played by the wife of the past and current Vietnamese Presidents, and then, with considerably more pride, the historical importance of women in Vietnamese history. She told Will of the role of the Trung sisters, after whom one of the main streets in Saigon was named. The sisters had led a rebellion against China two thousand years ago, and were national heroines. One of the sisters was "queen" of a section of North Vietnam for a time.

Will recalled that most of the translators in the embassy were women, and even allowing for American preferences for pretty young Vietnamese women, most were very good at their jobs.

Thuy asked him, "Don't you have women like that in your country—national heroes?"

He stumbled, trying to get out some names. "Uh, sure. Betsy Ross, the suffragettes, uh, Sojourner Truth and others who fought to free the slaves."

"But no queens or presidents?"

"Well, we never had a queen. And not yet a president."

Thuy smiled, and said, "Well, maybe one day. Maybe we could come and show you how to do it." Then she laughed, her small, sweet, tinkling laugh that Will had learned to love.

The biggest drawback to their relationship was how much they were isolated with each other. Most of Thuy's friends worked outside the embassy, and few had her English fluency, which made conversation difficult. They had met some of her friends for lunch a few times, but Will sat struggling to catch the few words of Vietnamese that he understood, feeling at times as though he was surrounded by a flock of lovely, twittering birds. The scenery was marvelous, but the sound effects were very frustrating.

Several of the Americans in the embassy were involved with Vietnamese women, but Will quickly found that the relationships were mostly arrangements of physical convenience. The enlisted men he had gotten to know from the BEQ would find the depth of his affection for Thuy hard to understand. Most of them had bar girls they were "close to," and he knew they would inevitably see Thuy in that light.

A few of George Diver's friends in the civilian mission had formed much healthier bonds with professional women or women they had met in their roles in the provinces, but it was difficult to connect with those civilians.

Yet in their first months together, being with each other was enough for each of them. Will's enjoyed Thuy's usually cheerful nature and her cultural "lessons," and Thuy in turn seemed to soak up as much second-hand American life as she could absorb from Will.

Thuy asked him many variations of the question, "What is your culture, Will?" Will was still struggling to give her a decent answer. He also knew that she was prodding him to talk about America because she wanted so much to go there. And he wasn't ready for that conversation.

"First let me tell you what I think about your culture. And then you tell me if I'm wrong.

"Your culture involves agriculture, and the importance of the river, and the mountains. You are much closer to your family, and to your grandparents and ancestors, than in most American families. Family rituals—weddings and funerals—are very important. In America, we sometimes use those rituals as part of our" –he struggled for the phrase from his college economics class— "our 'conspicuous consumption.' We show off—we show how much money we have. You do that here, but bragging is much less a part of Vietnamese culture."

He smiled, and traced the outline of her perfectly flat stomach. "And very few of you are obese. You are willowy, lithe, and lean."

"These words all mean skinny?"

He laughed, "They mean good-skinny, not fat, like some of our twenty-year sergeants and officers. And like many more back home."

One night Will found himself at an embassy party with some of the upwardly mobile embassy staff, diplomatic comers, some of whom he had known in classes ahead of him in graduate school, others who had moved in and out of California politics and universities. A sizable cross-section of the media heavies were also there, and Will reminded himself as he began drinking that he should be careful what he said to both groups. Will had been at another party where a very senior correspondent had ended up completely under the bed, passed out and snoring loudly.

He had gotten to know the senior reporters in both the *New York Times* and *Washington Post* bureaus, serious, hard-drinking reporters with national reputations and wide readership. They were friendly, having heard enough of his story to know that he had lived in a political world, and sensitive, most of the time, to his inability to tell them useful inside information—both because he was constrained by his role and because he really had little of what they wanted.

The drinking and the music intensified, and Will found himself in conversation with a senior FSO, Steve Jamison, who had graduated from Will's college a few years ahead of him.

"Always great to see a fellow Tiger out here, Will. How you doing?"

"Doing fine, Steve."

"Heard you were helping the Ambassador out a bit."

"Yes. Small stuff, a speech here and there."

"He's quite a guy. Wasn't sure about him, but that New England reserve helps with the locals sometimes, compared to some of the jumping up and down that we've had in the past."

"I suppose so."

"I'd pay to get into those sessions with Kieu and Nguyen Lo. This flinty old Vermonter and those wily snakes who are pretending to run the government. They think he's the naïve American and then he does what the New Englanders did to the Pequots—just negotiates them out of their shoes."

He looked at Will, and asked point-blank: "So are you going to sign up with the Foreign Service when you get out?"

The question surprised Will. "Uh, haven't thought about it much. Thinking more about politics, actually."

"Well, that's an option, I guess. But think about going FSO. You've had a hell of an experience out here, inside the embassy and all. It would move you ahead of some of the rest of the junior FSOs. It's not a bad life, travel, decent pay and benefits, chance to serve your country. Someday, who knows—you could end up an Ambassador yourself."

Will laughed. "Right. From the specialist 4 ranks of the enlisted man's army to the top rung in the Foreign Service."

Jamison smiled. "Not the craziest idea you'll hear, Will. And politics can be pretty savage."

"Believe me, I have a pretty good idea of that already."

"Yes, I heard they went after you. Stupid. But that's politics—you're always at the mercy of the biggest asshole in the game."

Will thought about the conversation as he rode back to the BEQ in a taxicab. He had thought about an international career before the political bug bit him. But for the moment, it seemed much more distant than the idea of going back to California and taking his shot at politics.

As part of his effort to understand the news translations better, Will had asked to be able to sit in on non-classified, lower-level meetings between Vietnamese agencies and embassy staff. He was told he could do so, but with the understanding that he was only to listen and not to speak. He agreed.

After attending a dozen or so of these meetings, Will had formulated his own perspective on US-Vietnamese interactions. The first thing he observed was that the Vietnamese were not monolithic. There were those who smiled and nodded and then went back and did whatever they wanted as long as the American funding kept flowing. Then there were those who frowned and quickly pointed out that American wishes were trespassing on national sovereignty.

A few, very few, in Will's experience, welcomed American expertise and cash when it was a means of improving their agency's performance— and knew where to draw the line and reject advice from eager-beaver State and USAID advisors who were off-base. Will witnessed one confrontation with USAID agricultural officials and a Vietnamese agency head who was trying to explain why rice grown in Louisiana and the Central Valley of California was not a substitute for rice grown in Southeast Asia. The Vietnamese official had patiently pointed out the differences in weight, color, and taste, but the USAID reps kept pressing for several thousand tons to be delivered. Finally, the Vietnamese official snapped, and stood up from the table, saying, "To us, it tastes like crap!"

In another set of meetings discussing agricultural assistance, the agenda was a review of falling rice production. The US military representatives patiently explained that the decline was due to banditry by the VC, while the USAID officials explained it as a result of villagers abandoning free-fire zones. The two sides could not agree, and the Vietnamese officials in the meeting seemed reluctant to alienate either side, so they mostly talked about the decline without addressing its causes.

After the briefing, Will went over and talked to one of the junior USAID staff. He introduced himself, explained that he did the weekly press summary, and asked if there was any study of the correlation between free-fire zones and rice production that supported the USAID claim.

In response, the USAID staffer pulled out some maps that superimposed free-fire zones and the percentage of rice production increases or decreases in the last harvest. As Will studied the map, the connection was clear— production had dropped in areas within or adjacent to free-fire zones. It was especially pronounced in the villages in the Delta.

"Where did you get these maps?"

The staffer looked around, making sure that no one was listening. Most of the rest of the participants in the meeting had filed out of the room, and he said to Will, "We asked the CIA branch chief for them." He went on. "We couldn't use them in the meeting because we're not supposed to have them."

Will had read an article in graduate school about what one theorist had called "Failure by Fragmentation," explaining how and why agencies in the US refused to work with each other. He assumed the tendency was either contagious or universal.

Will wanted to understand the country, and he wanted to understand Thuy. For a time, he believed that the first would follow the second, until he realized that Thuy was her own person, living in her own culture but already so marked by her time in the American military machine's embrace that she had become a hybrid of sorts. She was Vietnamese in all respects, but with a layer of American traits covering some of the deeper culture that had shaped her life.

Yet she had been a great guide into the inner depths of Vietnamese life, patiently explaining the foods, families, and history of her country. In his conversations with some of the embassy staff, Will began to feel that he had penetrated to levels deeper than some of the staff who had supposedly taken courses in Vietnamese culture. He often thought of the phrase he had first heard from Thuy—"the emperor's rule stops at the village gate"—as an explanation of popular disengagement from the South Vietnamese government.

Thuy had also helped him see how crass some forms of American behavior appeared to the Vietnamese. She responded with misdirection and polite ignoring to the crude overtures which were inevitable in a city filled with armed teenagers out of their element. He became newly sensitive to American bluntness in probing the personal recesses of the lives of friends and colleagues. He listened carefully to Thuy's interpretations of the nuances of the Vietnamese press as they revealed and concealed what was really happening in the tangled politics of her country.

She was at times child-like, asking him to describe the different cereals in American supermarkets—a fascination somehow imported by a cousin who had been to the U.S. And then, in her silences, she seemed ageless and distant, refusing to answer him sometimes when he asked her what she thought would happen in the war. Will wondered at those times how deep her sympathies with the North Vietnamese really ran, knowing it was impossible to expect that she had any respect for the clowns and thieves running her government, but unsure what she thought of the alternatives.

Gradually, in things she said and didn't say, he began to suspect that she was hoping to leave with him when he rotated home. He stopped talking about it, which made it worse as the weeks shortened and his departure drew near.

Finally the day came when she asked him, after a languorous time of love-making, "Will, are you going to take me with you when you go home?"

His pause was the answer, and she knew it. Then he blurted out, "It's too soon to talk about that." And then, knowing that was the wrong thing to say, he said a worse thing: "You really wouldn't like it there."

She just looked at him, silent. Then she slowly got out of bed, got dressed, and left. Will had no idea what to say, and simply let his ineptitude and ego work their damage.

Ernie Scott had called Will, having remembered his departure date from their first meeting. "You need an out-country debriefing, Specialist," he had said on the phone in setting up a farewell dinner.

They met at the Continental Hotel, Scott having suggested that Will needed to "get ready for American food with a serious steak."

After greetings and updates, Scott asked Will "What are you going to do next?"

"I want to run for office."

"Really? You seem…maybe a bit too interior for that kind of life."

"Interior?"

"Yeah. You're very self-contained, Will. You know who you are—much better than most kids in their mid-20s, in my experience. That's a compliment, kid. But politics—all that glad-handing and asking people for money and making sleazy deals. You sure that's what you want to do? Forgive me, pal, you don't seem like an outgoing, glad-handing kind of guy. Maybe you're supposed to be the greasy eminence, the guy behind the throne? Or the Sorenson, the idea guy?"

"Maybe. But the guy calling the shots is the guy who got elected. I think I want to try that. It's how you fix things, seems to me."

"Well, I grant you, it'd be great if there were a few more non-assholes in politics."

Will laughed and said, "There's my slogan: Vote for the Non-Asshole."

Scott said, "Great slogan. Tough to fit on a bumper sticker, though."

Then he looked serious. "Will, you know that story about the blind men and the elephant? Kid, you only saw one toenail on the elephant's left rear foot. But that's part of the story, so go tell your story. People need to hear what is happening here, and you saw a lot more than most of your generation who were out in the boonies or those at home with deferments."

Then he asked Will, "Did you ever see the movie *The Music Man?*"

"Yeah. Lots of singing, Shirley Jones. Good movie."

"My favorite part is where the salesmen—and most Americans are salesmen, Will, just ask Arthur Miller—the salesmen are singing a sort of patter song, and the refrain is *You gotta know the territory.* That is one of our worst handicaps over here, kid. We don't know the territory. There is something about us that makes us impose an American template on everything we see when we land in another part of the world. Our own territory was so vast and so totally overcome by the devastation that we brought along with the westward push, we never had to learn about another culture or worldview. You come into a foreign land, you overwhelm the natives, and then you start growing and building things. What's to learn?"

He looked out at the traffic in the night, and then said, "We may know where to drop the ordinance, but we don't know diddly about where the people live. And that costs us. That will always cost us. My agency tries to get US personnel to understand other places and local cultures—but it's a hard sell."

Will repeated the phrase, trying to understand it. "You gotta know the territory."

"Yeah. Don't forget that, Will."

"I won't."

Scott went on, chuckling now. "I suppose you've heard people talk about the teeth and the tail of the army, kid?"

"Yeah, I've heard that."

"Well, I've come to think the anatomy needs to be a little more precise. People back here in Saigon are the tail, all right. But some of them live just under the tail."

Will laughed. "The asshole, you mean?"

"Exactly."

Scott wished Will the best and suggested he look up a friend of Scott's named Sam Leonard who was a reporter Scott had gotten to know in Los Angeles. Will promised that he would.

It took forty-five years, but he finally did.

Will had received a short note from Thuy asking him to get to the apartment as quickly as he could after work because she needed to talk to him. He assumed that her anger at his unwillingness to take her back with him had worn off.

When he go to the apartment, she began speaking rapidly. "Will, I've heard the most horrible story, and I need you to tell me what to do about it." She was more disturbed than he had ever seen her, her hands shaking and her voice strained.

"Calm down, Thuy. What is it?"

She explained that a friend of hers—she wouldn't tell him who it was—had been doing some volunteer work with an orphanage north of the capital, Maison d'Enfants. The friend had accidentally come across some records of a special building set apart from the rest of the orphanage where older children, both boys and girls, were housed. When she looked at the records, it appeared that some of the children were being kept in the separate quarters prior to being sold into prostitution.

"Will, I couldn't believe her at first. But she said there were…there were priests involved, and what she called high officials in your army and our government!"

Will frowned and said "That's impossible. No one in either the Church or the army would be involved in anything that has to do with prostitution or taking advantage of children."

Thuy said, "Will, this is someone I have known for a long time, someone who is very careful about her life and her family. She did not make this up, and she told me she had details that she had copied and hidden in a place where no one could find them."

"All right. I'll ask around the USAID offices that fund some of these programs and see what they know."

"Please be very careful. She told me there is a lot of money involved and some very dangerous people. I don't want anyone to know she has discovered this—they might try to do something to her."

"I'll be careful, I promise."

Will's next step, after thinking about it, was to meet with one of the USAID officials in the embassy who was in charge of development assistance. He said it was for a story he was doing on recovery from Tet. He spent most of the interview asking about projects that USAID had funded, and waited until they had talked for a while before raising the question of orphanages. He was told that the agency funded several orphanages, and when he asked for the names, Maison d'Enfants was one of them.

"Do we audit these programs?"

The USAID official, whose name was Hilton, said "Yes, of course. We audit all of our grantees. Why do you ask?"

"I just wondered how we track all the funding with all these different agencies involved." He then changed the subject to other projects. Finally, at the end of the interview, he asked whether the official had ever looked into the rumors that government officials were involved in prostitution.

Hilton frowned. "We've heard that, but I've never seen any credible evidence."

Will had been in politics long enough, and had attended enough press briefings, to recognize that Hilton had not really answered his question.

So Will called Ernie Scott, who seemed a bit irritated at the question, but after a few days came back to Will and simply said, "This is a lot bigger than you think Will. We're going to look into it further, but you should drop it. Some heavy hitters may be involved. Stay away."

A few days later, an enlisted came into Will's office and said "A Monsignor Laflace called and would like to speak with you."

"I'll meet him after work at the Continental, in the restaurant."

The monsignor, dressed in black with a short red cape across his shoulders, greeted Will and asked him what he would like to drink. Then he began talking.

"Mr. Putnam, I appreciate your meeting with me very much. Good friends of mine have told me of your fine work for the Ambassador and your prior work in the government in California, and I am happy to meet with someone so young with such an impressive career."

His tone was smooth, almost silky, and he smiled throughout his remarks, his demeanor completely open and friendly. But Will heard the undertone, and marveled at how quickly and how well the monsignor had done his research.

He said, slowly, "Thank you."

"This is awkward. But we have been made aware of some unfounded rumors that may have come to you concerning some of our charities. I would be glad to answer any questions you may have, but I want to assure you that we have worked with our orphanages in this country for more than fifty years, and we have nothing but the best interests of these children in our hearts."

Will's mind was racing. He was trying to follow the conversation and the sub-text of what it meant. Among other things, it meant Thuy was at risk and possibly in danger. The only way they could have known that Will had information about Maison d'Enfants was if someone who had told Thuy had been forced to pass her name on to the perpetrators. Or, he realized, if Ernie Scott's inquiry had surfaced some digging that had turned up Will's involvement.

"Monsignor, I have indeed heard some disturbing reports recently. I'm afraid they also involved some Americans as well."

Now Laflace was frowning. "Mr. Putnam, I'm sure you realize that spreading rumors about the Church and also about senior officers in your Army could result in severe disciplinary action. We would not want that to happen to someone with such a promising career."

Will realized that he had just been threatened, and he didn't like it. As he thought about how to respond, an image came to mind. He remembered the blind girl at the orphanage he had visited with Congressman Bronstein and Yvonne Cohen.

He paused, long enough to make clear that he was speaking deliberately, and then said, "Monsignor, I am sure that no harm will come to any children or any officials who are caring for them as they should be. A few months ago, I had the opportunity to take a New York congressman and his staff aide on a tour of one of the orphanages here in the city. We had a very informative visit, and the congressman has become very interested in how US aid is being used by orphanages and other children's programs here. In fact, from time to time I am in touch with him about these issues. If anything were happening to children such as these rumors suggest, I am sure that he would be willing to come here to investigate with his subcommittee."

The monsignor smiled—without an iota of warmth. "That won't be necessary. As long as you understand that no harm is coming or will come to those children, I'm sure there would be no need for such an investigation."

Then, in a too-obvious gesture, he looked at his watch. "I'm afraid I must go now for a meeting with the archbishop. Thank you for your time."

As he walked back to the apartment, Will felt a great need for a cigar, or a drink, or both. Without understanding exactly what he was in the middle of, he had met a threat with a threat. But he had ignored Scott's warning, and he felt he was getting well out of his depth.

Thuy asked, "Are you going to tell one of your reporter friends?"

"I don't think so. That might be more dangerous. I let them know I was aware of the problem once they got in touch with me, which tells me your friend needs to be very careful. They know that I know, and you also need to be careful. Have you visited your parents recently? It might be a good time to see them,"

"Now I'm frightened. Can't you protect me, Will? Can't you tell someone about this so they can stop it and put away the people who are doing this?"

"I'll think about it. I already told them I would go to friends in Washington if I needed to. That's enough for now. Thuy, you've got to understand. I'm just a lowly enlisted guy. No one's going to listen to me. And I'm worried about your friend getting in very serious trouble."

She looked very troubled, but said nothing. Afterward, Will realized that his threat might not be enough to stop the abuse and trafficking, if that's what it was. But the risk in going further felt too great for him to take. So he did nothing.

A few days later, he told Thuy that he had taken care of it, and that she should play it safe by going to her parents' village. She did, and he felt better that she was safer. Months later, as he was preparing to out-process, he casually asked Ernie Scott in a phone call what had happened. He could tell that Scott was angry that he had brought it up again, because all he would say it that it was over and to forget it. So he tried to do that. But he knew he had failed Thuy, and worse, he had failed some of the girls and boys at the Maison d'Enfants.

He never heard from Thuy again.

Will Putnam was 26 years old, and he had been to a part of the world that many in his generation—most in his social and educational class—had avoided, ignored or stereotyped. He had learned that America was not the center of the world, and that other parts of the world included billions of people who never thought of Americans or, when they did, mostly disliked them. He had been immersed in another culture, as much as anyone in an artificial bubble of diplomacy and military command structures can be exposed to another culture in wartime.

All these things separated him from most of the people he expected to be with for the rest of his working life. So he wondered how he was going to talk with them about what he had learned. Or would he just have to drop the subject, excising this early part of his life from the rest of it? Would he have to forget it, along with what he imagined he had just begun to learn?

He had only been in-country for fourteen months, but they had been the months in which the war changed most radically. Not only the Tet offensive, but the reaction from the media and the American public, the failure of the bombing campaign in the North to crush its will to fight, counter-insurgency and free-fire zones turned out to be totally inconsistent battle plans, indecisive leadership at the top of the South Vietnamese government, and the repeated failure of the South Vietnamese forces to put up a real fight—all this happened during his time in Vietnam. Will was far from the center of things, but he was close enough to the reporting on the war and some of the most honest US civilians to see and hear much of what was happening.

As Will left, the number of Americans in Vietnam reached its peak, and slowly began to decline. Will felt certain that the decline would never be reversed. Within a month of Tet, the Secretary of Defense had resigned. Within two months, the President had announced he would not seek re-election. The end had begun, but it would take seven more years, more than thirty thousand more American deaths, and hundreds of thousands of Vietnamese deaths, before it was over.

Will had begin to read everything he could get his hands on that reviewed the war—an obsession he continued for many decades. As he prepared to leave Saigon, the lesson that came through his reading and his reflections was the tremendous momentum of bad ideas backed up with enormous resources. The money and the lives expended both made it all the more difficult for those in command to admit that they were bad ideas. Persistence, he had learned, was not the only value that mattered. "If at first you don't succeed, etc." had an opposite and, he thought, an equal mantra: *if the resources don't achieve the results, one of them has to change.* And it had become clear that a half million troops, thousands of tons of bombs, thousands of American lives, and more than a decade of frustration were the outer limits of the resources available.

After a year of listening to body counts in press briefings, Will had begun to think those were the wrong measures of progress. His own measuring point had gradually become steadfast, stemming from his earliest talks with Congressman Bronstein, their visit to the orphanage, and what he saw when he went out into the countryside. The touchpoint was *what was happening to the kids*. If the people are the prize, then their kids are the long-term payoff. He had begun to wonder if the flow of all the numbers could be distilled into a simpler, more valuable yield: Can the kids go to a safe school with reasonably competent teachers?

Once Will tried to explain his feelings about the "teeth and tail" distinction to a friend who was deep into the teeth side of the equation. Rob King was an African-American graduate of West Point who had been in Will's graduate school class at Cornell, and he had looked Rob up once he got to Vietnam. Rob had a Purple Heart and was up for a Bronze Star for his leadership of a platoon that had gotten into a firefight near the Cambodian border.

Will haltingly explained his regrets about being in the rear echelon, and watched Rob's face fill with laughter. "Shit, man, get over it. You're here. You got drafted, and you went through with it. Look, Will, in your college class, how many ended up over here—3 or 4, max? Out of 400? We're the 1%, man, the elite 1%. And if 30-40 % of us get shot at and the rest don't, so be it. You're here."

Will said "Yeah, but 10% of our age group got drafted."

"And 90% didn't. Leave it alone, Will."

Weinstein had come to see him off at the airport. As they shared a last drink before Will's plane was called, he asked Will, "So what memories are you carrying back, Will?"

"Memories? I don't know. A little blind girl in Saigon. A call from the Ambassador one day. Listening to some officers and civilians one afternoon on the edge of the Mekong River as they tried to figure out the war. Seeing a piece of the embassy wall that got blown up by a grenade. Reading Vietnamese editorials that longed for the day when the Americans go home." He paused and looked off at the airfield. "And reading in *Stars and Stripes* about one of my closest friends from basic training getting killed."

What he left out, Will realized as he walked to the plane, was Thuy, some abused kids at Maison d'Enfants, and his own sometimes clumsy dancing along the faded lines of his own ethical boundaries in working with the press. Thuy had given him gifts of understanding, as well as herself, and in return he had abandoned her. His courage had abandoned him when it came to the abused kids. And his "suggestions" to reporters had at times moved into the grayest of areas between the black and white lines of narrowed and larger loyalties. His anticipation of the next chapter of his life was dulled as he pondered what he had done and left undone in these two early chapters of his life—his movements at the margins of the war, and his move away from a commitment to Thuy.

Will had tried hard to understand his first war, but it was too big, too pathological, and he was too young to grasp fully how things worked and how things got screwed up. He had met some of the best Americans in Vietnam, and had seen the harm done by some of the worst. He had learned more about another culture than he had ever imagined he could, but there, too, he felt he was far out on the margins of really understanding the Vietnamese.

He had learned a lot, but he still had much to learn about war, and himself.

His next war would be different. And so would he.

As he flew home, he thought about the next chapters of his life. The embassy HR people had come to him twice and asked him to consider going FSO. He assumed Steve Jamison had put them onto him. But he knew he was still outside that orbit. He was certain that he'd never have the patience to slog it out in the Foreign Service, to do a consul's job in some obscure seaport, to serve time in the worst assignments or specialize in Russia or Brazil or somewhere in India.

He wanted to climb Disraeli's greasy pole—politics was what called him. It was what the friends he most admired in grad school were aiming at, and it had gotten him to Vietnam in the first place. He had met several others in Vietnam, officers and civilians, who all had some path to politics in view. He felt competitive with them already, envious of their deeper ties to states and towns with faster ladders than he knew he'd find back in California.

And so he had gone back to California, and after two more years as staff in the legislature, he had run for the Assembly when a spot opened up near where he had grown up. But it was too soon and his roots were too shallow. He had thought that being a veteran would help, but people were sicker of the war than he had expected, and he had gotten beat by a flashy kid with more money than brains whose uncle had held the seat twenty years before.

At the end of the campaign, after the votes were counted, his campaign manager had taken him aside for some quiet boosting up. He was an older graduate of Will's college and had known him for ten years, through college and beyond.

"Will, you have many gifts. It turns out that politics isn't one of them. You're going to be a success in any of a dozen other careers—and you're likely to rise to the top in one of them. But not this one. You're too much of an inside guy, and it's just too damn hard for you to reveal as much as most people want to know about their politicians. You went to those coffee hours and it was like you were suffering, waiting for the seminar to begin."

Will heard it, wincing internally, knowing it was dead right. He had never felt comfortable with it, working so hard not to talk down to people, but inevitably ending up lecturing them. Short of a personality transplant, it was not going to be a graceful way for him to try to make a living while making a difference. And he was honest enough with himself to face that truth.

And so he entered a time of wondering about his future. The career he had wanted was out of reach, and as yet, he had no idea what could take its place.

He returned home to Southern California and spent some time with his family. Will's sisters were more of an influence on him than he sometimes wanted to admit.

The eldest, Martha, was an emergency room nurse who had converted to Catholicism when she went to college. She was eternally optimistic, generous, and irreverently funny. She had aged marvelously, going from high-end cute to maturely lovely. She was really the center of the family, arranging continuing celebrations of the "five and zero" birthdays of the siblings, never failing to send the nieces and nephews birthday cards.

And she treated Will like a prince who could do no wrong—as long as he did what she said.

The next oldest, Peggy, had taken a somewhat different turn. She was a life member of the National Rifle Association, had two kids in the military, and approached foreign policy as essentially "nuke 'em or ignore 'em."

She and Will had decided long ago to have no serious conversations about his work or her politics. But she was ferociously loyal, and did a better job than any of the rest of the family staying in touch with Will as he bounced around between Cornell, Connecticut, Sacramento and Saigon. She wrote chatty letters that kept him posted on her kids, and the other nieces and nephews as well.

His youngest sister, Marie, had gone into police work, and had married a minister whom she had met in college. They had five children, and were very active in their church, which was a very progressive church that worked with immigrants. Her husband was from Mexico, and was also an excellent cook, always serving as the master chef at all family gatherings.

Will's brother was a school librarian, who loved research and computers. He'd married an artist, and they made a wonderful couple, despite their wide differences. When Will was with them, he marveled at how well they had negotiated their differences. They used the well-worn 1-10 scale, in which a couple had to be specific when they couldn't agree on something. Each issue got a rating: *is this a low-importance issue—a 1, or a Very Big Deal—a 10?* As a powerful form of shorthand communication, Will observed, it worked.

Each of his siblings had advice for Will, having suffered through his absence in Vietnam and then his campaign. Their advice more or less cancelled each other out in differing perspectives on his future.

What stuck, Will felt, was Peggy's telling him in typically blunt terms, "You have no idea who you are, and you won't figure it out moping around here. Get out on the road and see what you can find out in the world. There's a lot more of it out there besides Vietnam."

So he decided to travel, and chose a six-month fellowship with a nongovernmental organization that worked with children. The NGO would give him a place to live if he would pay for the travel, which he managed to do by taking out a loan from Martha.

He headed off to Mexico, India, and Kenya, hoping that somewhere along the way he would discover his destination.

PART TWO

Southwest Asia 2004-2008

Once upon a time, in a very dry, very brown country in Southwest Asia, a man in his late sixties walked down the stairs from a plane at an airport surrounded by military vehicles.

The man still had most of his hair, but it was almost totally white. Of average height, he lacked the paunch borne by many of his cohort, and his thinness was visible through the khakis and short-sleeved dress shirt he wore. But his eyes were bright and his demeanor was alert, watching, always watching.

He walked carefully over to a large camouflaged vehicle that seemed a failed compromise between a truck and a limousine. The driver nodded, said his name, and opened the door. The man stepped inside, out of the heat that was baking the airport runways. He sat on the soft leather seat, and allowed himself a soft sigh of comfort.

The vehicle drove off into a crowded city marked with domes, thin towers, and hundreds of concrete barriers, with brown hills surrounding its distant edges.

And as you've already guessed, perhaps, he was named Will Putnam. He had been posted to Iraq, the country where he had just arrived. Because of his prior service as Ambassador in Africa, he knew he would be given the honorary title of Ambassador, even though a civilian named Beemer had the Ambassador's post in Baghdad.

As the vehicle made its way through crowded streets, the Ambassador noticed two armed troop carriers moving just ahead and behind his own vehicle. He assumed there was a third vehicle somewhere less obvious. They drove a zig-zag route for thirty minutes and then arrived at a large compound surrounded by blast barriers, with guard posts every fifty meters. This was the American Embassy.

"Ambassador Putnam, welcome to the embassy. Ambassador Beemer has a full schedule today, but he'll be able to see you for a half hour tomorrow morning at 7."

Will Putnam knew that the game had begun, the game of putting him in his place. He was merely an Ambassador at large, which usually meant someone back at State wanted him in country. But the team already there definitely wanted him safely off to the side, out of their hair. He was ready for it, and had mentally packed extra helpings of patience. He knew he would need it.

He looked out the window at the adjacent buildings, looming up several stories high, with marble fronts and minarets along all sides of the building. The former dictator's palace had been occupied by the US senior embassy and military command from the earliest days of the invasion, and he assumed most of his meetings would be there.

The aide showed him to an office, which was not so small that it would be insulting, but located on a floor removed from the main action on the top level of the building. He had noticed a penthouse garden on the corner of the building's roof, and assumed that was Beemer's area. He also assumed the embassy security team had lost the argument about the garden's vulnerability.

"You will be staying in the diplomatic guest house, Ambassador. Ambassadors Loomis and Sydowski are in there as well, but I think you'll find it comfortable."

Putnam had known there was at least one other FSO who had held Ambassador rank who was assigned to the embassy, but the bonus diplomats reminded him that there were some embassies where the American mission included four former ambassadors. *Ambassador creep,* he thought to himself, as he walked with his carryon bag behind a cart pushed by two civilians who had loaded his suitcases onto it.

Putnam walked quickly, quicker than a man in his very late sixties normally does, and the aide had some difficulty keeping up with him.

Putnam had always walked rapidly, and those with enough standing to complain about it usually did. His response, when pressed, was to say that he hated walking and so he did it as quickly as possible. The nearer truth was that he knew he didn't get enough exercise, which his cardiologist pointed out annually, with little effect. So he excused himself by accelerating his infrequent walks.

It was one of the many compromises he had comfortably reached with himself: smoking cigars, but giving up liquor; admiring women greatly, but rarely engaging with the time and effort it took to move past idle chatter. He had been in so many negotiations, both within the Department and across tables around the world, that he welcomed negotiations with himself because he knew his adversary so well.

The diplomatic house turned out to be a modular building with two bedrooms and a study that had a bed in it. The latter was to be Putnam's, and he was pleased to see it had a decent-sized desk and an entire wall of book shelves that was only about one-third full.

The aide, whose name Putnam had not caught, said "Mr. Colletti said he hopes you don't mind having a bedroom office, but the others were already taken, sir."

"Thank you. Not a problem. Who is Mr. Colletti?"

"He's the chief of staff to Ambassador Beemer, sir."

"Fine. This will be fine." He added, "I'm expecting a shipment of books and other materials. Just bring it in here when it comes."

"Yes, sir."

Left alone, Putnam began unpacking. His first move was to reach into a pocket in his suitcase and pull out a small piece of concrete, marbled on one side. Then he tossed some ancient, well-worn military dog tags next to the rock. He carefully placed both items in the middle of his desk and looked at them for a long time. Then he returned to his unpacking.

As Putnam settled in, he reflected on the career choices that had brought him to Iraq

Once he found that a political life was not meant to be, Will Putnam returned to what he'd originally thought of as his Plan B. He took the Foreign Service test, passed with a high score, and did well in the Foreign

Service Institute. His first assignment was consular duty in Indonesia, which he enjoyed, mildly concerned that he was going to get pigeonholed as an Asian expert. That problem was soon solved by a three-year stint staffing the Assistant Secretary for African Affairs, followed by a posting in the economic affairs section of the embassy in Nairobi.

He had done well enough to be able to choose his languages and selected Arabic while in Indonesia, continuing with it in Kenya. Then he began working on Mandarin, struggling with its tones, but calling on long-ago practice with Vietnamese.

Soon he found himself in his late thirties, working on the China desk back in Washington, and married to a woman he'd dated in college. The marriage lasted five years, doomed by his assignment as consul in Harbin and his wife's refusal to travel outside the US, combined with her determination to make far more choices of her own than the wife of a diplomat was likely to be given. What had seemed charming assertiveness in college turned out to be unending contentiousness fifteen years later, and he finally gave up. By that time he had experienced difficult international negotiations, and decided that endless negotiations at home were beyond his tolerance.

The China assignment came during a period when the White House was convinced it would be able to benefit politically from the economic boom that was under way in China, and on his return from China he found himself detailed to the National Security Council staff. Working in the White House—actually in the Old Executive Office Building adjacent to the White House—gave him great cachet with the group of FSOs in his 'class.' His normally taciturn nature fit well with the classified content of his work, and he kept quiet about his role and his assignments when he connected socially with the FSOs he had gotten to know during his prior assignments.

He spent a good deal of his time in the NSC role shuttling between the OEOB and the Pentagon, since the China assignment included assessing the ever-shifting balance between China's emerging economic leadership and its military. He also saw more than he'd like of Langley and the CIA officers who handled China.

Neither the generals nor the senior CIA case officers impressed Putnam as much as he would have expected from his earlier experience watching both of them over-ride State in the frequent four-sided negotiations among the White House and the three agencies. He found the generals typically full of themselves and the CIA often preferring clandestine methods even when openness would have worked better. And he soon recognized that the colonels under the generals in the Pentagon were about evenly divided among three groups: comers who were on the way to their star, time-servers who would never make general, and those who should have but for their willingness to tell those already wearing stars when they were wrong. Putnam spent as much time as he could with the latter group, attracted to their iconoclasm and their ease with the kind of dry, acidic humor he used and welcomed.

In each of his overseas postings, Will added to his store of knowledge about diplomacy and other cultures. None of them was as intense as Saigon had been, but he had learned something in Saigon about how to listen and watch, both inside the embassy and out in the country, and the lessons came in handy in his rounds of foreign capitals and consulates. He served as senior political officer in two embassies, and then was given an Ambassador-rank posting in an African country that was far from a U.S. priority, but allowed him to head up a full mission for the first time.

He learned that he had a knack for the inside games that went on within the embassies, when to insert his point of view and when to be quiet, waiting for a chance to get a higher-up to make his point. He became skilled at memo skirmishes, polishing his writing to a point where he could persuade in a few paragraphs where other, wordier colleagues would go on for pages and pages of stiff bureaucratese.

And when he could get out into the countryside, he became the journalist he once thought he was meant to be, making notes, interviewing officials and grass-roots people, listening and watching for the undercurrents of culture and habit that made up such different parts of the world he was coming to understand.

And gradually, he realized that one of the great divides was how differently cultures responded to education. The abject fear shown by Islamist extremists who opposed allowing girls to go to school was impossible not to contrast with the broad acceptance in Asia that learning is the ladder out of the villages and into the cities. He knew that some Asian cultures valued education too little, and that some women in some

Islamic countries had made huge strides in getting girls into primary and secondary education. But he could see that the broad currents of fear of and longing for education were distinct and opposed, with profound impact on the cultures in which these currents flowed.

And then the second war swept down on Will and his career.

He had been called into the Secretary's office, and knew that it was going to be about his next assignment. This kind of meeting was usually handled at a lower level, so it meant he was going somewhere that wasn't routine.

The Secretary was typically blunt. "We need you in Iraq, Will. You've got the Arabic, you did tours in Muslim posts. And I'd like someone who has a bit more history with the military than most of our guys. And gals," he added, as the Assistant Secretary for the Middle East, Sheila Zakarias, coughed quietly into her hand. "I'm raising you to Ambassador-at Large rank so Beemer and the rest of that crew will think twice about pulling rank on you. How soon can you leave?"

"I ought to be able to wrap things up in a week, Mr. Secretary."

"Terrific. Keep me posted on how it's going. Sheila will brief you on the details. And thanks. I know this won't be the most fun you've ever had. Maybe after this one we'll find you a nice quiet spot back here."

Putnam smiled. "Looking forward to it, Tom." He'd decided he'd switch over to first names, having known the Secretary when they both worked in the White House and in Vietnam. And they both knew the assignment had the potential to be a massive PITA—pain in the ass. Having the Secretary owe him wouldn't hurt a bit.

Sheila Zakarias was one of the sharpest career officials in State, and Putnam had great respect for her. They settled into comfortable chairs in her office, and she picked up a thick briefing book that had clearly seen a lot of use.

"Will, you'll get a copy of this, which we update all the time. But a few words of warning, if I may. Beemer will try to isolate you. I would suggest that you not take him on when you first get there. I know you can hold your own, but we don't need any early pissing contests with either the White House or the Pentagon. Pick your shots and let us know what you think is happening. And what isn't."

"Get to know Sydowski, I've worked with him and he is very solid. Quiet guy who soaks up a lot of information. He works with the Agency, so know that and take care. But he's very level and not a guy who leans on the secret stuff just because he can."

She paused, and looked at him, choosing her words carefully, he thought. "Will, more than anybody around, you can help us think about what this means in light of the Vietnam experience. Tom wants you there because you were in Saigon. The Pentagon thinks they've digested all that, but neither they nor we have. The Secretary would welcome any thoughts you have on what you see, and you should feel free to address them to him eyes only."

She stood up. "There'll be a code in your briefing book that will reach me directly. Use it as you need to." She came closer and gave him a hug that was as much personal as professional. "Good luck. And Will?"

"Yes?"

"Try to get laid if you can—but be careful."

He walked out of her office chuckling.

And then, semi-randomly, he remembered Ward Just's definition of a diplomat: "A connoisseur of the counterfeit and the inexplicable."

After unpacking, Putnam checked out his hardware. He had what looked like a fully encrypted desktop. Seeing no speakers, he made a note to get to the PX as soon as possible, knowing that sound systems were one of the essentials that U.S. troops have available in most military installations. He assumed an installation this large would have a fine selection.

At 7:00 the next morning, Putnam checked in with the colonel stationed outside Ambassador Beemer's door. "Morning, Ambassador. Mr. Beemer is on the phone to Washington, but he'll be right with you."

"Right with you" meant ten minutes of waiting, and as the colonel showed Putnam into Beemer's office, he saw Beemer hang up the phone on the top of his vast desk. Beemer rose and shook hands, saying "Welcome, Ambassador. Nice to have some diplomatic experience out here to help us civilians."

In one sentence, Beemer had managed to remind Putnam that Beemer was a direct White House appointee who was neither career military nor

State Department. Beemer was tall, young-looking—Putnam knew he was 45—and had a remarkable tan which went well with his brown combat boots.

Beemer's "wall of fame" included the predictable pictures of him with various Presidents, generals, and foreign leaders. The other message sent by his décor was that he was a short-timer, because one whole wall was covered with pictures of his native Texas, including a huge photo of the front wall of the Alamo. Putnam refrained from noting the outcome at that famous landmark.

As they talked about Putnam's assignment, Beemer urged him to spend his time looking at the performance of the civilian agencies of the U.S. presence in Iraq. "We need a better handle on what USAID and all these NGOs are doing in-country. Building schools and hospitals and training agency staff for the new Iraqi government that we're going to install next year. Doesn't seem to be any coordination. I've talked with the State people about this, but they don't seem to have any overview. Couldn't even get them to give me an inventory of all the projects going on in-country that are sponsored by the civilian groups."

Putnam, listening as always for what wasn't said, heard *stay out of military issues.* Beemer's view of the world with an artificial division between military and civilian was going to be a problem. *Strike One*, he thought.

"I could look at that, Ambassador," Putnam said. "I'd also like to see what the military units assigned to reconstruction teams are doing. How it affects the counterinsurgency effort."

Beemer frowned. "Sure, sure. But that hasn't gotten much emphasis lately. It's more about clear and hold these days."

"Understood, Ambassador." But Putnam thought, *Strike Two: he thinks local counterinsurgency is BS. Which it may be, if it's done wrong.*

They talked further, Beemer doing most of it, telling Putnam what they had been doing to work with "the locals," as he called the Iraqi officials. Watching the clock, Putnam rose at the 30-minute mark, wanting Beemer to get the message that he was not a loquacious old fart who needed to talk.

"Thanks, Ambassador. I'll get back to you once I've learned the ropes."

"That's great, Will. Thanks." Beemer seemed relieved, and Putnam could tell that he'd been warned about Putnam's being somewhat difficult and outspoken.

As he walked back to his office, he replayed the conversation. Beemer had seemed intent on showing that he was in charge, trying to carve out safe areas to keep Putnam enclosed, avoiding possible conflict. Beemer knew that Putnam had a good relationship with the Secretary, and for all his posturing about being a White House appointee, Beemer couldn't feel completely comfortable with a new, very senior, well-placed FSO roving around.

Putnam suspected that Beemer's discomfort was unlikely to decrease.

The next morning, Putnam attended his first meeting of the Executive Council. Beemer introduced him with ample praise, Putnam thanked him, and then remained quiet for the rest of the meeting.

Putnam had mastered the art of meetings long ago. He no longer needed to study the attendees; he could quickly classify them into one of the several categories he'd refined during the roughly twenty thousand meetings he'd attended in forty years. The leadoff hitters, the cleanup guys, the counter-punchers, the weather vanes—he could listen to the first few words of somebody's contribution and easily fit the speaker into the slot where they belonged.

Beemer, predictably, was a cheerleader trying to be a coach. Putnam had learned long ago that the distinction mattered: cheerleaders just jumped around, while coaches—if they were any good—could persuade people to do hard things. The persuasion came more by showing than talking—you had to believe that the hard thing was doable, and that the coach had done it or knew damned well what it took to get it done. Cheerleaders rarely convinced anyone that they had more going for them than mobility, good bone structure, and yelling a lot.

This meeting was about "metrics." Putnam had learned that this was a new way of talking about how to measure progress, both military progress and progress in what they had once called the "hearts and minds" side of the war. As he listened, he marveled at how familiar the discussion was, though with new labels on many of the old subjects.

Beemer pressed for numbers that quantified insurgents killed or captured, bridges rebuilt, schools and food warehouses constructed, oil flow and electricity hours increasing. And as the numbers rolled out, Putnam recalled the same presentations in Vietnam, with the same overlay of confidence that we were "winning."

But he stayed silent, knowing that the time had not yet come for history lessons, and that he could easily get typecast as the old guy reminiscing about the old days.

As the meeting broke up, Putnam noticed an old friend, the military press liaison David Johansen. They went all the way back to Vietnam, where they had first met. They exchanged greetings, and then Johansen, who had always been blunt, got right to it.

"Why are you here? Who's your sponsor?"

Putnam frowned. "Sponsor? I don't need no stinkin' sponsor."

"Very funny. The question stands."

Putnam stared at him for long enough to make it uncomfortable. Then he responded. "Several people at State and elsewhere"—he knew Johansen would assume he meant the White House—"rely on me for occasional advice. I don't have one special sponsor. As you know, the Secretary and I were in Vietnam at the same time, and we've stayed in touch over the years. I have forty years of working with some of these people, civilian and military, so they listen to me and I listen to them. Doesn't mean we agree. Sometimes they take my advice, sometimes they ignore it. Dorothy Smithson— staff head of Senate Foreign Relations—and I served together in the consulate in Harbin many years ago, and we became good friends. She calls, we talk."

Then his tone changed. "Look, Dave, like I said, I know a lot of these people. They tend to understand my point of view somewhat better than they do the former advance men from the last campaign who seem to make up a good part of Beemer's staff. We speak the same language. That's all."

"You can see how that might be a little threatening to those advance guys, though."

Putnam laughed. "They wouldn't know Dottie Smithson if she walked up and grabbed their crotch. Those poor guys aren't smart enough to be worried by some old fart wandering around the embassy."

"That's not what I hear."

"Oh?"

"Beemer is a bit nervous. Worried that you're here to check up on him. His press has gotten a lot worse lately and most of the press people like you."

"Except for the ones that detest me, yeah."

"You know what I mean. You're a threat, Will."

Putnam smiled and said, "Only to those who should be threatened." Then he changed the subject. "When are you going up to Kabul?"

"Next week. Want to come along?"

"I may just do that."

"That will calm Beemer down. Nothing much happening up there right now."

Putnam frowned. "That's the problem."

Johansen kept at it. "What's your ask, Will? What do you really want them to do here?"

"I don't want some bloody little pilot project that is supposed to divert me into running something to keep me out of their hair. I want the damned policy to change. I want our troops to be safer, to stop pretending that they are winning hearts and minds, and I want fewer dead and ignorant kids in this country. That's my *ask*. And I hate that term, because it sounds like it can be satisfied with some little fix."

"Will, I'm just trying to get you to focus on what your priorities are."

"If we hadn't worked together off and on for forty years, that would really piss me off." Then he calmed down, knowing Johansen was trying to help. "Look, Dave, I'm just trying to make up for the worst of the shock and awful planning these clowns have been doing. Priorities? Our kids safer and then their kids safer. How about that for a mission statement?"

"Not sure Beemer's boys will get it."

"Me neither. But I'm going to try."

Putnam had been assigned a young FSO as his aide. Mike Petrosian was from Fresno, part of the great Armenian diaspora, Putnam assumed. It was his second assignment, his first having been in Egypt. His Arabic was far superior to Putnam's and he had strong ties to a Guard unit from the California Central Valley that was stationed a few hours south of the city. He asked good questions and wasn't afraid to ask Putnam for deeper explanations than the surface answers he sometimes got from others in the embassy. Putnam knew he'd gotten lucky with the young FSO's assignment, and tried to mentor him from time to time with nuggets of context and history.

Over the years, Putnam's introversion had mellowed out into what he considered, with a measure of rationalization, an appropriate reserve. He was not overly formal—he could be riotously humorous, among close friends or family. But he could easily put up barriers, establish distance when he wanted to, while having learned how to remove it with a disarming remark.

It helped that most of the people he dealt with were younger, which happens to older professionals. It made his reserve and distance easier to invoke, with an unspoken message when he reached out to them that said *I'd really like to talk to you, but it will be about what I'm interested in, and your questions had better be on point.*

Putnam put down the facsimile copy of the *New York Times*, shaking his head. Petrosian noticed and asked, "What is it, sir?"

"Old memories. Last year's candidate for President is complaining about the media, and says they cut him up. Says he never wants to run again because of how badly they cut him up."

"So what's the memory?"

"I had the exact same conversation with his father forty years ago in Saigon. He said the media cut him up—used the same phrase—'they cut me and cut me.' So why is the son surprised?"

"It's a tough business."

"Yes, it is. But I'd rather have an unfair media than no media at all. After reading the pitiful excuses for local papers they have here, our press doesn't look so bad. Lesson for the day, Petrosian: If the media can make it look bad, they will. It goes with the territory. Know *The Music Man?*"

Petrosian recognized the refrain. "And…" he paused "'you gotta know the territory.'"

Putnam laughed. "Now you've got it."

Putnam enjoyed sometimes shocking Petrosian with his tastes. The young man occasionally came to Putnam's private quarters in the morning if they had a meeting outside the Zone. One morning, he entered the office while Putnam was listening to the Doors on his Bluetoothed Ipad.

"You like the Doors, sir? Excuse me, but that's very different from the classical stuff—uh, the classical selections you usually have on."

"Kid, I'm surprised at you, not knowing the history of the Doors. That's Vietnam music, strange days music, my boy. Just because they've come back—and I congratulate you on your taste, compared to the C-rap your colleagues seem to prefer—just because the Doors are now popular again doesn't mean you should overlook their pedigree as classic, late 60s, doper musicians. Classic too, in its own way."

Early in their shared assignment, Petrosian asked Putnam for the backstory on his career. "I mean, I've read the bio, sir. But I'd be interested in knowing why you made the choices you did."

So Putnam told him a somewhat expurgated version of the story. "I grew up, I guess. I had been in Vietnam, and had seen the embassy up close, and thought that BS was what it was all about. I got back to the States, and took an ill-advised shot at politics, and that didn't work out. So I traveled for a year, and along the way I saw some of the best—and worst—of what we do when we go out in the world. All those roles we play: The caretaker, the nanny, the salesman, the imperialists. The experience in Vietnam had blinded me, I guess, to all the rest of what we do and who we are outside the US. I knew I could do diplomacy and negotiations better than we were doing it in some places, and it looked like a good way to make a contribution. So I took the test. The rest is a sort of career."

"Hell of a career. Someone told me you were a secret soft power guy."

Putnam smiled. "Not so secret. But," he added, "I'm not afraid to let the hardware guys loose when there's a good reason for it. We play good defense. I'm not too wild about our offense, though."

"Meaning what?"

"We go in and try to re-arrange countries that aren't direct threats to us, step into civil wars where we have no clue who hates who—that's offense. We take out Al Qaeda whenever we find them planning another 9/11—I call that defense."

"And where does the soft power come in?"

"I'm not wild about that label. But if it means we worry about other people in other countries and how they live their lives, whether they have enough to eat and somewhere to learn, and whether that keeps them from hating us, I'll take the soft power label." He was quiet for a while. "A long time ago I figured out that it made more sense to count kids who are learning and eating better than to add up the people we killed. The body count thing in Vietnam." He shook his head, frowning. "Unforgettable. And a big part of why we lost."

Before he left for Iraq, Putnam had paid a visit to George Diver. He had stayed in touch with Diver over the years, finding him one of the most enjoyable companions he had ever met. Behind his outsized Texas personality was a generous, highly intelligent lover of life. He had returned to his native South Texas roots and managed over the decades to marry a succession of progressively wealthier Mexican and Texas women. Ending up with seven children, Diver had somehow stayed close with all of them, and even more amazingly, with his ex-wives as well.

Putnam had arrived at Diver's ranch three days before he was scheduled to leave for Iraq. They spent the time catching up on each other's recent doings, smoking cigars, and reflecting on the patterns they both saw in the war they had shared and the one Putnam was headed for.

"Will, I can't for the life of me figure out whether this rodeo you're headed for is the same god-awful swamp we tried to wade through all those years ago, or a totally different kettle of fish. Just when I think I see a parallel, I read about drones or satellites or some dammed thing we never dreamed of in our war."

"It's different, George. And it's the same. Search and destroy—same. Build schools and dig wells—same. Knowing next to nothing about the culture, despite a boatload of anthropologists and sociologists stumbling all over each other—same.

"But, George, I've got to give credit where's credit is due. The military and the IT geeks and the satellite guys have made it a hell of a lot safer for civilians when the chickenshit insurgents hide out in their villages. Collateral damage—still going on, but on a very different scale, I'd have to say. In our war, we wiped whole villages out and never thought twice about it."

"Yeah," George said. "But all that goes to hell in this war whenever we blast some poor wedding party into eternity. Or when some dumbass rednecks torture prisoners on camera."

"Right." Putnam was quiet for a while, watching three of George's kids in the swimming pool with the flags of Texas and Mexico painted on the bottom.

Then he said, "The biggest difference, in some ways, is the draft that was the great faucet that turned out a half million troops in our war, and the volunteer army that's over there now. It's a better army now, as near as I can tell.

"But the saddest difference, maybe, is what they briefed us on at the Pentagon a few weeks ago in the orientation sessions. Deaths from combat—way down. Life-long disabilities—way up. We save a lot more of those kids, but we're leaving a hell of a lot of their arms and legs all over the battlefield and the streets where those poisonous bastards we're fighting have planted their IEDs. That's far worse than our troops ever had to deal with, even with all the mines and ambushes. Another thing that's pretty much the same: The FATA safe haven along Pakistan's northwestern border is Cambodia."

George asked, "What about this guy Beemer and the rest of his staff? And what about the generals? I read where Easton is now in charge. I remember him as a captain in the next province over. Not too bad, not too great."

"Not sure yet. I'll let you know. But the article the other day about all the political types—former advance men now working in the embassy—really pissed me off. There was no one like that in the embassy in Saigon. Knowing how to set up a rally in Des Moines isn't very useful in Fallujah."

He shook his head. "Somebody told me in one of the orientation briefings that some of the Provisional Authority staff actually have T-shirts bragging about the President's re-election campaign. Somebody else said half of the little bastards never had a passport before they got their jobs with the Provisional Authority. George, it may be the most incompetent embassy I've ever been part of anywhere in the world."

In his first few weeks, Putnam took his "assignment" from Beemer seriously, spending a good deal of his first few months reviewing the embassy's relationships with the NGOs and the USAID projects under way in the country. He met with several of the project directors, building a file on the scale of the projects, gradually distinguishing between those that were counting heads and those that had some idea of what their projects were actually accomplishing. He began working to introduce the idea of alternative measures that would begin to assess the effects of the projects. It seemed like a new idea to many of the Council members.

He made an interim report on his findings to the Executive Council, watching the military contingent as they seemed disinterested, until he mentioned the provincial projects undertaken by the joint military-civilian teams. Once he had moved into their turf, the brass became more animated, asking for the sources of his information, which was partly complimentary and partly critical. He was careful to call his report "preliminary," in the bureaucratic formulation that would allow him to revise the conclusions later on to add more positive or negative findings.

Beemer was right—there was no overall inventory of projects. As a result, at times some provinces had two duplicative projects under way while others had none. The lack of coordination, which Putnam had always believed to be a symptom of confused missions, was widespread, revealing the urgency given to funding mainly to show the American presence, rather than making coherent efforts.

Putnam had heard about a parallel investigation under way by a GAO team that had been sent out in response to a congressional request for information about funding that had "disappeared" or could not be accounted for in regular reports. One choice nugget from that investigation involved the amount of cash that was sitting around in embassy and military safes, including one notorious tip that several hundred thousand dollars had been hidden in waterproof bags in an office toilet when no safe had been available.

Since Putnam had learned unofficially that a substantial portion of that cash was going to buy off heads of clans and tribal groups that had been part of the insurgency, he left the topic for the GAO investigators.

Putnam was talking with Petrosian about the Abu Ghraib abuses that had just become public. "This is so sad and so reminiscent of My Lai 40 years ago. The guys who reported what really happened were some of the real heroes of Vietnam. They finally gave the DFC to Hugh Thompson, the helicopter pilot who reported the massacre to his chain of command. His crew got Bronze Stars. But that happened only after they were attacked by some of the US media and the Chairman of the House Armed Services committee."

He shook his head, saddened at the memory. "You learn a lot about people when something like this happens. Colin Powell, who was a major at the time, ran an investigation of My Lai that ignored the brutality charges. And Barry Goldwater was one of only a few members of Congress who replied to the soldiers who wrote Congress telling them what had happened at My Lai."

Petrosian said, "If only we could remember what we have forgotten."

Putnam laughed, and said "Right. We need to recall our amnesia."

Then he had a thought. "You check in from time to time with that unit from the Valley that's based near here, don't you?"

"Yes, sir. I have two cousins in that battalion and I promised their mothers I'd try to stay in touch with them."

"Let me know next time you're headed out that way. I'd like to come along with you. Get a little closer to the reality of all this."

Petrosian was pleased. "I'll do that, sir. I try to get out there at least once a month, and I'll let you know as soon as I can schedule it with the security detail."

Putnam had agreed to meet with a delegation of women who had worked for the Iraqi government agencies, most of whom had been removed by the American occupation. They were requesting hearings on their status and had prepared a roster of each of their names and former positions. As they introduced themselves, he paid special attention to a woman who announced herself as Aisha Araden. On the roster she was listed as the former Assistant Minister of Women's Affairs in the Ministry of the Interior. She was one of the four women selected to speak by the delegation, and when she spoke, she looked at each of the ranking attendees, including Putnam, and asked that the women be given work appropriate to their qualifications.

She said, "We know that there is a great amount of rebuilding to be done, in our cities and our institutions, and we are here to ask that we be given a role in that work. Your country is known throughout the world for giving women a greater measure of opportunity than in most other nations, and we would hope that you would do the same here. Each of us has played a role in our nation's agencies, and we want to continue those roles. Right now, we are being used solely as translators. We would appreciate the chance to have assignments that are more challenging."

They continued to talk, and he promised that he would do what he could to upgrade their roles.

After the meeting, he was able to slip Aisha Araden a note through a staff aide that simply said *I was very interested in what you had to say. If you would like to discuss this further, please call my staff at the embassy. Thank you for coming.*

She called a week later and arranged to see him in his office. When she arrived, he was struck at her dignified bearing compared with most of the local staff in the embassy. She was dark-haired, covering her head casually with a blue-green scarf. Her features were softer than many of the women of Iraq, with an oval-shaped face set off by large brown eyes that were lightly made up. Her usual expression was unsmiling, but when she spoke, it softened and when she wanted to be persuasive, a broad smile broke forth and lightened her entire visage. Her voice was lower than most women, almost musical. She was tall for a Middle Eastern woman, about 5'6", he guessed, with a waist somehow visible beneath her loose-fitting overdress. His guess as to her age was likely to be wrong, given his small experience with women of the Middle East, but he imagined she was in her early forties. She wore a wedding ring.

After an initial discussion of the meeting she had attended, and assurances that he had spoken to Beemer about positions for her colleagues, he decided to learn more about her.

"Your English is excellent. Have you been able to travel much?"

"Yes. In my former position with the ministry I attended several international conferences, in Geneva and New York. I enrolled for a year as a fellow at Hartford Seminary in Connecticut, which has an active program of exchanges with Middle Eastern universities and organizations."

"Ah, New England, It's where my family's roots are. Araden—where does that name come from?"

"It's Aramaic, Ambassador, the language Jesus spoke, and the language of the original Talmud." She added, with some detectable pride, "It means land of Eden. Our roots here are very deep."

Then, as lightly as he could, he asked her, "Would it be appropriate for me to invite you to dinner? To continue our discussion of roles for your group?"

She smiled, but guardedly, he thought. "It would be appropriate, Ambassador, but it would not be very safe for either of us, unless you want me to come here—in which case it would only be unsafe for me. I came here today through a very roundabout way, concealed in the back of a vehicle until we got to your gate where I showed them your invitation."

"I'm sorry to have inconvenienced you."

"It is a reality of the present time. Your invitation was surprising, and I wanted to see if we could have a useful exchange."

"And did we?"

She smiled again, warmer this time, and said, "Yes, I believe we did."

They had several dinners, arranged with care due to their shared concerns about both security and rumors. Putnam found her very easy to talk with, her time in America and in international settings having made her very comfortable with Americans and the American sense of humor. Always, there was an appropriate distance. They talked about the war, but never directly about the American presence. Putnam was careful never to put her on the spot and invite criticism, but felt it appropriate and even necessary to tell her of some of his own reservations about the war and American policy.

Gradually, she was more forthcoming. In their first meeting, she had shared her background with him, and it helped him understand more about her independence.

"May I ask your place among the many groups in this country?"

"I am Chaldean, Ambassador. We are Christians of the Middle East. We have been here for nearly two millennia, and there are more than a million of us in this country. Our Archbishop has been threatened by terrorists, and many thousands of my fellow Chaldean Christians have left the country since your…" she paused, "your troops came into our country, because it has become so dangerous for us now."

"And your husband?" He gestured to her wedding ring.

Unsmiling, she replied, "My husband worked for the former press spokesman for the dictator. We have not lived together since he took that position. I believe he is now in one of your military's prisons." She looked down at the ring. "I wear the ring because I believe he is still alive and that means we are still married in the eyes of our church."

Putnam found himself enjoying both her company and how much he was learning from her about deeper currents of local culture and attitudes than he had been able to pick up from official sources. Without formally agreeing to a routine, they tacitly continued their dinners, always aware of security and his position in the embassy.

Petrosian had been able to schedule his visit to the Valley troops, and the negotiations with security had resulted in their being able to accompany a supply convoy. They left at dawn, trying to avoid the heat.

On the edge of the city, as the desert opened up, Putnam looked out the Humvee window and saw three men watching them from a first floor window of a three-story building. As they drove by, Putnam thought he saw one of the men raise a cellphone to his ear. He glanced back at the second seat and saw that the sergeant with the security detail was watching the same building.

The battalion's base was a two hour ride south of the capital, and they arrived as the final round of hot breakfasts was being served. *Another difference*, Putnam thought. *Our guys almost never had hot food in the field in those days.*

Petrosian checked in with the command office and introduced the Ambassador to the colonel in charge of the unit. After a brief exchange, Petrosian asked the colonel for permission to look up his cousins and was told where to find them.

The battalion was housed in tents next to a few containers where the weapons and ammunition were kept. One was used as a rigged-up jail, with an air conditioner stuck in a window that had been cut in the side of the container. The front of the container had been removed and bars had been welded in front of what looked like double-strength glass. Putnam saw two prisoners in *dishdashas* sitting on the ground, glaring as the group walked by.

"Who are they?" Putnam asked the captain who was escorting them.

"Couple of guys we caught trying to drive off with a truck of cement," he answered. "They keep trying and we keep catching them. It's like it's a game. We let them go after a few days. Then they send someone else in on the work detail, and they give it another shot. Hell, we're giving the stuff away if they have a halfway good proposal for reconstruction. But they'd rather steal it, I guess. So they can re-sell it."

Petrosian's cousins were part of a scout unit that had just gotten back from a night patrol. He had called ahead and told them he was coming, and they were sprawled out napping after their patrol. As they rose, Putnam could see the stocky, dark Armenian origins they shared with Petrosian, along with their confident bearing.

After the usual profane, family-fueled man-hugs, Petrosian introduced them to the Ambassador. Seeing his pressed fatigues without any insignia other than his name, they seemed confused until Petrosian explained Putnam's role in the embassy.

Putnam said "I appreciate taking a few minutes of your time, fellows. Tell me what you can about your patrol. I understand you just got back."

They looked less confident, shooting a look at Petrosian. He smiled and said "He's cleared guys. He sees stuff that's classified so high God can't read it."

The shorter of the two, who was a Spec 5 and whose nametag read Marajian, said "It was fairly routine, sir. We patrolled outside a village 20 clicks from here that's been giving us some trouble. We got some rocketing from there a few nights ago and thought we could find where it was coming from. Got some good coordinates from one of the overhead teams. But when we got there we found it was a school building. We went inside and poked around but couldn't find anything. Locals told our translator they hadn't seen anything. Pretty quiet night."

Putnam asked, "Any of the local troops go with you?"

Marajian laughed without humor. "They were supposed to. But when we got to the rendezvous point their major was there with one other guy.

Said they had a local festival come up and his guys had to attend it. So they left."

Putnam pressed the point. "What do you think of those troops? What's it going to be like when we clear out of here?"

Marajian shook his head. "No way of knowing, sir. But I wouldn't want to trust them to protect anybody I care about." He was quiet, and then added. "It's like they're still waiting to see who wins between the Sunni and the Shia, and when we leave, I think all hell is going to break loose. These people just don't like each other." Then he looked angry. "Reminds me of what our grandfather used to tell us about the old days in Turkey."

Riding back, Putnam asked Petrosian, "What do you think about what your cousin said? Is this like the Turks and your people?"

"I think it's worse here, sir. As bad as things were in the genocide years, this crap has been going on here for centuries."

"So what ends it? Say you're Ambassador here thirty years from today. Is it going to be the same?"

Petrosian said, "Not if the players are the same. Sir, I know we're supposed to be building a nation here—or helping the locals do it. But I think they really want *two* nations—maybe three with the Kurds. So why should we keep that from happening?"

"Maybe because those nations would just keep fighting each other across their new borders. They'd fight over the oil, or the religious differences, or something else." He sighed. "I don't know either. But I do know that risking those kids' lives every night on patrol makes zero sense to me right now. If the locals won't do anything about assholes who shoot out of school buildings, why should our guys take the risk?"

They had come to the city's outskirts. Putnam noticed the driver of their Humvee reach up and flip a switch over his head. The captain with them leaned over and explained. "Counter-measures for cellphone IEDs. Sometimes it works."

They had come up to the building where Putnam had seen the man with the cellphone. As they drove by, the captain murmured, "God bless the nerd who invented that sweet little machine."

In one of his occasional eyes only memos to the Secretary, following Sheila's advice, Putnam had written about Vietnam and Iraq.

My first observation is not a new point, but it needs repeating: Occupation wipes out pacification. You can't pacify people when you occupy their country. You can dominate them, for a while. You can suppress them, for a long time. But to call that pacifying them is a perversion of the language. They are not pacified, peaceful—they are simmering, waiting for their chance to strike at you, waiting for their Gandhi or their George Washington or for the bastards next door in Iran to ship them some weapons to start their insurgency.

Too many of these places were colonial outposts, and they have long memories. They haven't forgotten what it feels like to be part of someone's empire, and just because we don't have red-coated troops doesn't mean we don't look like imperialists when we come marching in. Or even when we hover invisibly thirty thousand feet up and then drop our bombs into the middle of their villages.

Once you make a huge, world-class mistake, you face a very messy cleanup game for a long time after. And if you persist and refuse to admit that it is a mistake, either the cleanup gets harder—or you just pull out when it's convenient or when you are losing much more than you are winning. And you really do lose credibility.

Yet Reagan pulled out of Lebanon within days after the bombing of the marines. No one questioned the move, and everyone agreed they shouldn't have been there with lousy security in the first place.

The rivalries and hatreds in this country are millennia-old, and some of what we are doing worsens them instead of working past them. It is our concrete barriers that have gone down to divide the capital into areas much more sectarian than they were before we arrived. Part of that resulted from all the weapons that were stolen by both sides when we let the rampaging run free for the first two weeks after we got here. But we made it worse, Tom. That doesn't help anything, and it looks a lot like the ethnic cleansing that went on in Bosnia.

Petrosian once day asked Putnam if he had ever missed having children. Putnam smiled and said, "Your premise may need revision, Petrosian." Smiling at Petrosian's quizzical look, Putnam then told Petrosian a story very few of his friends and colleagues had ever heard.

Twenty-two years after returning from Vietnam, while on a desk assignment in State, Putnam had received a call from a young man named Steven Jefferson who said that Ernie Scott had suggested he meet with Putnam to discuss his graduate school plans. Ordinarily Putnam would have referred the young man to his staff, but Scott's name was still a door-opener for Putnam, and he agreed to see the student.

When the young man came through the door of Putnam's office, Putnam had a strong sense that the visit had little to do with Ernie Scott. The young man was a handsome, well-dressed Eurasian with a ready smile. He shook hands and settled into the chair Putnam had indicated.

"Sir, I appreciate your seeing me. Ernie Scott, who knows my parents, had suggested I get in touch with you. I just finished my undergraduate work at the University of Colorado, and I'm applying to Cornell for graduate work. Cornell seems a good fit with my interests in agricultural assistance programs."

"Well, I could write something for you, Steven, but I'm afraid I don't know enough about you to be specific, which is what they're usually looking for."

Jefferson smiled and reached into his coat pocket, handing Putnam a picture. It was a picture of Thuy Thieu and Putnam taken at a base exchange photo shop. As Putnam looked at it with amazement, Jefferson said, "I'm Thuy Thieu's son. A year ago, when I turned 21, she told me that you are my father."

"Thuy is here—in the US? Your father? I never knew... she never told me..."

"I know, sir. She married an army captain, Bill Jefferson, who retired from the army after they came to live in Colorado. He teaches in the ROTC program at the U, and she's an advisor in the international relations program at the Korbel School at the U. Sir, I think of Bill Jefferson as my father in every way that counts. But my mother wanted me to know my full history, and so she told me about you. My father knows I'm here, and he's fine with my asking you for this help."

Putnam was still struggling to sort out his emotions. Relief that Thuy had gotten to the US after all. Amazement that after many years of having no children, suddenly he had a rather extraordinary one. And even a little pride that he had something to do with the life of this remarkable young man.

"I am… I'm glad you came to see me, Steven. I'm sure you can understand that I'm a little overwhelmed by your…your news. And I'd be delighted to write something for you to Cornell. Tell me more about yourself. I assume you want me to write as a reference, rather than as …as a family member."

"Yes, sir. My mother told me she never told you she was pregnant before you left Saigon. And then she and my father decided they would tell me about you once I was 21. I'm glad they did."

He went on, watching Putnam's reactions carefully. "I think they've had a good marriage. My mother has been back to Vietnam twice, and she took me with her five years ago. We visited the village where she grew up. I want to go to Cornell for the agricultural programs to see if I can help villages like that."

"That's a great goal. Your father must be a remarkable man." Putnam realized that Bill Jefferson had married a woman with a child she had had with another man, and then raised that child.

"He is, sir. And he really respects how much my mother wanted me to give something back, both to this country and to hers—her first country."

They talked for an hour, and Steven told Putnam about his life growing up in Boulder. After Thuy told him about Putnam, he had looked up Putnam's ancestry online and found that Putnam's great-grandfather was buried in Boulder, after a remarkable life of his own, serving as a judge in Missouri and then as a founding trustee of the University of Colorado. In the family legend that Putnam had heard as a boy, his great-grandfather capped off his career in the Old West as Billy the Kid's lawyer during the Lincoln County wars in New Mexico. The cemetery where he was buried was only a few blocks from where Steven had grown up in Boulder, and he showed Putnam another picture of himself standing beside Putnam's great grandfather's—his own great-great grandfather's grave.

As he walked Steven to the door, Putnam was still sorting out his reactions to the visit. He was filled with a kind of quiet joy at discovering he had a son, and at the same time realized he had just acquired some new responsibilities to be whatever the young man wanted him to be in years to come.

Petrosian was quiet at the end of the story. "Sir, that is an unbelievable story. Do you ever see him?"

"He's done a very good job of staying in touch. He came down from Cornell a couple of times and interviewed me for some papers he was doing, and we've spent some time at my place in Connecticut. He's in Bangkok now, passed his FSO a few years ago and got an assignment working with the agricultural missions in Southeast Asia. Almost the perfect first job. And I'm pleased to say I had nothing to do with it. He got it on his merits."

"So you do have children—a child anyway, but you missed all the child parts."

"Yes, and I have very mixed feelings about that. Not sorry to miss the diapers—but I missed a lot of other things as well." He was quiet for a while, and then added, "He's a fine young man and I'll take whatever I can get."

"Have you ever gotten in touch with his mother?"

"No. It seemed best to let that alone. So I have."

Loomis and Sydowski, Putnam's housemates, were both at his rank, Ambassadors at large. Loomis was from the economics side of the State Department, and had been assigned oversight of the reconstruction efforts that involved large scale projects, including oil production and highways. Sydowski had been introduced as being from INR, the Intelligence and Research staff arm to the Secretary. He had served as Deputy Assistant Secretary in INR, but his reticence in describing his exact functions reminded Putnam that he was either CIA or CIA liaison.

Loomis was outgoing, from Iowa, a former dean of the Business School at the state university. He had some political connections that were never spelled out, but that Putnam assumed had something to do with the state's unique role in presidential politics. Sydowski was much more taciturn and blunt, from Georgia, with a twenty-year Army career after graduating from West Point. He was a veteran of Desert Storm and had several postings to Middle East countries, including Israel.

There were few opportunities for the three of them to use the living room of their residence for informal talk, but on one such occasion, they had compared notes on their careers and postings. As the conversation warmed and the bourbon his roommates were drinking worked its impact, Sydowski opened up a bit on life in the Green Zone.

"Will, you'll get used to it, but this is a pretty insulated setup. Those seventeen-foot blast walls do more than keep people out—they keep us from knowing what we're doing, sometimes. My advice is to get outside as much as you can, within limits, of course. I sometimes think we're flying blind here, cooped up in this place. Loomis here goes out with the contractors, and their security is pretty fierce. But I prefer to go out with as small a detail as I can get away with."

Putnam said, "I appreciate the advice. When I got here and saw the PX inside the walls, along with the Green Zone Bazaar, those shops run by locals, and a fully equipped computer store, I thought for a moment that I was in suburban Arlington."

Sydowski laughed, and said, "Yeah. Bizarre is right. We really have a lot of people in here who never go outside. They're sitting in their offices in the old palace writing constitutions while people are getting blown up outside and the electricity goes off at 5 pm in the rest of Baghdad."

Loomis frowned, "I'm not sure I'd be so negative about it. We're getting hundreds of miles of highways built that are going to connect parts of this country that have never had good roads. And we're putting thousands of the locals to work with good jobs."

Sydowski said, "Yes, but what happens when we leave and the funding for all that cuts off? What are those guys going to do then?"

Loomis said, "We have plans for the next ten years, and we're projecting a 10% growth rate of the national economy. The oil development alone is going to be able to pay for a lot of additional reconstruction."

"Yeah, but most of the oil is up in Kurd territory, and they're totally at odds with the Shia political types we're going to turn the government over to next year."

The conversation trailed off, and Putnam could tell that the two had had this disagreement often enough that they had decided not to pursue it in any depth. It echoed some of the discussions Putnam had already heard in the Executive Council, although Sydowski had not been as blunt about his reservations in those sessions. Putnam assumed his conclusions were going straight back to the Agency, and wondered if they were having any effect.

Will had stopped drinking several postings back, after a night in which he had gone too far at an embassy party in a country whose vice-president was widely known to be the protector and beneficiary of opium smuggling and, it was also rumored, trafficking in prostitution. Will had considerably more bourbon that he should have, and referred to the vice-president as the "pimp-in-waiting."

The remark had traveled rapidly and Will received an angry cable from an Assistant Secretary of State whose job, as nearly as Will could figure out, was chief apologist.

So alcohol and Will had parted company. He clung to his cigars all the more fiercely, scoping out the allowable and semi-allowable smoking areas in the embassy and living spaces he inhabited. And every chance he had, he consistently argued for an end to the Cuban embargo.

As Putnam continued his dinners with Aisha, she assumed the role of tutor, because Putnam's questions about Iraq had begun to come so fast that she had stopped him and said she was going to try to organize what he needed to know in small bites. So she walked him through the history and what she felt were the most important things he needed to know about culture and the strengths of the Iraqi worldview. She never held back from criticizing what she felt was wrong with Iraq, but she helped him understand much more than he could have gotten from any other sources. She wanted him to try to understand about what Americans didn't grasp, and he worked hard at justifying her effort.

She talked about what it meant to live, in her words, "at one of the busiest intersections on the planet." From the Greeks on, she told him, the kingdoms and caliphates and tribes of the Middle East had been invaded, especially those in what was now Iraq. Alexander, Rome, the Persians, the Mongols, the Crusaders, the Ottomans, the British—the waves of invasion led to a historical paranoia that was well-justified.

"You are merely the most recent of the invaders," she said. "And so we are naturally suspicious. Invading us to do us some good—that is what they all said."

She described the second layer of paranoia that flowed from the threat of Western values, the fear of the new, of innovative technology that brought new ideas and new attitudes and, inevitably, new variations of power. "What is new," she told him, "is for many in the Middle East the most threatening force imaginable."

She said, "Innovation, *bid'a*, is in Islam the greatest heresy—to suggest something new in the face of what is established by the Prophet. It originally meant innovation in religious doctrine, but it is an easy slope down from that to fear of innovation in other things. And then tradition becomes all, and we risk becoming a backward people, closed to the new, to science, to evolution in human thinking."

The hardest part of it for Putnam was understanding the treatment of women. He had explained his refraining from alcohol to her, and so she used that experience to try to help him understand what Americans inevitably saw as misogyny in Arab culture.

"Will, it's not in the religion, it's in the culture. And some of it comes from the history, from a twisting of the history of the Middle East. Some of the women who are writing now about the future of Islam are reminding us that the origins of Islam included much better treatment of women than in most countries in the Arab world today. It has been perverted by a kind of addiction."

"Addiction?"

"Yes. An addiction to male power. The philosopher Bertrand Russell wrote somewhere that power is an addiction just like alcohol or drugs or tobacco. Our males learn from their earliest days that girls and women are to be protected, which inevitably makes them inferior. And when you are insecure about being from a backward part of the world, this gets perverted, into a kind of addiction to power. Some men have internalized the view that we hate the West for the power they have had over us and for their technology and the sweep of their popular culture. And so some men and religious leaders cling to the certainty that they will always have the power to dominate their women. They will justify it by talking about the sanctity of the home. But in the final analysis, the point is that women are not to be given any power."

"So it's our fault—the imperialists?"

"No, but the lust for power is very strong, and when you lose it in one part of your life, you sometimes go looking for it in other parts. When you add the lure of sex to the lust for power—the ability to control getting what your biology compels you to seek—you end up with a very addictive drug."

Putnam smiled, but cautiously. "It is, in a way, an adolescent male's dream—to have power whenever you have the urge."

"Yes, I suppose so. But the other side of that is that the family will protect their own women from that urge at all costs. Driven by the certain knowledge that men seek to dominate women—most men," she smiled, "the men of the family suspect all outsiders. And that adds to the fierceness with which women are hidden away, and to the demand that males must have the power to hide their women from the worst ravages of other men outside the family."

She smiled, adding, "And some of your religious denominations have the same patterns, Will. At times, here, it is justified as an exaltation of what is seen as precious in womanhood, her supreme status as the giver of life, which must be protected above all values. *Umma*, the people, the community, comes from *umm*—mother."

She went on. "And when your culture roars in with nearly naked women in your magazines and your videos and your movies—you threaten us at our core. Satan is the tempter—and that is why the ayatollahs call you the Great Satan. You are infidels by definition, but you are threatening not because you are infidels, but because your culture threatens to shatter ours."

"And so we're seen as crusaders for sexual depravity."

"Exactly."

"So what will happen? When you add it all up, what's most likely?"

"In the final analysis, it is up to Iran and Turkey. Iran because of history and the Shia. Turkey because they will decide whether the Kurds will be given a nation or enough autonomy to have a virtual nation. And Iran matters most. The word *Baghdad* is Persian, Will. If Iran is able to solve its nuclear problem with the US and emerge from sanctions, it will soon be powerful enough to decide whether the east of our country will become essentially a western province of Iran. Whatever you do, you will have little influence on that decision once you agree to lift sanctions. They are too close and too powerful to resist, despite your trillion-dollar adventure here."

Putnam couldn't help but wonder what the Executive Council would make of their discussion.

Putnam was back in his study, talking with Petrosian.

"Mike, you said the other day you hang out with some of the Air Force guys."

"Yes, sir."

"Could you get me a session with them? Totally off the record, I just want to understand better what they do."

The session was arranged at the air base that was adjacent to the capital. Petrosian had arranged for an informal conversation with a Captain Marty Wang, an Air Force Academy graduate who had flown four tours in C-130s in Iraq and Afghanistan. They sat in the flight bay on foldup chairs.

"Captain, tell me how the review works for firing on a target."

"Sir, we go through several levels." Then he paused. "Maybe you should talk to the brass about this. They aren't wild about us going out of channels."

"This is off the record, and I will never use your name and what you are telling me. I just want to understand the process better."

"All right. We have to get authorization to fire after we get a target from ground troops or from our spotters—or the overhead assets."

"The satellites and drones, you mean?"

"Yes, sir."

"How long does that authorization take?"

"It comes from the Ground Force Commander. He has the authority on his own to authorize strikes—and with which kinds of weapons. The timing varies depending on what we're targeting, sir. It can be a few seconds if our guys are taking fire and in serious trouble of being over-run. Or it can take a lot longer if it is a target we're trying to identify as a threat. Or if he's asking for heavier ordinance."

"And in your experience, how many times has that authorization been mistaken?"

"Mistaken, sir?"

"How many times has it resulted in your firing on civilians who are not part of the targeted forces or commanders?"

The Captain was angry now, seeing that Putnam was questioning his judgment. "Sir, with respect, you have no idea what we do or how we do it."

"I know that and I totally agree, Captain. That's why I'm talking to you. Collateral casualties come up here in the embassy all the time. And I need to understand our side of the story." Then he played a card he knew would work. "I don't know how many other embassy staff have sat down with you and asked these questions."

Grudgingly, then with a smile, Wang said, "You're the first. We talk to the chain of command about this all the time. But never on the civilian side." He continued. "We've made mistakes. You'd have to get the number from USAF command. But when we do, it's usually because we're responding to an urgent request from ground troops under fire. We would never know if civilians were in the line of fire until after the incident is over. The rules are different in those cases. I'm sure you understand that, sir."

Putnam said, "Of course. War isn't perfection—any more than diplomacy is. And when our guys on the ground want help, your job is to give it to them as fast as you can. I get that. If I had your job, I'd always make a mistake on the side of protecting our guys."

Wang went on, calmed down. "It happens more than we'd want it to. There's no reset button. You fire, and then—for some of us—you pray. For the rest, you go on to the next target." He looked away. "Praying takes time."

"Thank you, Captain, That's what I needed." He paused, wanting to end on a higher note. "I was once part of a war where those controls barely existed. This is infinitely better. Not perfect, but a hell of a lot better."

"Thank you, sir."

Wang then looked at Putnam and said, quietly but with great intensity, "One more fact you might want to take down, Ambassador. The latest UN report says that three-fourths of all civilian casualties are due to insurgents firing on civilians or suicide bombings in crowds. Three-fourths. That's a UN report—not ours."

"Noted. And you can be sure that'll be pointed out in any discussion that I'm part of, Captain."

Putnam and Aisha had had lunches and dinners for a month, and had become much more comfortable with each other. Each had told their story, and responded to gently phrased questions about their marriages and their families. Putnam had told Aisha of his son, Steven, and she had explained that she had determined to have no children once she saw who her husband really was.

They were at her apartment, and had finished a leisurely dinner. Aisha was sitting next to Putnam on her couch, and she leaned over and kissed him, and then said, in mock-solemn tones, "I think it is time we moved to the next stage of our cultural exchange."

Putnam tried not to show the full measure of his pleasure, and said, adopting her formal tone, "I agree completely. I believe you can never understand another culture until a full and frank exchange has taken place with no barriers between the parties."

"Such as clothes?"

"Exactly what I had in mind."

Love-making with Aisha was of a slower, more graceful kind, far from the feverish grasping of the young. She was a generous, full-bodied lover, blending intimate talk with even more intimate touches and embraces. At one point she actually giggled and said "You do know that the Kama Sutra is not a part of our culture."

To which he replied "You could have fooled me."

Once he smiled at her during an interlude in their lovemaking, and said, combining an apology with a claim, "As you can see, I am not here to conquer you."

To which she replied, after a lingering kiss, "Nor am I here to be conquered, beloved."

"Graham Greene once said age is as good a card to be played in the sexual game as youth."

She laughed softly and said "Ah yes, but the games are played less frequently in those leagues, I am told."

He slowly reached over and stroked her hair. "Let's see about that."

There had been a painful confrontation with the embassy security team when Putnam told them he would be spending some of his nights with Aisha outside the Green Zone. The security head insisted that he take a detail with him, which Putnam refused.

"I am not having some kid blown up because he is standing outside an apartment building in the same place every night thinking he has to protect me."

"Every night? This is now a permanent thing, Ambassador?"

"My nocturnal habits are not your concern, Colonel, You—"

The colonel interrupted. "The hell they aren't my concern. I'm the one who gets demoted and sent home if you get assassinated, Ambassador. Try not to forget that."

After they cooled off, they negotiated. Putnam explained, "This woman is a close friend, and she is a major asset to our mission. She has contacts and knowledge that are invaluable to me in doing my job. I need to see her on a continuing basis, just as the CIA agents see their contacts on a regular basis."

"'Seeing her,' as you put it, is fine. But leaving the Green Zone to do it is a problem. I would suggest that you bring her here, if you must, and that you visit her where she lives no more than two nights a week, on a completely random schedule. I will send plainsclothes troops with you, only two, and two local police who are trusted. And I will ask you to sign a statement that you understand the risks you are taking, and the risks to those troops."

Putnam agreed, feeling he had no choice, and wondering how he would explain it to Aisha. When he did, she simply shrugged and said, "I understand. You are worth the risk, beloved, and we will be careful."

The security problem had finally been worked out with a set of elaborate arrangements in which Petrosian and another translator would trade off taking Putnam to Aisha's apartment and bringing Aisha into the Green Zone. Petrosian had some contacts among former students in the US who had invited him to teach an evening class on international relations at their university in the capital. After the class, he would pick Aisha up and drive her to the Green Zone. Using nondescript older cars, the transport worked well over a period of five months. They were together two or three nights a week, on average. Loomis and Sydowski were very discreet about entering Putnam's space when Aisha was there, and she stayed in his room as much as possible.

She was graceful in every movement; he would not have doubted it if she had told him she had been a dancer in an earlier life. Her lustrous dark hair curled carefully out from under her scarf in public, but in his apartment, when she slowly slipped it off, in a movement that he found totally seductive, it billowed around her head. She had full lips, large brown eyes set off by a larger-than-usual nose, and cheekbones that suggested some Eastern European had wandered by at some point in her genetic history. Her body spoke to him in joyous curves, lovely breasts, a still-visible waist, and hips widening to ample curves of still-firm flesh. The total effect was simple: it said *Woman, gracefully mature, knowing much of life's ups and downs.*

The Executive Council continued to meet weekly. At every meeting, sooner or later someone made the point that Putnam had come to think of as *the TIN-V moment*—the point at which someone said or implied that "this is not Vietnam." The way the point was argued varied from speaker to speaker, but the point was always to show how different things were.

The geography was different, the religious factions were different, US technology and war-fighting tools were different—anything that could divert the discussion from someone saying that it was the same. To admit that Iraq was at all like Vietnam was to open the door to considering how it ended in Vietnam. And that was the one memory that was deeply etched in the minds of most of the embassy senior staff, whether they had been in Vietnam or not.

But it *was* the same, Putnam had come to believe. Or enough like it to make the parallels much more important than the alleged differences.

The argument that was masked as a discussion was very rarely stated directly. No one said *we screwed this part up in Vietnam and we're doing it again.* It was much more subtle, which was why Putnam wasn't.

He had decided five or six months into the job that he had by then learned enough to see what parts of the war and the endless negotiations with the local government really were repeating themselves. He came to feel that those were the parts of it where he needed to speak out.

If he had been as indirect in using the nuanced language that most of the Council used when they talked about the war and its effects, he would have blended in. But finally, he had decided to stop trying to blend in. He had sent more memos to the Secretary, but little had happened as a result, so far as Putnam could tell.

A meeting had put the transfer of power to the Iraqis on the agenda, and after an hour, Putnam had finally heard enough. He looked over at Beemer, indicating that he wanted to talk. Beemer seemed a bit surprised, but nodded at him.

"Let me ask a few questions if I could. First, do we agree that the government here is deeply involved in corruption and nepotism, to a point where it jeopardizes our efforts to get their ministries working again and projects built? Second, do we agree that the current level of civilian casualties, despite our best efforts, is unacceptable because of its effects on recruiting insurgents and our eventual human rights liabilities? And finally, what is the answer to the question of why we are asking our troops to patrol in hostile areas when we are preparing to withdraw and let the Iraqi troops take over?"

Beemer, leaning back, said through steepled hands, "Interesting questions, Ambassador. General Easton, perhaps you could take the second two questions and then I will try to respond to the first—to the extent that it needs a response."

Easton was able to contain his anger, but not to conceal it. "I understand you were briefed recently by Air Force personnel on our protocols for firing on insurgents, so let me see if I can answer any specific questions you have."

"My specific question is whether we maintain a running total of civilian casualties that were preventable and include them in after-action reports."

"*Preventable*, Ambassador? What you construe as preventable and what troops under fire think they needed to beat back an attack may vary a great deal."

"Use whatever definition you like. Do we keep such records?"

Easton knew that if he said yes, the next question would call for review of those records over time, which he could not allow for fear of leaks. If he denied they existed, the callousness of not even recording civilian deaths or injuries would be obvious.

"I'll bring what we have to our next meeting, Ambassador, and we'll see if it meets your standards."

"Very well. And the other question, about what we are asking of our troops during withdrawal? How can we keep our troops safe without shooting at civilians?"

"We are naturally being more cautious as we withdraw from forward positions. But we are still in some very dangerous positions, and we are defending them as we reduce our numbers in country."

"My question is why we are in dangerous positions at all if we are withdrawing. Why don't we rely on the local forces we have been training?"

By now Easton had lost it. He raised his voice and said, through gritted teeth, "We are under fire because this is a bloody dangerous country, Putnam, and you damn well know it. We're not going to retreat to our bunkers and wait for the transports to come, whatever you may want. We have a mission and we're going to carry it out, even if it means we get shot at. That's what we get paid for. And that's what we're going to do."

"General, could you explain how the incident in Bar Hazah relates to that approach?"

Easton replied, "The insurgents retreated to a school—a school which we had built, I might add. And after verifying that no children were known to be in the building, we fired on the insurgents' positions."

"General, why didn't we surround the school with local forces if we had the insurgents pinned down?"

"Because the local forces were not in position. The bastards had retreated to safe locations once the firing started. It is a pattern that is all too familiar, I'm sorry to say."

"But these are the troops we are expecting to replace us, correct?" He paused, ready to call on history again. "I remember how much we hoped the Vietnamese troops would be able to pick up the slack as we drew down our forces, but it just didn't happen."

Easton shot back. "I was in Vietnam too, Ambassador. And I guess I was a little closer to the front lines than you were able to get."

Putnam answered quickly, but softly. "I'll guarantee that you were closer, General, but I saw what we told the American people about those front lines. They didn't buy it. And they didn't buy our alliances with the poor excuses for a national government we were stuck with. You know as well as I do that we never had a local horse to bet on that was worth a damn, General, and it feels to me like we're in the same dead end here. Drug dealers, Shia thugs, and Al Qaeda wannabes. This is the nation we're trying to build here?"

Beemer couldn't let that go by. "Will, that's unfair. There are hundreds of senior officials in the government whom we work with every day. They're honest and they want to overcome the sectarian battles that have plagued their country."

Putnam answered, his tone much quieter. "Agreed. I don't mean to say there aren't honest, hard-working officials, and I know they are our best hope."

Beemer stepped in again, using his *now let's stay calm here* voice. "I'd like to respond to your first question, Will. There are definitely elements of the government here who are skimming from our grants and contracts. We have repeatedly warned the administration that they must get rid of these appointees, or they will risk cutbacks in our aid to those parts of the government that are implicated in this kind of corruption."

Knowing the answer, Putnam pressed harder. "And have we ever cut any funds?"

Beemer frowned and said "No, but we remain ready to do so if needed. Some of the implicated officials have been removed. Others are on notice that they will be if they don't cease their practices."

"They aren't just implicated. They're padding their Swiss bank accounts every month with their profits."

"And how do you know that?"

"Treasury is using new technology to watch funds transfers, and they have detected unmistakable transfers."

Beemer was seething, furious that Putnam had gotten knowledge about Washington-based operations he had not been briefed on. "I don't know your sources, but I haven't heard that."

"I'll await your checking my sources out, Larry. But I think they're very reliable. The bottom line is that these guys are ripping us off and they're moving their profits outside the country."

Then he smiled and said in a much quieter voice, "Look, I appreciate this exchange and I don't want to take any more of the Council's time. Perhaps we can table this discussion for now and come back to it when the information has been compiled."

He had backed down. It was too soon to burn his bridges, and he wanted to build a stronger case. He had gotten his opponents to reveal their arguments, and he could prepare his responses with new evidence, while seeking the alliances he knew he would need to win the next round. For the first time, they were going to have to report what they had been ignoring. Plus he had identified new allies. He could hear it and he could see it, watching the body language and discomfort at Easton's arguments.

As Putnam expected, Beemer asked for a private meeting. This would be the predictable "let try to get along, don't rock the boat so much" speech that the occasion called for, and it would buy him some more time to marshal his forces. The only real challenge would be concealing his disdain.

"The corruption thing is killing us, Aisha."

She smiled and nodded. "Yes, it is. I can see that. The latest study of your congressional fund-raising turned up amazing correlations of legislation favoring the firms that gave the most. It's extraordinary."

Putnam was usually pleased that Aisha kept her English current by reading the *New York Times* and the *Washington Post* online every day. But not always.

Trying not to let his irritation show, he said, "So you're saying that our corruption is the same as yours?"

"Not at all. Yours is much more lavish than ours. Somebody steals some concrete from one of your construction sites here, or the permits for the project have to be lubricated with cash. That's our kind of corruption. But giving thousands of millionaire farmers subsidies not to grow their crops? Letting companies deduct the costs of their corporate jets from their taxes? That would be the envy of our thieves if they could ever understand it. I believe even your Republican members of Congress call it 'crony capitalism.'"

She went on, watching his frown grow deeper and deeper. "Corruption. Yes, that's a big problem. But it's deep in history, isn't it? Tammany Hall. 'Honest graft,' as George Washington Plunkitt labeled it. Abscam—such a pungent way of referring to Arabs."

She was smiling, knowing that this was not the discussion he had wanted to have, and at the same time knowing that she had impressed him with her familiarity with American ways of legislating.

He shook his head, and said "You never cease to amaze me. Fortunately the officials we deal with don't have your cultural mastery of our strange ways."

Putnam had arranged to meet with two of the non-governmental organizations—widely identified as NGOs—that had been working in Iraq long before the US troops arrived. He was continuing to work on Beemer's proposal that he explore better coordination among the many NGOs working in the country, but he also wanted to understand how these groups worked with children and with each other.

The two executive directors quickly accepted an invitation to meet with Putnam in the Green Zone, and both arrived a few minutes before their agreed-upon meeting time. The country director for Rescue the World's Children was a late-middle aged man who was somewhat overweight. The head of Apostolic Charities was a younger woman of Middle Eastern origins, dressed in civilian clothes except for a head scarf with a design that appeared to Putnam to be a pattern of clouds.

They met in one of the embassy's conference rooms that had walls covered with maps of current and proposed projects.

Putnam began saying "Thank you for meeting with me. I know you meet regularly with the USAID team, but I wanted to understand your work and how it affects what we're trying to do with the development and humanitarian agenda."

"We're glad to have you talk with us, Ambassador."

"Let me ask a question, if I may. What measures do you use to judge your impact?"

The Rescue director said, "Ten years ago that would have been a very difficult question for us to answer. But now we have developed new metrics for measuring not only head counts but some of the longer-term effects of our work. I can get you copies of those annual reports if you like, Ambassador."

The other NGO official spoke up. "We also work with some civil society organizations, smaller, more grass-roots agencies that are sometimes working in a specific area of the country or on more narrowly defined issues, such as birth registration, child labor, and gender equity."

"How are they funded?"

She smiled. "Some of them are very strict about not accepting any US government funding, for fear it will identify them too much with US policy and the military. One of the most effective is a group called the Nineveh Institute for Learning. They sponsor schools for girls, and they work very hard to show their independence of US policy so that their schools can stay open. They work in some of the most traditionalist areas of the country. They work through a national organization here and a parallel group based in Minnesota that does fund-raising. The local staff go into a village or a region and meet with the elders and then with the local women's groups where they exist. The women talk with their husbands and fathers, and then they talk with the elders. It's sometimes very slow work, but they have made remarkable progress in increasing the number of girls attending school."

Putnam said, "Help me understand something. The biggest question about NGOs, it seems to me, is whether we have hit the ceiling of our generosity, or whether government and private charity, along with much larger trade and financial flows, could break through what we've been doing with token projects and move up to making changes at scale." He smiled, dialing down his intensity, which he could tell was beginning to concern them.

He continued. "A long time ago, I worked as a summer intern in the State Department on a project that was supposed to identify the products of the poorest nations. The theory then was that we could lower tariffs in ways that affected the poorest workers in those countries. It had nothing to do with foreign aid. It was trying to affect the flow of foreign *trade* to help the developing countries. Do your groups ever get involved in those issues?"

The head of the Rescue group said, "Our national organizations have lobbied for those kinds of changes, Ambassador. It makes sense, as a companion measure to what we are trying to do with private aid."

"But most of your funding now is from the government, right?"

It was a point he had deliberatelynot begun with, because it was so at odds with their carefully cultivated image of fund-raising from private donors.

"A sizable portion is, yes. We operate as contractors, because the State Department, as I'm sure you know, has cut its own staff and hired contractors to deliver most of its programs. So we bid on those contracts, and we're proud to have been awarded some of them."

Wanting to change the subject, he added. "I'd like to bring up a rather difficult subject, Ambassador. Some of our workers have been targeted in some of the rural areas where your reconstruction units have been based. The military does an excellent job building roads and schools, sir. But when these units in uniform work on local projects and then leave, the civilians who follow them to work in those schools sometimes have been attacked because they are seen as closely linked to the military. Militarizing foreign aid risks making foreign aid workers into targets."

Putnam frowned. "I see your point. Does it make any difference when the workers are Iraqi instead of foreigners?"

"Not always. The building remains American—your units leave American labels on them. That makes anyone who works there a target."

"And the local police and military are no help?"

"In our experience, Ambassador, they cannot always be trusted."

Then the woman from the children's organization asked Putnam a question. "Ambassador, I'd like to ask, if I could, how much is our embassy's position on human rights informed by what we have learned lately about brain development in children?"

Seeing his quizzical look, she added, "I'm asking because recent research on neurodevelopmental damage makes clear that there are lasting effects of the harm that many of these children face as they grow up. War is one of them, of course, but so is abuse and neglect. Children's brains change in response to these toxic effects. Ambassador, I attended a lecture recently where the speaker asked us all a very provocative question: what would we do if we knew that four hundred million children were being poisoned in ways that affect their brains? That's the number of children who are abused or who suffer profound dislocation in their lives—sometimes by their parents, sometimes by others. Girls, of course, are the main victims of sexual abuse as a result of early marriage and gender bias in many cultures. Including our own here in Iraq, at times."

She had made her point at length, with passion, but without hectoring Putnam. He said "I'm fascinated by what you're telling me, and I confess I know almost nothing about it. Could you give me some references to look into? And tell me who in our government or at UNICEF or other agencies is framing the issue this way?"

"I'd be glad to send you a reading list. It's a human rights issue—children's rights, really. But I'm afraid there are very few people who have yet put those pieces together. The human rights people are over here," she gestured with an outstretched arm and a pointed finger, "and the child development and neurodevelopmental people are mostly over here," and the other arm went out with the same gesture.

Putnam had steered clear of most of the media—the word "press" had been replaced with media and he usually remembered it—because he knew it would make Beemer and his acolytes anxious if stories began to emerge that might be sourced to Putnam. But he knew too many of them to be able to duck all contacts. Some of the media in Baghdad were reporting to editors who had been his peers in Saigon, and that also made it difficult to totally avoid requests for interviews.

So he went through with some innocuous interviews, stressing his role in the assignment Beemer had given him reviewing civilian agencies and the NGO role. A few of the reporters pressed him on his views of the war, and one or two even knew enough of his history to ask him for comparisons. But Putnam had learned long ago how to answer the question he wanted to answer rather than the one the reporter sought, and he was able to parry most of them.

Except for Cassie Gillis. Cassie Gillis and Putnam had first met in Washington, during his assignment to the White House, and since she was covering Capitol Hill at that point, there was no formal bar to their seeing each other. They had been together, off and on over a five-year period, which ended when he was assigned back overseas. Neither had wanted any kind of permanency, and they had parted amicably, Putnam thought.

Cassie had been involved in some of the Pentagon reporting immediately prior to the invasion in 2003, and had been one of the reporters who was persuaded by Iraqi expatriates that weapons of mass destruction existed. Once assigned to Baghdad, she did everything she could to vindicate her earlier reporting, which became more and more difficult once the WMD myths began to appear impossible to document.

She called Putnam with a request for an interview within a few days of his arrival. He told Johansen about the call, but not about their prior relationship. Other than warning him about her obsession with WMD, which Johansen assumed Putnam would avoid, he urged Putnam to go ahead and make contact with her.

"It's more of a story if you duck her, Will, so sit down and just bore the hell out of her. I know you can do that."

"Thanks, Dave. Appreciate the vote of confidence."

Gillis came in, and Putnam did all he could not to marvel at how well-preserved she appeared based on his memories of her fifteen years earlier. She was tall, about an inch or two taller than him, with ample endowments, still-blonde hair worn short, and fitted khakis that were definitely fitted well.

They gave each other a perfunctory hug, and she sat down at the small conference table in Putnam's office in the embassy. She began by asking about his current assignments. Putnam told her about the civilian NGO agencies he had started to review, and she made notes as if she cared about what he was saying.

They fenced, and it soon became clear that they had somehow gone past their once-physical rapport to a purely professional encounter. Putnam was mostly grateful that he was not going to have to deal with complicated enticements as an undercurrent in the interview, while the deepest male part of his mind still regretted the passing of the possibility.

Gradually, she tried to move the topic over to the military side of reconstruction and then to security for the civilian projects he had mentioned.

He couldn't help but admire her craft in trying to shift the focus toward WMD. Finally she went all the way. "Will, what have you heard about whether the security forces have gotten any intel on chemical supplies that may still be around? Might that affect some of the reconstruction efforts?"

He looked at her, drawing out the silence, letting her know how transparent her tactics were. Then he asked her, "Did you know Lee Bernard?"

She was surprised at the abrupt change in direction, and said, "Uh, yes. Globe reporter. He was in the Washington bureau when I was on the Hill. Good guy, smart. Retired a few years ago. Why do you ask?"

"Something he told me in Saigon long ago. He told me that in some stories what isn't happening in country is more important than what is."

Then he stopped, not wanting to touch the WMD topic directly, so that he could say he hadn't discussed it.

But she knew instantly that it was a put-down, however veiled. She glared at him and closed her notebook. "Screw you, Putnam. You want to stonewall me, fine. I hoped you might bring some fresh eyes into this thing, but I guess not."

"Cassie, I really can't help you out. I know what this means to you, and I know you'll get past this to dig out some of the mistakes we're making, and even some of what we're doing here that matters. I'd like to help you with that if I can."

He had softened his tone both because he didn't want her to leave angry and because he wanted somehow to honor the comfort they had once given each other.

She was quiet, watching him. Then she smiled at him, and he knew she hadn't given up on a story, even if it wasn't the story she had come for. "One more question, Will, for old times' sake. Does this take you back to Saigon, or is it totally different?"

"Can I go off the record?"

She laughed, and said, "I'd negotiate for background, but you're the only one who was really in both places who could answer that question in any depth. So they'd know it was you. Sure, off the record."

"Thanks." He paused, wanting to answer her question with more than slogans. "It's painfully similar, in too many ways. And yet it's obviously different. We're different, all of us. The world is different. We buy $25 billion a year worth of imports from Vietnam now, going up every year. Our ships dock there, we did joint military maneuvers with them last year. We're caught in a terrible cross-fire here that goes back a thousand years."

He stopped, wanting to withhold what he was beginning to slide into, realizing how much he wanted to talk to somebody about all that was tragically similar in the two wars—but not to a reporter. Not yet.

She read the pause, and knew she had gotten what little she could get on this round. "Can we talk about that some day? I know you well enough to know you've thought about that a lot. Not now, but some day?"

"Yes." He smiled. "They'll soon figure out that I'm just an old windbag and tune me out. And I'd welcome an audience at that point."

"Oh, I doubt they're going to tune you out, Will. Not you." Then she leaned forward and touched his face. "Still have your music?"

"Yes." And as they parted, this time the hug was far from perfunctory, and Putnam began to be very grateful that his deepened relationship with Aisha would prevent any further confusion about Cassie Gillis.

Putnam finally arranged for a second trip to one of the villages near the capital, one that was far enough out that it wasn't part of the capital's sectarian cross-fighting and one where there were no US forces nearby. He had to negotiate for a protective detail with the Embassy security and then separately with the military side. After rejecting a helicopter ride and escort, the two security authorities agreed that he could ride in a Humvee with a troop escort of only three, negotiating down from a whole platoon. A major from the civil reconstruction detail was assigned to head up the detail.

He also asked for and was given approval to take Aisha as his translator. It had been her suggestion originally, and he was glad she was coming. The plan was for them to visit an orphanage, a school for girls and boys, and meet with the village elders to review reconstruction plans.

The road out of the capital to the village took an hour, even though it was only thirty kilometers north of the city. The buildings of the capital grew smaller, and then the road was open, paved recently, with signs announcing that US funds had paid for the paving. The signs were almost totally obscured by slogans in Arabic. Aisha told them that most of them were anti-American.

They passed through US checkpoints, Iraq army checkpoints, and provincial checkpoints, all requiring inspection of the vehicles. Putnam was patient, but could tell that Aisha was even more impatient. She turned away from the checkpoint staff until they asked to see her identification papers, and then she handed them over quickly, watched them carefully, then accepted a nod from one of the ranking officers.

As he looked out the window of the armored vehicle, Putnam tried to recall his college professors' brief recounting of the dozens of armies that had swept across the deserts and nearby foothills that were coming into view. Hittites and Assyrians, Babylonians and Mongols, Persians, Greeks, and Romans. Millennia of conquerors, passed on into history.

He murmured "Ozymandias. 'Nothing beside remains.'"

The major looked over and said "Excuse me, sir?"

Putnam smiled and said "Just a poem."

The major gave him a strange look, but said nothing.

They arrived at the orphanage and were met by the couple who ran it. They gave them a tour of the run-down buildings and sat down in the cafeteria. The lunch meal was being prepared, which seemed like a stew that was long on vegetables and short on meat.

"How many children are here?" Putnam asked as they began talking.

"About 50. Not all of them are orphans. Some have lost one parent, some both. Some of the surviving parents just gave up and brought them to us, hoping that we would be able to keep them safe in here."

"How are you funded?"

"We have funding from UNICEF, USAID, and our own fund-raising in the US and Europe."

"Any funding from your national government?"

"Very little."

As they talked, the children began to file in by classes for lunch. Most of them seemed to be under the age of ten, walking in careful lines. They were much quieter than Putnam imagined children of that age to be, looking with curiosity at the visitors. A few smiled at Aisha, who nodded back at them with her own soft smile.

Then one of the younger girls came over and spoke to Aisha. She was shy, but seemed determined to say something. Aisha bent down and spoke to her quietly, then stroked her arm gently. She asked Putnam to pose for a picture with the little girl, and after she took it, she patted her on the back gently and sent her back to the group.

She turned to go, and then she came back and said, in halting English, "Thank you for coming, Mr. Ambassador." Then she scampered back to the group.

"What did she want?"

"She asked if the Americans—you and the rest of the group—could send them some books in English. She said she likes reading very much and wants to travel to the US sometime, so she wants to learn to speak and read English much better."

"What is her name?"

"Amira."

"Petrosian, let's see what we can do back at the embassy library and with the USAID education people."

"Yes, sir."

As they left, Putnam noticed a sign on the front of the wall surrounding the orphanage. He looked at it for a moment, and asked Aisha, "Isn't that the Arabic word for child?"

She said, "It says Children's Home."

"Children's Home." Then he murmured "Maison d'Enfants."

"What?"

"Just an old memory."

They moved on to the village school. They were met by its principal, an older man who frowned when he saw Aisha but was polite in welcoming the group. The armed detail had left their weapons outside with a sergeant who stayed with their vehicle, which was parked just outside the front of the school.

The building was concrete with a tiled roof, better-constructed and maintained than most of the buildings in the village. When Putnam complimented the principal on the looks of the building, he received a wry look, and the flat statement, "It has been rebuilt several times."

Putnam asked about that history, and the principal sighed and said, "The Rescue NGO first built this school twenty years ago. It was then destroyed in a tribal battle between warring clans. It was rebuilt by our own government, but an earthquake collapsed it. Then it was rebuilt by one of your reconstruction teams when they had a base nearby. But the rebels came into the village one night after rocketing the base, and your planes bombed it when the rebels refused to come out after they had been surrounded. It was last rebuilt by another reconstruction team."

He ended by saying, "We are very glad to have the school, and we hope it lasts this time."

Aisha quietly pointed out the near-equal mix of boys and girls in the school as they left through the courtyard, where some of the children were playing soccer. She said to Putnam, "That ratio is not always the case."

As they got back into their vehicle, the major accompanying them filled in more of the details. "I've heard some stories about that school. It's fairly well-known. When he first took command, the colonel who was in charge of this area two years ago called in the elders and the heads of the two major militias in this area. He made them an offer he assumed they couldn't refuse. He would give them the money to rebuild the school— four or five times the amount it would really cost. They could hire whoever they wanted for the project. And in return they would agree to lay off the troops and the national police in the area. The deal stuck."

He added, "Ambassador, I'd appreciate your not using my name if this information is helpful. I think it's the wrong way to do business, because it creates an expectation of buyoff that we're not going to be able to sustain. But it got that colonel through his tour with minimal casualties."

Putnam was silent. Then he said, "I've heard similar stories from other parts of the country. And I'd agree it's not the way we should be doing business."

As they entered the room where he would be meeting with the village elders, Putnam was at first mildly surprised by their apparent comfort in dealing with Aisha as their translator. Two of the elders even came up to her and nodded, murmuring greetings to her.

She spoke to Putnam as they were taking their seats on the floor, the ubiquitous cups of tea in front of each of them. "They know who I am. My grandfather was from this area. Many years ago, he was the only go-between trusted by both Sunni and Shia to be impartial, because he was neither."

Again Putnam felt dwarfed by the weight of history that was so powerful in local cultures. Ancient hatreds, trusted mediators, neutral ground—all invisible and mostly unknown to Americans.

He fell for a few moments into a reverie, imagining a reversed occasion, wondering about the impact if one of the elders had been dropped into a New Hampshire town during a presidential primary and asked someone to explain what was happening.

As an occasional history buff, Putnam had been to Dixville Notch in northern New Hampshire during three presidential campaigns. Dixville

Notch was the small town near the Canadian border that had long ago been given the right to vote at midnight on election day. He wondered what one of these elders would think if they were transported to the basement of the Balsams, the classic old hotel where the balloting was held every four years. What would they make of the strange customs of the two dozen or so townspeople entering their own personal voting booths to cast their votes in the primary, then emerging to the glare of television cameras and reporters waiting to broadcast the results out to a nation of more than three hundred million. *Local culture*, he thought. *Opaque, incomprehensible to outsiders, and fascinating.*

In their discussions with the elders about security in the village, he got little sense that they were likely to open up. He asked about the local police force and received a very non-committal response by one of the elders to the effect that "We are glad to have them here."

On the ride back, he asked Aisha, "What do you make of the visit?"

"I think that is a fairly typical slice of village life, although they are more insulated from the cross-fire these days because of the base that used to be out there." She was quiet and then added, "It was good to see the makeup of the school as equal as it was."

"The elders were fairly quiet."

"Yes, they would be after only one visit. It would take a long time for them to open up to you. And they would test you first to see what you could do for them."

Putnam was quiet. He was wondering the same thing.

The vehicle was making good progress, and then, as it rounded a corner, it came to an abrupt halt. Fifty yards ahead, two small trucks with mounted 50-caliber weapons were sitting in the middle of the road. A dozen men were lined across the road, their AK-47s all pointed at the Humvee. On top of both trucks, men had trained the barrels of the machine guns on the Humvee.

"Lock and load, guys," the major said quietly. "This is not a regular checkpoint."

The clicks of the clips slamming into their weapons were the loudest mechanical sounds Putnam had ever heard. He said, "Looks like they knew we were coming."

A bearded gunman came forward from the band of men and stood by the window of the Humvee. He grunted a few words, motioning for the group to get out of the vehicle.

Aisha leaned forward from the back seat and spoke quietly and intently to the gunman. He glared at her for a long moment, then turned, spat on the ground, and then motioned to the rest of his band. They walked over to their trucks and drove away.

As the Humvee started up, Putnam, recovering from his amazement, said "What did you say to him? I made out some words about your relatives."

"I told him that my cousin is the clan leader—you would call him a warlord—who has dominated this area for fifty years. He's Sunni, and just speaking his name is a threat. I told him that if any harm comes to those in this vehicle, my cousin, who knows I am here, will hunt him down and torture and kill all of his family. Four months ago a Taliban raid wounded another cousin, and the next day the warlord destroyed the entire camp where the raid was based. Burned it to the ground and killed thirty men living in the camp."

Putnam said, "Unbelievable."

The major said, "Thanks, ma'am."

She was quiet, then said. "We live by threat and we die by threat. It is a terrible way to live, but sometimes it preserves life."

Putnam was quiet all the way back into the city. He was thinking about the incident, and how easily Aisha had dominated the action by her threat. Once again he had glimpsed the swift and deadly currents of power that ran beneath daily life in Iraq. And he thought *What on earth makes us think we could do something called nation-building here?*

Johansen had arranged the trip to Kabul that he had promised Putnam, and it was set for the next day.

They arrived in Kabul on a supply flight, corkscrewing down into the airport and then racing to the embassy. The streets were a bizarre mixture of ruins from past battles, new construction, and crude shelters of the bricks covered by the ubiquitous blue tarps that the US and the UN had left all over the world.

They received a briefing by a joint diplomatic-military team that made a valiant effort to explain away the obvious neglect that the Afghan front was receiving from both State and Defense.

For Putnam, the highlight of the briefing was what seemed to be a low-key, fact-loaded segment on what was called "the critical distinction between Ghilzai Pashtuns and the Durrani Pashtuns."

At the end, Putnam dared to ask a question, and wished he hadn't.

"How do you tell the difference between the Ghilzai and the Durrani?"

"Ambassador, there are many factions within each and clans within the factions, which makes it difficult. But a prime difference is that the Durrani tend to speak a Persian dialect."

"Persian? So they are closer to Iran?"

"Oh, no. They hate Iran. They were conquered by the Persians, but they hate Iran." And then he smiled, with an edge to it that essentially said *You visitors will never understand the nuances that we have mastered, so don't even try.*

Putnam thought to himself, *Utter complexity. Like trying to explain Wall Street and Main Street Republicans, with the Tea Party thrown in for good measure.*

Once, many years before, he had convinced himself that he could become Putnam of Indochina, Lawrence's successor. In the Middle East, he knew better. He'd learned how Lawrence's fantasies and British and French clumsiness in drawing neo-imperial lines through the deserts of the Middle East had created generations of failed states, foolish statesmen, and second-rate dictators. And there were maybe a half dozen US diplomats who knew their way through the thickets of complexity. He knew he wasn't one of them. But he knew that his questions were a better grade of questioning than most of his colleagues, thanks to Aisha, and that would have to be enough for now.

Johansen had arranged for a helicopter flight to a nearby Provincial Reconstruction team outpost, and they were dropped into a compound that was far more primitive than anything Putnam had seen in Iraq. Several dozen Marines were visible on the outer edges of the compound, watching the surrounding countryside through ports in the walls. They were on alert, much more battle-ready than Putnam had seen when he visited the Valley-based team in Iraq. An Afghan unit was encamped outside the perimeter.

As the captain in charge of the unit showed them around, Putnam noticed a young man who was doing some of the translation for the Afghan officers who accompanied the tour. He was thin, dressed in the typical jeans and sweatshirt of the older youth, clearly a local, but with barely accented English.

Then the young man spoke quietly to the captain, who nodded. The young man, who had been introduced simply as Ahmed, addressed Putnam. "Sir, may I speak?"

"Yes, go ahead."

"Sir, I have translated for your reconstruction team here for the past year. I attended Maplewood High School in New Jersey and then my parents sent me back here to live with my relatives. So I know this village, and I know what your team has being doing. They are brave men, and they are trying to help the people here." He took a deep breath and said, "Sir, it is not working."

Putnam could tell that he was very nervous, and knew that he feared losing his job with the team. So he said, "Go on, son. I appreciate your telling us what you think."

"Sir, what we call pacification—what we are trying to do by providing security in a way that will win loyalty to the government here—is lived as daily humiliation by people in this village. We humiliate them when they want to leave the village with checkpoints where there were none, we humiliate them when they come back, we humiliate them when there is a gathering of more than a few people by sending a patrol of the local police over to investigate. We are in their faces all the time—and we call that pacification? The word means peace-making, sir. That is not what we are doing. It is humiliation. It is occupation. They are proud people, sir. And they want us to go away more than they want the insurgents to leave them alone."

He glanced at the captain, knowing that he had crossed over a boundary, but then quickly looked back at Putnam and Petrosian, sensing that they could make it all right.

Putnam said, "Thank you. I know what you say is true, because I have heard it from others here and in Iraq. We will continue to try to work with the local people in different ways that keep both our teams and the village safe. And thank you for the help you are giving us and the village."

As they walked toward the helicopter taking them back to Kabul, Putnam asked the captain, "Will he be OK, captain?"

"Yeah. He's a good kid. I actually encouraged him to speak out." He smiled. "He went a little further than I expected, but he's been great working with us and knows a lot more about us than most of the translators we've worked with, because of his time in the States."

Then he got a worried look. "He's a marked guy, though, and I just hope we can keep him protected. He sleeps in the compound a lot of the time, and moves around when he isn't with us. His relatives here more or less kicked him out when he started working with us."

"Let me know if we can help with any of that."

"Thank you, sir, I will."

They were silent on the flight back to Iraq, reflecting on what they had seen. Afghanistan was a backwater in the war, but what the young translator had said was even more basic than the neglect of this front. Everything he said applied to Iraq as well as it did to Afghanistan. And to Vietnam.

Putnam occasionally attended sessions that weren't strictly Executive Council business, given Beemer's vague mandate to look into civilian reconstruction. One afternoon at the Embassy he sat in on a review of aid projects. The USAID mission chief had just made a presentation to Beemer on schools and health facilities that had been built with U.S. civilian and military assistance.

Putnam said, "This is very impressive, and I appreciate the briefing, especially the emphasis on girls' education."

He paused, knowing the next part was going to be thorny. "What do we have on the recent Human Rights Watch report? They say that based on their surveys up to 40% of the girls in parts of Iraq are still getting mutilated and that honor killings are still going on all over the country."

The USAID mission chief, who had transferred over from an Army Corps of Engineers position and was known for his bluntness, said with a frown, "It's not our job to protect little girls. You're always talking about the local culture, Ambassador. That's the rotten culture they have here—they cut up little girls and they kill women who have sex before marriage. Some culture."

Putnam said, "No, protecting girls is probably not your job. But we are still congratulating ourselves on all of our achievements on women's and girls' rights. Maybe we should stop these self-congratulations until the locals start enforcing their own laws."

Beemer spoke up then. "We don't put much credence in HRW materials, Will. They tend to be propaganda."

"What's wrong with their data, then? Do we have any data of our own?"

The frowns around the table were expected. He was probing again, poking at the outer edge of inside dissent. It was the age-old question of how far to go in official circles in pushing beyond an easy consensus, bringing new information into play.

He knew he was bordering on PITA status. But as a seasoned student of body language, Will saw some barely perceptible nods from the back row of staff, including one from a Navy commander with Medical Corps insignia on her uniform.

The USAID official said, "No, we really don't have that kind of data."

"Perhaps we could discuss how we could get such data at a future meeting."

"Noted."

As he left the room, the Navy officer brushed by him and murmured "Thanks, sir. We'll keep trying to raise that issue."

The Executive Council had been meeting on the counterinsurgency campaign for several weeks. The Ambassador had attended nearly every session, and had said little. But he'd been told that this would be the decisive meeting, and he was ready to make his own position clear, finally. He assumed he'd lose, but he knew he could chip away at the weakest parts of the plan.

The briefer opened the meeting with PowerPoints. Putnam detested PowerPoints. He collected articles and an increasing number of studies that had proven that PowerPoint briefings inevitably oversimplified the content of whatever they were trying to explain. He was somewhat notorious for stopping halfway through a briefing and taking apart some obscure bullet point. He'd ask, looking anywhere but at the briefer, "But what does this really mean? What's behind that bullet?" They had to brief the briefers about his WBB moments—what's behind the bullet?

The now-familiar "metrics" were reviewed. Oil production, electricity, insurgents detained, insurgents killed. Then Easton said, "We are still trying to gather the information you requested, Ambassador Putnam, but we don't have it all collated yet."

"General," Putnam began, "I respectfully request that this effort be accelerated. Whether we call it counter-insurgency or pacification, the question still seems to be how do we keep from destroying the villages we are saving? How do we keep it from turning into Operation Phoenix," he added, knowing that some of the attendees would have no idea what he was talking about. "Except for the drones and the satellite surveillance, how is it different?"

General Easton smiled and said, with only the faintest tone of irritation, "We appreciate the history lesson, Ambassador. But this effort is designed to take advantage of everything we've learned in the past forty years."

Then he let the anger show. "It's totally different. You know what the overhead assets," he meant the satellites and the C-130s" allow us to do, to discriminate targets in ways that were impossible forty years ago."

Putnam knew that the refrain of "forty years" was aimed at destroying his credibility as outdated and irrelevant. "And so the thirty people in Al Homs were a computer glitch?"

Two weeks earlier an incident had resulted in mistaken fire into a village that was sheltering insurgents.

Easton said, angry now and not trying to conceal it. "No, that was not a glitch. We engaged insurgents in buildings our troops were taking fire from."

"General, the Pentagon has already said we can't kill our way out of here. As we've seen in two or three of the provinces, the insurgents sometimes can be bought off. And some of them can be neutralized when they go too far in trying to run villages where the elders have broad support and resent outsiders coming onto their turf where the same family has been running things for a few centuries. I just don't see the difference from the issues that plagued us in rural villages in Vietnam."

"I'm getting a bit weary of your historical references, Ambassador. I'm not sure your time in the embassy those long decades ago is very relevant to what's happening here. The realities on the front lines were a bit different, I suspect."

Putnam said, smiling tightly, "I was very rear echelon, General. But no one died defending a useless hill on my watch."

The general blinked once, then went silent as the room watched. Finally he said, quietly, "Fuck you, Putnam."

Beemer quickly said "Gentlemen, this is not getting us anywhere. You both have ample experience to debate our policies, but right now we need some decisions."

Putnam saw his opening. "Ambassador, I would propose that the key decision is placing on the agenda for our next meeting the issue of civilian casualties, with a review of the report that General Easton has said he will be bringing in."

Easton quickly said, "I said it wasn't collated. I didn't say we were bringing it in."

With excessive politeness but a steely voice, Putnam asked, "When will it be available, General?"

"When it's done. We have a lot of missions more important than counting dead civilians who were where they weren't supposed to be."

"That's exactly what we said in Vietnam about what we used to call free-fire zones. But most of the studies showed that recruitment for the NLF from such areas was twice the level of other areas."

Scornfully, Easton shot back, "That's because those zones were where the NLF was based, obviously."

Beemer intervened again, "Gentlemen, litigating the lessons of ancient days may not be the best use of our time here. We need to—"

Putnam interrupted for the first time. "We need to set a clear agenda, Ambassador. If pacification and counter-insurgency are becoming an occupation, and occupation undermines the mission, we risk triggering more insurgency that isn't aimed at Sunni-Shia rivalries, but at our troops. And that is an unacceptable risk. We can ask for guidance from Washington if placing this on the agenda can't be resolved here."

As Beemer glared at him, Putnam knew he had picked the right moment to finally invoke whatever clout he had and take Beemer on.

There had been rumors that he was going to be replaced, and Putnam was at a point where he cared more about getting his views into the debate than observing protocol.

Beemer said quietly, "I would agree that we need to review the agenda. Let me draft the agenda for the next meeting and send it out."

Putnam knew a deft punt when he saw it. "Larry, I request a decision now on discussing civilian casualties at the next meeting."

Beemer glared at him, and then said, "My decision is that it will be on the agenda. Now *let's move on.*"

Putnam had raised Beemer and Easton and then called them. And they knew that whatever the decision Beemer would make, it would be appealed within hours if Putnam disagreed.

Aisha and Will were together in his quarters after a dinner at the officer's club, during which Aisha had been quietly amused by the glances that came her way. They had made love, and Putnam wanted to talk. They were sitting on his couch, listening to softened guitars playing Bach in the background.

"How does this"—he gestured to the disheveled bed—"fit into your religion?"

"Like yours, I suspect, my religion values physical joy when people can share it with each other. God did not give us bodies that fit together so well in order to keep us apart when we want to be close to another human being."

"But you cover yourself—after a fashion."

"Yes, I do. I live in a culture where women cover themselves, and I do not want to call attention to myself that way. I believe your phrase is 'pick your battles.'"

She went on, smiling. "Will, I went out to California for a week when I was enrolled at Hartford Seminary. I spent some time on the beach in Orange County, after visiting some of the big software firms up north."

She laughed, "I felt like I had gone from Silicon Valley to Silicon Hills—the cosmetic surgeons must be very wealthy out there. Now tell me, Will, do you disagree with the evidence that American men are fixated on breasts?"

He asked her, gently, "Aisha, what language was the Song of Solomon written in?"

She threw her head back and laughed as long and as hard as he had ever heard her laugh. "I surrender. Quoting scripture at me—*you're* the fundamentalist!"

And then, not satisfied with his rare victory, he reached over and began reading from his deskside Bible,

Why should I be like a veiled woman, beside the flocks of your friends?...A bundle of myrrh is my well-beloved unto me, he shall lie all night betwixt my breasts...Thy lips are like a thread of scarlet, and thy speech is comely...thy two breasts are like two young roes that are twins, that feed among the lilies... thy stature is like to a palm tree, and thy breasts to clusters of grapes...now also thy breasts shall be as clusters of the vine, and the smell of thy nose like apples...I am a wall, and my breasts like towers, then was I in his eyes as one who found favor."

He paused and said, "And you want to talk about the beaches of Southern California?"

He often played music for her when they were in his room. When Aisha realized how much the music meant to him, as he played the tapes and CDs he had brought, she asked him why it was so important. He became more inarticulate than he usually was, because there were levels of his love of music he simply lacked the words to describe.

Carefully, because he had learned that she could detect the slightest hint of his condescending to her, he tried to answer her.

"A lot of it is deep in my childhood. My mother played the organ in our church, and I heard wonderful music at a very young age. We had a record player," he paused to make sure she understood that ancient technology, "and she played music when she was home with my sisters, my brother, and me.

"So music as spirituality—as something above the daily, greater than the random noise of life—was part of growing up in our home. Then later, I was able to spend time studying it. I graduated to less familiar music, and learned about forms of music that my mother had never played."

"Church was very important to you, then. But you don't go to any of the churches here."

He smiled and gestured to his music players and speakers. "That's my church. There are twenty or so masses I have learned note by note. I even have the sheet music for some of them. That's where I worship. That's how I acknowledge something greater than me—the higher power that people talk about.

"I guess I more or less gave up on organized religion the more I understood what was happening to children around the world." He shook his head. "Kids and organized religion—the scandal of the millennium. Global institutions of pedophile protection, fundies who think kids should be beaten regularly, madrassas that teach children to hate the West so much they put on vests and blow themselves up. In Russia the Orthodox Church refuses to support any kind of child welfare system because it would trespass on the rights of the parents to raise their kids any way they want. Think about it—this hugely centralized state refuses to vest any power in the central government to protect children, with hundreds of thousands of them in orphanages and living on the streets. The Church says that's a problem that should be left up to parents—when the parents have already abandoned those kids."

His anger and disgust had risen, and he knew he was showing it. He allowed himself one final dismissal. "Religion? If Jesus came back, he wouldn't go after the money-lenders—he'd go after the churches for what they've allowed to happen to children."

He wanted to lighten the mood, and so he told her with an air of superiority, "You know, translators are going to be obsolete soon."

"Really?"

"Yes. With the advances in software," he explained with some pride, "voice recognition translation is about to take off." He pulled out his cellphone. "It's all in here, Aisha."

She reached over and took his phone, and then quietly spoke a few words of Arabic into it, so that he couldn't hear her, and handed it back to him.

He quickly touched an icon on the phone and in a few seconds, the phone said in a halting, mechanical voice, "He is a rapid horse."

Aisha whooped with laughter, and Putnam quickly said "What did you really say? What did you say?"

She finally got out, through peals of laughter, the words "I said 'you are a wonderful man.'"

Putnam joined her laughter. "Not quite ready for prime time."

"Not quite."

Beemer had sent around a notice to the Executive Council that a congressional delegation would be visiting the capital city and one of the nearby bases during the next week. Putnam knew that such visits were a more frequent occurrence than most of the embassy staff and military brass would have wished, since it meant normal operations had to be set aside for a show-and-tell with the visitors. In his prior posts, he had briefed and entertained his share of "congdels," as they were called, and he was usually able to set aside his cynicism. In all his time as an FSO, he'd only met one or two members of Congress who had any sophistication about the rest of the world, and he resented but understood the time it took away from conduct of the war and contacts with the locals.

This group included two of the more notorious congressional blowhards, including a Vietnam veteran who had been very critical of the administration's failure to "go all out" to win the military side of the war. Beemer was unusually nervous as he briefed the Council a few days before the visit. And even the generals seemed anxious about how their reports would be received.

The delegation, made up of members of a subcommittee of the House Armed Services Committee, had flown in the night before, and as the group sat down around the table in Beemer's conference room, Putnam could see that some were not coping very well with the time change very well. Beemer presided over two hours of briefings by civilian and military staff, and by the end, Putnam could tell that half of the group was struggling to stay awake and the other half was struggling to conceal their frustration with the content of the briefing.

The chairman of the subcommittee, Representative Edgar Morrison from Arkansas, seemed to be in the latter group. He frowned throughout the briefings, and asked the first question once Beemer invited reactions.

"Ambassador, no one here has said anything that adds up to the bottom line. Are we winning or losing?"

"We've made a lot of progress, Congressman. We have a ways to go, but we've also come a long way, as the briefings tried to make clear."

"Ambassador, with respect, that's weasel-wording horseshit. And it sounds to me like no one wants to say we're winning. That means we're losing." He stated his conclusion as if he was expecting applause, but instead he got frowns back from most of the group, with the exception of Beemer, who was still smiling but with a somewhat frantic look on his face.

"Congressman, most of the metrics we use to measure progress are trending up. I hesitate to call that 'winning,' but we are definitely in better shape than we were a year ago."

Morrison scoffed. "At the end of the game, if the coach told the media they were in better shape, they'd laugh and look at the scoreboard. Now, you've told us all about your 'metrics,' which I guess is your scoreboard. But having twenty little scoreboards still doesn't add up to an answer to my question."

He changed direction, and said, "I'd like to meet with a few of your top people separately. I understand Ambassador Putnam served in Vietnam, and I'd like to sit down with him for a one-on-one. I'd also like some sessions with the generals."

Putnam knew Beemer was stricken at the suggestion, but he hid it well. "I'm sure the Ambassador has time for that. Will?"

"Absolutely. I'd welcome the chance to talk."

The Congressman and Putnam sat down in easy chairs in Beemer's office, which he had offered to them as a meeting place. Morrison sipped a diet drink, studying Putnam over the top of the can. Then he asked, "When are the Iraqis going to get this budget thing resolved—the deal on who gets how much from the oil sales that all the groups are fighting over?"

"Congressman, we're hopeful that those issues are close to being resolved. Some serious horse trading has gone on and the oil-rich provinces and those with much less are close to an agreement."

Then Will had another of his *what the hell* moments and added, "Sir, with all respect, when we were pushing one of the top legislators in the Iraq parliament on these issues the other day, he did point out to us that our own Congress has been unable to pass a budget on time for the past ten years."

The congressman blinked, and then smiled in a way that made Putnam glad he didn't have to deal with the chairman very often. "Well, maybe he has a point. But that Congress he's criticizing has so far managed to fork out about five hundred billion dollars for this sand pit masquerading as a country. So I'm not sure these pissants are in a position to second guess the Congress of the United States."

Then he pointed at Putnam, and said, "They tell me you were in the embassy in Vietnam. You must have some ideas about whether we're sloshing around in the same swamp we were in back then. What do you think?"

Putnam was silent, watching the congressman's half-hooded eyes, wondering whether he should try to answer the question and stray off the reservation, or whether that was something the congressman wanted—or would understand. He decided to answer the question.

"Sir, as you know, many books have been written about Vietnam and what we did right and wrong. I think there are some important parallels—and some big differences. I wish, though, that we had more people asking that question, because I'm not sure we still understand what leaving Vietnam meant to our country. We've tried to forget it, and maybe that was the biggest mistake we're making here—trying to forget what we screwed up back then."

He went on, seeing that Morrison was listening for a change.

"What's the same? Congressman, when you put hundreds of thousands of American troops in a country—any country—you change the dynamics. You change them totally. And then whatever brought us to that country, whether it makes sense or not—stopping communist expansion, finding weapons of mass destruction, overthrowing a rotten dictator—any of those missions become less important than what it takes to protect and equip our troops. That's what changes for us. What changes for the locals is that hundreds of thousands of young Americans and their officers are rotating in and out of their country, moving through their streets, flying through their skies, shooting and dropping ordinance. And then *we* become the issue, whatever the original issue was."

He paused, seeing if Morrison was following him. Morrison nodded, and said "Go on."

"I'd say the weakness of the local government and army is pretty much the same, too. We had lousy allies in Vietnam, congressman. Kennedy said it's their war, but we got caught between having a half million troops deployed in their country and saying at the same time that it's their war. If it's their war, their leaders matter—a lot. And there was no one in Vietnam who had the respect of the average guy out in his rice paddy. So far as I can see, there's no one here who rises above the religious splits and the warlord history of the place.

"What's different? We're taking better care of our troops. Medical, food, comms back home—it's better. It's still atrocious for those guys out in forward operating bases, but it's better for the rest. Once we got a Secretary of Defense who cared about the troops, the troops got some of what they needed."

Morrison frowned, but Putnam knew he wasn't going to want to defend a former secretary whom the congressman himself had eviscerated on several occasions.

"The religious stuff is different, too. We faced nothing like the Sunni-Shia history in Vietnam. So our troops get caught in the middle of hatreds that have been around for a thousand years, and whichever side thinks we're favoring the other guys makes us the target of the day."

Morrison interrupted, having reached his listening limits. "So you're basically saying the mission is impossible. We should pack up and go home?"

"No, sir. If we did that, we'd just be repeating what we did in Desert Storm. The Shia and the Kurds thought we'd protect them, and when we pulled out, all hell broke loose." He paused, wanting him to understand the next part. "What we never did in Vietnam was to stand down and really see what the locals could do on their own, after we gave them the tools and the training to do the job."

He continued, watching Morrison carefully. "Sir, we bought our way out of Anbar. We fought like hell, and then we bought a few leaders who would stand up to the insurgents. That may have worked once, but you can't run a whole country that way. And the idiotic lines that we and the Europeans drew in the Middle East after the world wars were phony as hell, pretending that this is a country. That's not clear to me, congressman. Maybe it's two countries—or three. But we can't decide that, any more than the French could decide how to run America just because they helped us defeat Cornwallis."

And then he decided to extend the history lesson to make one more point, "Congressman, I know you know this, but I think sometimes some of us forget. *We* funded the Taliban when they were fighting Russia. *We* funded Saddam when he was fighting Iran. This stuff about surrogates fighting our wars for us isn't working out too well for us lately."

Morrison's smile got tighter, but he remained silent.

Worrying that he was exceeding Morrison's quotient of American historical understanding—Aisha's recurring point—Putnam quickly added, "Congressman, let me wrap up by repeating a story we hear a lot over here. Forty years ago I heard the Vietnamese version of it. We capture an insurgent leader, and we're interrogating him. He's having a rough time of it, but he keeps smiling, looking at the clock on the wall. Finally somebody asks him why he keeps looking at the clock. Guy smiles again and says Americans have clocks. Many clocks. But we have time."

Letting the point sink in, Putnam finally said, "Congressman, we're running out of time. Protecting these people from the worst of their countrymen is going to take more time and money than I think people back home are going to want to put up." He smiled, "But that's your territory, sir, not mine."

"What about Iran? We pull out, Iran wins the war."

"With respect sir, places we pull out of tend to do pretty well standing up on their own. The Vietnamese are an economic power in Southeast Asia, and the Chinese know it. Japan and Germany aren't doing that badly these days, either. I doubt Iran's own problems are going to let them take over countries that have hated the Persians for a long time. Iran and Turkey—and Israel—are going to be powers in the Middle East for decades to come. But that doesn't mean they get to run the place. The Saudis and the Gulf States have some other ideas and a few resources of their own."

"Still sounds a lot like you think we should fold our tents and come home, Ambassador."

"Not that easily, sir. But we are not doing ourselves or the people here as much good as we intended. And our young men and women out there do not deserve to get caught in the crossfires we put them in. We have no right to do that to our troops—or to the civilians who live here, either. You want a bumper sticker of my position, sir, here it is: stand down and see who stands up. Bush said it—maybe the only thing he got right. But he never called the question. Kennedy said it in Vietnam: if it's their country, see if they'll defend it with the tools we've given them. If not, I say send our kids back to Little Rock with all of their arms and legs."

Morrison kept looking at him, silent. Then he stood up, and said "Thanks, Ambassador. I appreciate your straight talk. I wish there had been more of it in that briefing we got."

Putnam stood, and then said, "One more thing, sir. We tend to think of these people as backward. But it turns out that there's a lot of evidence that Muslim traders from Africa were in the Caribbean long before Columbus. Look at the map—weather comes from Africa, so ships could easily have come with it. A large percentage of slaves were Muslims from West Africa. The three million or so Muslims in the US—estimates range up to seven million—include wealthy doctors, lawyers, and software moguls, African-Americans who converted, and families who left the Middle East much more recently as its wars made them refugees."

He frowned. "But we've done a disgraceful job of protecting and supporting the translators and many others who worked for the US here in Iraq." He paused, reflecting. "Just as we did in Vietnam. We abandoned people who had worked for us, and they ended up in work camps—if they were lucky. That's one of the most important things we have to get right this time, Congressman. We have to protect the people here who worked for us. Otherwise we're really nothing more than hit and run drivers."

Morrison thanked him again and walked back toward the conference room where the larger group was meeting. As he walked back to his quarters, Putnam knew that some version of his apostasy would get back to Beemer and the military brass. But he realized, once again, that his value depended more than ever on his honesty. And he also knew that he felt a lot better than he did when he had been part of the show and tell routine.

Putnam also knew, of course, that most of the decisions were still being made back in Washington. But he saw that as the war and the attempts at decent withdrawal terms wore on, the role of the people in the field would increase in importance. And he was still convinced that he would be able to move the overall embassy position a few steps closer to his own position, both with what he could do in Baghdad and what he was able to send back to State.

That was enough, for him, for now.

A press conference was held as the delegation prepared to leave for Washington. Putnam stood in the back until he was asked to provide a brief summary of NGO operations suitable for press consumption. He made his presentation and then returned to the back of the room.

After the press conference, Will walked out with the CIA station chief, the official he assumed was Sydowski's boss. They had worked together in Indonesia long ago, and had stayed in contact over the years.

Will asked the station chief, a New Englander whose name was Lexington, "Did you see the young reporter?"

"Oh, yes. She was taking notes as if you were revealing state secrets."

"I was elucidating."

"You were pontificating."

"She was entranced with the nuances of my complexities. Or perhaps it was the complexities of my nuances."

"She was lovely, actually. And she had *une derrière formidable.*"

"Yes, she had."

They laughed, that both of them had checked and noted.

"But she is *dalit.* Untouchable. Not in the Indian sense but in the dangerous sense."

"Yes. *Dalit.* But still, *quelle derrière.*"

"Yes. But hardly the *grand tetons.*"

"No. But still, rather shapely *tetons.*"

The station chief frowned. "You realize that if we were recorded, we would be reported to HR within ten minutes of this innocent conversation on aesthetics."

"Yes. Probably quicker. But I was not objectifying her. I was greatly admiring her, merely sharing my views with another connoisseur."

"You were taken, as I was, by the techniques and thoroughness of her note-taking, revealing as it did her innate intelligence and sensitivity, regardless of all the other, more earthly features."

"Yes. That too."

Beemer had arranged for a professor who had been working under contract to USAID as an anthropologist to brief the Council on "Gender and Culture Collision in the Middle East." Putnam was not optimistic about the session, but decided to attend anyway to see what she said.

After several of the inevitable PowerPoint slides, the professor summed up. "The cultural collision is easily defined as the conflict between full realization of the potential of girls and women and the desire of men to exercise male power over women, family life, and reproduction. The corollary is that children—all children, both girls and boys—are affected by the outcome of this conflict. They hear and see equality, or they learn male dominance."

She continued. "I am not saying, however, that Western culture is necessarily more evolved than those that subjugate women. There are many ways to keep women caged, and just because some of the cages are invisible makes them no less powerful.

"We need to understand when we see women denied their rights in this society how widely this is still accepted, here and around the world. A majority of women in many cultures that allow men to dominate women accept and even encourage that domination. In the US, for example, Mormon and fundamentalist Christian women often accept male domination.

"That is not what this war is about. But it is partly what the insurgency is about. Taking Western culture at its extremes—as we often take Islamic cultures at theirs—can lead an outsider to that culture to magnify and thus detest our pornography, the glorification of sexual appeal in marketing, and acceptance of gay and lesbian lifestyles not as normal but as preferred, in ways that threaten the family. These misperceptions can be powerful forces fueling insurgents' hatred of Western values—especially when combined with abuses like Abu Ghraib and colonial history."

Putnam was torn by his reactions to the professor's near-pedantic tone and his agreement with some of her points about the deeper strains of culture that most Americans in Iraq failed to understand. Too much of it was true to reject fully, but too much of it seemed to be a reverse stereotype for him to accept it all.

So he decided to offer his own wry version of summing up. "The threat we fear most is another 9/11. The threat they seem to fear most is a Victoria's Secret store opening in their marketplace."

The professor did not join in the muffled laughter that went around the table.

Will decided to press the point. "And so is objectifying women universally wrong?"

"If it diminishes their potential as individual actors able to shape their own lives, yes."

"So the critics of our sex-crazed culture and the critics of the Middle East's misogyny are morally equivalent?"

"No. Cutting a little girl is worse than Playboy magazine. No one makes you buy or read Playboy. But a whole village will hold that little girl down while some one cuts her if her family tries to resist, unless she has the good fortune to live in one of the hundreds of villages that have now ended the practice. We supposedly fought for freedom in Iraq, and nearly half of the girls in some parts of this country are still getting cut. That's wrong—absolutely wrong."

"But we can sit eight thousand miles away and condemn it and then wash our hands?"

"No. Your troops can't stop that, but your dollars could, by supporting the locals who are trying to end the practice."

"You and I both know that wasn't why we invaded Iraq."

"Of course it wasn't. But it could still be one of the best things that happened as a result, if we put some of our money where our mouth was when we bragged about bringing democracy and private enterprise to Iraq. We both know that private enterprise isn't helping those little girls much, so far."

Will agreed, mostly, and so he remained silent.

Putnam asked Aisha if she could bring together some of the people she had worked with in the ministries for an evening of informal talk. He asked her, "Sunni, Shia, all of them. Is it possible?" She agreed, and they set a date.

The group assembled, after the usual protests by the embassy's security and Putnam's protests in response to the proposal to surround the block where the gathering was being held with armed vehicles and troops. A neutral location at the university was picked, invitations were sent out by

Aisha and a cleric who was known for working across Sunni and Shia lines, and about a dozen people agreed to attend.

As the group gathered, Putnam saw that Aisha knew almost all of them and was treated with respect by most, despite her known identification with the embassy and, he presumed, with him. Coffee, tea, and refreshments were set out, and troops from the national army and the local police force were unobtrusively located around the building, which was inside the university gates.

Putnam opened the meeting by thanking them for attending, telling them he had no agendas or message from the embassy other than wanting to become better educated about "you and your sense of your futures."

The first round of comments were mostly abstract, expressing thanks to Putnam, indirect references to the harm done by US troops, and vaguely expressed hopes for the nation's future after the US troops departed.

Then the cleric who had convened the group, Abdullah Charbadi, spoke up. Slowly, in less elegant English than the others who has spoken thus far, he said "I appreciate this chance to meet with you, Ambassador. We need to help you understand how important it is for us to escape from our 'liberation.' We can blame you, we can blame the Saudis, we can blame Iran, our powerful and unpredictable neighbor. But really, Ambassador, it is us. Somewhere in our past, maybe long ago, maybe during the dictator's time, we lost the ability to think of each other as fully human."

He smiled, sadly. "You have helped us slightly in the last few years with your…I am going to use the word *occupation* because that is how we see it. The occupation united us, if briefly, in hating what your country did to ours. First you shamed us by removing the dictator in a few weeks, which we had failed to do in decades. And then you shamed us by forcing us to try to work together, which we are also failing at doing. What I mean when I say we must escape from our liberation is that we have not yet decided to move past your doing things for us. I believe the American phrase is 'to take the training wheels off.' That is what we must now do, and talking like this may help us do it.

"You will not be here forever, not in the way you are now. And we will have to decide whether we are one country or merely many tribes plagued by many thieves. We are the oldest nation on earth, and yet we may have lost the right to even call ourselves a nation."

It had been a longer speech than the others, and the group was silent. Putnam decided his response was going to be less important than the group's, and was also silent.

Then a man who had been the Deputy Minister of Economic Affairs spoke up. "I am not so pessimistic. I believe we will move past the occupation as we have moved past dozens of occupations—and dozens of our own conquests over our neighbors. These tides flow in and out, even in the desert. And we have endured and will continue to endure. We have natural resources and an educated population that compares favorably with any country in the region. You will leave, and we will be left with each other. And I believe we will find more that unites us than what divides us, despite the efforts of the devils who want us to fight each other forever."

He went on. "Maybe one of these countries in our region—or a piece of a country that secedes, as your South tried to—will finally understand what you call pluralism. That there can't be any real winners if there are real losers. Winner-take-all has been the rule throughout most, but not all of our history. But maybe somewhere, Tunisia, the Emirates, even Israel—maybe one of these countries with sizable Islamic populations will come to understand what sharing power is like. Maybe even here, one day. It is not an alien concept, after all. Cyrus in Persia, Akbar in India—there have been rulers in this part of the world who understood that sharing power creates new power. Why not again?"

A professor from the university who had been quiet then spoke. "Something to remember, Ambassador, which I am sure you know. This room is filled with English-speakers, nearly all of whom have traveled widely. But our country is filled with millions of people who are content with their own dialect in their own city or village. That is really all they know, and all they want to know. What we could perhaps agree upon within this room could not be as easily agreed upon in our villages or even our city's neighborhoods. We lack the forums and occasions for meetings like this. Our legislature is a sham, and there are very few places where we come together across the lines that you see here tonight." He paused and shook his head, frowning. "We have a long way to go before we can be optimistic. But your leaving will help," he smiled then, "as long as you leave some dollars behind."

Putnam laughed and said, "We tend to do that, based on the past record. Along with a hell of a lot of hardware." Then he changed direction completely, asking the group, "What do you see as the chances for non-violent action to pressure the government into more democracy and less sectarian conflict?"

The Deputy Minister smiled and said, "There tends not to be much history of that approach in the Middle East, Ambassador."

"No? I would say that in Tunisia, in Lebanon in 2005 when Syria was forced to withdraw, and in the first rounds of the continuing changes in Egypt, non-violent action was very powerful. Studies of non-violent resistance compared to violent insurgencies show that non-violent action often produces better and more lasting results."

"Perhaps. But Egypt can tell us a great deal about how quickly the tyrants return to power when they choose to—and how little the US does to help those who seek greater democracy, despite all your promises and slogans. Perhaps President Wilson meant make the world safe for a *little* bit of democracy, occasionally."

One of the faculty members smiled and said "May I ask you a question, Ambassador? I know you have heard more than once that people in our country wonder why you have difficulties with our tribal warriors when your country was so efficient in destroying your own tribal resistance." He smiled again, but it was not friendly this time.

Putnam responded, "Yes, though it wasn't quite that easy. The Comanche were generally considered to be the fiercest of the tribes, and they fought for nearly a century against the…I suppose you would call it an occupation." Then he added, "There are still some important battles going on, but they happen more often in courtrooms than on the battlefield."

"Sir, why haven't you hired some of those tribes to patrol your borders as you did with the Sunni in Anbar, who are now patrolling the Syrian border?"

"Stay tuned. Something like that option appears to be on the table."

As they drove away, Putnam thanked Aisha profusely. "I did not expect unanimity, and there wasn't much, but it was very helpful for me to have an exchange like that. What did you think?"

"As with the elders in the village, Will, it would take many more sessions and gallons of tea before they opened up. They were freer with their talk than I expected, and you played the listener part very well. But there were no stakes on the table yet, so it was an easy round."

Back in his room, they continued to talk about the session, and Putnam briefed her on some of the worsening violence in the provinces.

"How can I—how can Americans at their most thoughtful—understand a culture that disintegrates into mindless religious violence like that?"

"Being neither Sunni nor Shia, I confess I find it difficult, too. Although you might want to look into Northern Ireland or much of the history of Europe before you judge us too harshly on religious bloodshed, Will. And you might want to check out the Mormon part of your history, and your own civil war. And as the professor noted, please be careful how you describe our tribalism, given the history between your country and the tribes that were already there when most of you got there."

Putnam shook his head in amazement. "How do you know so much US history?"

"When I was in the US, I was spending time with some of the American students, and I soon found out that they knew very little about their own history. They wanted to learn Arabic and a bit of our history, but they knew little about their own. So I started using translations of books by Howard Zinn and Nathan Philbrick and others who have thrown some light into the darker corners of American history."

She smiled. "In a meeting here in the embassy a few months ago, one young man who had been—do you call it advance person?"

"Advance man. Someone who arranges visits for a candidate in a political campaign."

"Advance man." She sighed. "Such a great qualification for coming to enlighten us in the Middle East. This young man was deeply offended when I mentioned American tribalism after translating a session he was having with one of our professors.. He knew almost nothing about your versions of genocide or the Indian wars. I quoted him the racist phrase 'The only good Indian is a dead Indian…'" He said that was just a saying, and I had to tell him that General Sheridan and President Roosevelt—the first one—had used it repeatedly as a summary of national policy."

She smiled, "Before you came, I sometimes made a game out of it, because I was often bored. I would talk about Sunni-Shia and other more tribal conflicts here, and then slide in references to slavery and your Indian tribes."

"You liked being oppositional, in a subtle way."

"Yes, I guess I did. It was their constant righteousness and ignorance that bothered me so much."

"Aisha, I know you know this, but I need to say it: you have taught me a great deal about your country and your culture, and you have often done it by reminding me about ours."

"Thank you." She paused and went on. "Will, the history here *is* as important as yours. We didn't draw those insane boundaries after World War I that pretended that there were nations in places where there were only dozens of tribes. Sunni and Shia got sliced up in stupid Western lines. That happened just because Winston Churchill and Lawrence of the Saudis and all those other geopolitical illiterates decided those stupid lines looked good on a map."

"So just redraw the lines around the tribes and the sects and let it go?"

"No, of course not. But it will take years of education to make it possible for different groups to come together to see what nations are possible—for our young people to see what they have in common instead of what ancient hatreds divide them."

She frowned, and continued. "There was a university president who was here before you came, Will. He was close to all the neo-cons in the White House, and they sent him over here to remake our universities into models of higher education. And he tried, and tried, and first Beemer blocked it and then the Pentagon blocked it and then the budget came up short and all he was able to do, finally, was teach a few classes and hire a few of our professors to write a plan no one read. Because somewhere in a university you have to let ideas battle, and none of your policymakers or ours really wanted that kind of freedom. And then he quietly went home. Another well-intentioned American, frustrated by what he found here— but really blocked by his lack of any real power back home."

She looked at him, sad, almost pleading. "You could have won the whole game if you had sent us scholarships and hired our best minds, Will. Invade us with universities, Will, not tanks. Kidnap our young people with scholarships, rather than imprisoning them in the dictator's rotten jails.

"Do you know where I learned English? My father sent me to American University in Beirut, before Lebanon collapsed. And I was so grateful for what happened there, for the flow of ideas and openness. It was like finding a large pond in the desert, fed by ideas flowing with the water.

"Will, let us send our young men and women to your universities to be educated instead of sending yours here to be blown up. Or build universities here instead of concrete, walled-off embassies. Soft power, as Secretary Clinton called it. Ninety percent of our students would take scholarships to come to the US, and fifty percent would be brave enough to attend a US-backed university *here*. You've spent hundreds of billions in our country, and there isn't a single first-rate university with American credentials to show for it."

Putnam was irritated, despite agreeing with most of what she said. "There's one in Kabul, actually. Laura Bush has been justifiably proud of it. The American University of Kabul. There's another one up in the Kurd regions that's going well. Who knows how long they will last, and how dangerous it will be to attend classes there. But someone got the message about education. At least in a few places."

He frowned, and added, "Too few, though. You're right about that."

Petrosian came slowly into Will's office, and it was clear that he had very bad news.

"Sir, the Valley unit we visited got hit last night. An Iraqi police unit went rogue, shot the place up and then someone threw satchel charges into the camp. We lost six guys, two more barely hanging on." He choked out the last words, "Two cousins. Gone. Both guys I played with a lot when we were kids."

"I'm sorry. I know those guys were close to you. Take some time, go on out there if you think you can do some good. I'll sign off on it."

As Petrosian began to leave the office, Putnam said, "And try to figure out what kind of screening they do that lets some crazed bastard get that close to our guys. If we can't trust the local cops we're training, this whole thing just isn't working."

"Yes, sir."

Putnam had arranged a briefing on the NGO programs for a group of legislators from the recently formed Iraqi parliament. He spent the first hour of the meeting reviewing aid projects, and then shifted to a wider range of subjects. He had mentioned some of the difficulties of working across the religious barriers in aid programs that the NGOs had told him about, such as the unwillingness of Shia administrators to work with Sunni staff and their preference for service organizations with Iranian ties. Then, deliberately addressing his remarks to one of the legislators from the Sunni quota, Putnam said, "With respect, Minister, some people have recently suggested that you're on your way to becoming a western province of Iran. I assume it's not what you had in mind."

Frowning, the minister said, "You are insulting our sovereignty, Ambassador."

"I've heard that before, Minister. You're welcome to your sovereignty, and your people deserve it. Really, it is because you have such a long history of independence that some have expressed concern about a Persian eclipse of the re-dawn of the Iraqi sun."

Without waiting for the translation, the Minister nodded. "A very skillful evocation of our long history, Ambassador. We have, of course, considered carefully our relations with Iran. And we will continue to do so."

The Shia delegates were silent, but seething. Putnam had not made any new friends, but perhaps, he thought, he had sent a clearer message about what at least some in the embassy were thinking.

And then he thought, *what the hell* and added, "Legislators, let me say one more thing. If you were only liberated to have the freedom to try to kill the people you couldn't kill under the dictator—you never got liberated at all. And *that is not our fault*. With us or without us, the dictator would have fallen. It is the nature of the world that sooner or later that happens. And if your primary response is to start killing people who are different from you, who live in the same country, then you may have wasted your liberation on mere vengeance. That too, is not our fault. You can blame a lot on America, but your hatred for your fellow countrymen is not our fault."

The Minister glared at him but did not respond. The head of the delegation then changed the subject back to aid projects.

He was telling Aisha about the meeting with the legislators. "You could see their unease with each other. They sat, almost all of them, according to their sects. We had cards with their names on them, trying to mix them up, and they moved around before we sat down and shifted the cards so they were sitting with 'their own kind.'"

He shook his head. "There is this moment in the film *Lawrence of Arabia*" he interrupted himself—"whom I know is one of your least favorite characters in history," noting her emphatic nod, "where Peter O'Toole says to the sheik played by Omar Sharif, 'So long as you fight tribe against tribe, so long will you be a little people, a silly people—greedy, barbarous, and cruel.' A true reflection of what Lawrence believed, but such an arrogant thing to say. And yet…"

She was angry. "Yes, it is arrogant. Especially coming from the product of a continent whose own tribes, sects, and religions spent much of the past two thousand years trying to kill each other."

"All true, my dear, but 'you're one, too' is not an adequate response in this case. The dead of European strife are long gone, but the dead from your brand of sectarian hatreds are piling up outside in the streets every day."

He went on. "It is not just the religious stuff. It is the blindness about dismissing half the country as irrelevant. How can you—how can any of us—reconcile the pressure for change in rotten governments—Egypt, Syria, elsewhere—with the terrible realities that nearly all of the rebel groups would cut back rights for women?"

"Will, you have your Tea Party fundamentalists, and we have the madrassas and the worst of the imams and the Revolutionary Guards in Iran. They are dangerous maniacs. But, Will, you empower them every time you fire into a mosque."

"So we just disappear and they lose power?"

"It depends on what you leave behind when you leave."

She continued, becoming more intense. "Will, when I was in the US I saw a movie on TV that was as good as a year's advanced course in understanding America. It was called *The Way We Were*. And in it this sort of golden boy American writes a novel with the line 'he was like the country he lived in. Everything came too easily to him.'"

She looked at him, almost pleading with him to understand what she was trying to say. "That's part of what happens when you Americans go out in the world. You think things will come as easily as they usually have for such a fortunate people. And then they don't, and then you either double your firepower, or you try to buy your way out of it—or you just pack up and go home."

She smiled. "Let me tell you another story about what I learned in America. At one point I decided I needed to learn more about your country. And I felt I could learn more by studying your games, your sports, which seemed a very important part of American life. A whole section of the newspaper was all about sports. So I persuaded a friend who was at the Seminary with me to attend baseball games—I think they called it the Cape Cod League, playing in the summer in New England towns. I bought a book on the rules so I could follow the game. And so I understood it when one of the professors used the phrase, talking about wealthy people, who were, as he put it, 'born on third base and thought they had hit a triple.'"

She smiled, trying to soften the criticism. "That is your country, beloved. Americans were born on third base, and you thought you deserved it. All that land, protected by two vast oceans, possessing enormous natural resources, blessed with some of the world's hardest-working and smartest immigrants—you thought all that was the natural order of things. Few Americans ever realize that no other country on earth had those benefits.

"So you come into a place like our country, and you imagine that a bill of rights and some traffic lights and new generators will bring order to a place that has suffered thirty years of a dictatorship that made us all afraid of speaking the truth. And then you set up quotas for Sunni and Shia on the governing bodies and assume that will lead to a nice neat system of checks and balances—when that idea is as foreign as baseball to us."

Putnam chuckled. "You could always teach a seminar on the US called 'Love Us or Leave Us.'"

Then he got serious. "You're right, of course, about the difficulties we have going out in the world with our ideas about who we are. 'The indispensable nation,' a recent Secretary of State called us. Maybe."

He fell silent, then murmured, "But you gotta know the territory."

"What?"

"Another movie—song from a movie, a musical. It says you have to know the territory—the culture—when you're trying to sell something. You're saying it's very hard for Americans to do that—to understand the rest of the world. And so we mess things up."

"Sometimes. You do wonderful things, but sometimes you make a mess, yes."

The Executive Council was meeting again, but with changes happening. Beemer's departure had been announced and the handoff to the national government of Iraq was scheduled for the next month. It was a time of flurried activities, but with no clarity about the priorities of either the US leadership or the new national government, since in neither case were the actual leaders appointed or agreed upon.

Putnam realized that he would have to make his case all over again with Beemer's successor. Bremer had reportedly had a blowup with the Secretary of State, the White House had not backed Beemer this time, and he had been dismissed on a timetable not of his choosing. Putnam wondered whether his report to the Secretary had finally had an impact, but had no way of knowing. Easton's successor was also being rumored to be near announcement.

So the meeting had become a flock of lame ducks quacking at each other, able only to lay down tracks for the record, but unable to force any decisions.

Easton had apparently decided to let someone else take Putnam on. His deputy, a Marine two-star named Garnett, jumped right into it as soon as the agenda moved to the civilian casualties issue.

"All right, Ambassador. Let's pursue your point. You keep telling us over and over that we don't know enough about the culture here. Let's assume we agree, and we spend more time trying to *get* the culture. Then what?"

The Ambassador was familiar with the ploy the General was using: *Say I agree with you—then what?* Impatient with the tactic, he shot back, "Then, General, we reverse our spending priorities from supporting our troops to supporting their troops, and their cops, while we're at it. And then we wait and see how they perform."

"Their troops are mostly cowards and their cops are mostly corrupt."

"Then, accepting your premise, which I don't, there is no way we can achieve the mission here, is there, General—unless we stay here forever?"

"So we just go home?"

"Absolutely not. We make it clear to the national government now coming into place that unless they set up measures of their troops' and cops' performance—their measures, not ours—and release them quarterly, we are going to stand down except for our own bases' safety."

"So you're going to respect their culture by backing them into a corner? They'll start screaming about their sovereignty being compromised."

"Let them. They can be sovereign if they want. Their culture will respect us a hell of a lot more if we draw that line than if we keep shielding them from reality. Reality right now is that this government has the support of only one-third of the nation. And they're the horse we bet on?"

"Ambassador, I still don't see what your problem is. What do you want to change?"

"It's really very simple, General. My problem is what you are asking of your troops and what you are doing to civilians. You are asking brave men and women on our front lines to serve as an occupation force, and we are alienating and harming too many people who want to be left alone."

"The Taliban and Al Qaeda will never let them alone, Ambassador. Can't you see that? We are the only thing standing between those civilians and thugs who want to take this country back to the dark ages."

"If we are, then it is hopeless, because we don't live here and they do. When I go out to those villages, I see elders and others who hate the insurgents as much as we do. But we keep recruiting for the bad guys, breaking into houses, getting in the middle of tribal battles that have gone on for centuries. And if the leadership of this country can't use our money to make things better, then they don't deserve our troops. There is no way we are going to stay here long enough to build security in those villages without somebody in their government picking up the security. And that just isn't happening."

"So pull out?"

"No, but for now, pull back into safer places and let people decide if they want to stay in their villages or move to safer places where their own troops and police can take over."

"We called those enclaves in Vietnam."

"Yes. And they called them strategic hamlets before that. But whatever we called it, it was stepped-down occupation. And when we are the occupiers, we become the targets. They turn on us. General, these aren't dead-enders, as a recent Defense official once labeled them. These are the former troops of the dictator, combined with the militias of the sectarian forces. And they are all shooting at us or planting IEDs that maim our troops. For what? Security for a nation that sees us as occupiers, not defenders? Have we lost or forgotten *all* of the lessons of Southeast Asia?"

For the first time, Sydowski spoke up, agreeing with Putnam in part. And then, so did Johansen, pointing out the public relations problems they were having with civilian casualties. Putnam realized that it was the first time he had been joined by open allies.

But Garnett wasn't backing down. "These aren't lost lessons, Putnam. We talk about them every day. The Vietnam syndrome almost kept us out of this war, and it would have been a mistake if we hadn't come in."

"You and I could debate that for eternity, General, and I doubt we'd convince each other. But what's real is that our guys are getting shot at by both sides here, and it was only by the damned VC and the NVA in Vietnam. Our so-called allies stink here, and they stunk in Vietnam."

The general sneered. "So cut and run. That's your answer, Putnam?"

"No, General," carefully using his title although the general had refused to use his. "But have the balls to tell these thieves that we're done with their hiding behind our troops. It's time they go out and fight for their own country. Kennedy said it first about Vietnam—it's their country. Not ours."

"Easy slogan. And their troops have gotten better."

"Yes, when we pay them and when they greatly outnumber the insurgents. But who's going to pay them when our kids are safe at home?"

Then he softened his tone. "General, I don't know as much as you do about military strategy, I'll admit that. But you and I both don't know as much as we need to about local culture and why these people hate each other almost as much as they hate us. Our troops don't belong in that cross-fire. Until they get past their thousand-year-old civil war, it's like telling our troops to go back in time and get in the middle of the wars between the Catholics and the Protestants in Europe. Those wars went on for centuries, General. Why should we be in the middle of that?"

"Simple. To deny them sanctuaries they can use to pull off another 9/11."

"Not convincing. If we'd stayed with it in Afghanistan, we'd have solved the sanctuaries problem in 12 months, according to military people I've talked with up there."

As Putnam built to a conclusion, he began to feel a drift in his thinking. He struggled to get back in control, but he continued to fumble with finding the right words to make his case. He realized that he had forgotten the point he was trying to make.

He struggled to continue. "We need to focus our…our efforts on the… the safety of the areas we control."

Impatient, Easton got back into the discussion and said "We do that every day, Ambassador. I'm not sure what you're trying to say."

"Forgive me, I haven't been sleeping well. I'm just saying that we need to get our efforts under control."

"I'm sorry you're not sleeping well, Ambassador. Perhaps we can return to these issues at our next meeting."

Beemer, having watched the back and forth long enough, intervened. "That's enough, gentlemen. We've got decisions to make, and speculating about European history probably won't get us there." He went on to lay out the latest agreements between the White House, State, and the Pentagon, ignoring Putnam's frowns and slight shaking of his head.

As he walked back to his room, he knew he shouldn't have brought up sleeping, given the inevitable rumors about his relationship with Aisha. It had been a slip, and along with his fumbling for words, it worried him. It was not the first time his memory had skipped a beat. But it was the first time it had affected his performance,

He had unexpectedly shown a weakness that he knew his opponents would try to take advantage of in the next rounds. But he had also mobilized others who could carry the ball further, and he began to feel he could leave in good conscience.

The COIN-dinistas, the search and destroy cabal, and the rent-a thug crew were all on the defensive. That left only the conventional war forces, and sooner or later they would notice that their army had mostly gone home.

Easton's successor and Beemer's would continue to try to buy their way out of trouble, but much of their money was going to the same gang of thieves that had drained so much of the reconstruction funds. One of his sources on the Hill had told Putnam that the Inspector-General of USAID was preparing a report about diverted reconstruction funds, under pressure from the appropriations subcommittee on the Middle East. The report was expected to be a bombshell, and Putnam would let that fallout make his case on the corruption front.

He had come back to his office from the Council session, pleased at some of the responses he'd gotten, but irritated at what he judged to be his own ineffectiveness in selling his argument.

Sydowski was in the kitchen making coffee, and when he saw Putnam walk in, he said "Will, do you have a minute? I'd like to kick around something you said in the meeting."

Gratified that at least someone had listened, Putnam said, "Sure."

"Want coffee?"

"Thanks. Black is fine."

Sydowski brought him the cup, sat down, and said, "Tell me a little bit more about what you were saying about the occupation and counterinsurgency. I've read everything I can about what the Army thinks about Vietnam and here, and of course I've read Field Manual 3-24 on counterinsurgency—the COIN stuff. But you were suggesting that we haven't really learned those lessons. What did you mean? What are the differences you see? Very few people here have the range of exposure you have, and I'd really like to know what you think."

Trying to conceal how rapidly he was upgrading his estimation of Sydowski's competence, Putnam began. "In Vietnam, we weren't replacing a dictator who had kept a lid on things for thirty years. We were trying to prop up—to energize—a weak army and lousy police force to get security for the people. The people were the prize—we got that part, same as here. But the insurgents were supplied even better than the ones here; they had a border to hide behind, just like here, and they had a supplier in the North. But then we got sucked into trying to wipe out the supplies and the troops coming in from the North, and they seemed inexhaustible, they just kept coming, even when we bombed the hell out of the north and we used all our firepower in the South, And we were wiping out villages all over the place, search and destroy failed because we were destroying as many civilians as insurgent troops and irregulars."

He paused, watching Sydowski, who was nodding and following him closely. *He's feeling me out, and I wonder why,* Putnam thought.

He went on. "There were so many of us in Vietnam that the security support role inevitably became an occupation. Pacification to improve security inevitably becomes occupation. We had to bulk up because the South was so weak. We made a huge target, and of course, we make a big target here, too. I've never understood why the insurgents here didn't try for a Tet. In Lebanon, one terrible bombing and we went home. Occupying a country is a long uphill slog, and no one thanks you for it."

He laughed, wanting to lighten the atmosphere a bit. "Sometimes I think we should just let the Chinese run it again for a few centuries. It will drain them and they'll never understand how much the rest of the world hates their Middle Kingdom BS. Ugly Americans? You ain't seen nothing until you've seen Chinese contractors hit a third world country with checkbooks, bringing in their own workers, along with their own hookers, refusing to eat the local rice. The Middle Kingdom comes to town.

"But you know, I've also seen some of their kids, young college grads we brought over to work as interns at State and in other agencies. They are just amazing, mostly young women, many from villages that haven't yet been touched by the explosion of the economy. They're incredibly hard-working, comfortable talking about their country's flaws—and even more so talking of ours, with an incredible sense of humor. There's only one woman on the supreme governing body now, but I'd be surprised if there aren't a lot more in years to come, And then watch out. If we had any foresight we'd double the scholarships going to those kids to study here, and we'd send just as many of ours over there. Every scholarship for a Chinese student in this country is an investment that will repay itself a dozen times over."

"Soft power."

"A bit softer, yes."

Then he asked Sydowski a question. "Have you heard the stories about our senior military in the provinces making deals with the warlords not to attack us in return for cash for supposed reconstruction projects?"

Sydowksi made a face, more disgust than anything else. "Yeah, more times than I'd like to. We take it to the military and they say it's not a deal, it's pacification."

Putnam nodded, agreeing. "The argument about search and destroy vs counterinsurgency and pacification is sort of phony. In Vietnam, we did both, with a lot more resources going into the firepower side, obviously. But one set of facts is indisputable. We killed three million civilians from 1954 to 1975 in Vietnam. And not many hearts and minds get won that way."

"No drones in those days. We just dropped 'em and went back to base."

"I'm afraid so. B-52s don't discriminate the way the C-130 gunships and the drones can—sometimes."

"So that makes counterinsurgency easier?"

"No. It makes search and destroy on the ground less necessary, as long as you have somebody on the ground who can tell you where the bad guys are. Somebody who either believes that the bad guys should lose—or somebody you bought and paid for."

Sydowski frowned. "But if we bought them, somebody else could buy them. Or they could take our money and just wait until we leave and then choose sides all over again."

"Right." Then Putnam decided to challenge Sydowski a bit. "So what about here—is special operations the answer? Forget major operations and go after individual bad guys, terrorize villages where we know they're holed up?"

"I think you guys called that Phoenix. How'd that work out for you?'

"Killed a lot of Vietnamese, some of whom were VC. Some weren't, we found."

"Special ops makes sense when you know exactly who you're going after. But when your local sources are just trying to get us to knock off their rivals, you're flying blind again."

Putnam laughed, but without any humor. "We're a couple of optimistic guys, aren't we?"

Sydowski smiled and said, "I guess not. But maybe we see things more clearly." He paused, watching Putnam's reactions. "Here's how I'd sum it up, and I know you won't quote me. The premises we came in with were more than half wrong. Premise 1: they have a dangerous dictator. Premise

2: the dictator has weapons of mass destruction. Premise 3: we can make things better for ourselves and for the people who live here, in ways that last.

"Only the first premise was right—and he was less dangerous than we thought because premise 2 was wrong.

"Then based on what you've said, think about the logic of Vietnam. Premise 1: the fall of Vietnam would strengthen worldwide communism and therefore threaten us. Premise 2: we can succeed where the French couldn't. Premise 3: the people of Vietnam will rally to their government and as that happens, we can protect them from the North and the insurgency. Near as I can tell, those premises were *all* wrong. I have yet to read a convincing argument about what the 58,000 on the Wall died for. So we can have joint naval operations with the current government of Vietnam? So we can buy cheaper clothes at Walmart? So we could get two million or so hard-working Vietnamese to come to California and Texas?"

Then he asked Putnam, "Did you ever know Watkinson in Vietnam?

"State liaison up in I Corps?" Sydowksi nodded. "Yeah, I met him once or twice. Unpleasant guy, as I recall."

"Bad old Watkinson. He spoke to a group out at the Agency once, after he retired. He had a clear policy, whatever happened. He was fundamentally a racist bastard. 'Blame the dinks,' he'd say. Give the guys on our side good weapons and then stay out of the way. If you can rig the weapons so they won't work after five years, so much the better. Then we won't risk getting them used against us later on."

"Because the guys we backed were nearly useless."

"Right. Blame the dinks."

"Not that culturally sensitive. But when everybody is blaming us for everything, maybe a corrective of sorts. Strip out the racism, there's some real accountability there. As Kennedy said, it's their country."

Sydowski had one more question. "Tell me again what you have been saying about our metrics and the kids."

Putnam said, slowly, "I've tried over and over to make it clear. What I've tried to say is that the only metric that really matters is whether children in the villages are safe. It's the linchpin, the keystone—use whatever metaphor you want. Safe kids in schools, is a proxy for village stability, for how girls are being treated—even for corruption, give the number of places where teachers and cops are getting paid but don't show up for work. If that isn't happening, the locals aren't holding ground, and it's our war. If it's our war on their ground, we lose."

Sydowski stood up. "Thanks for the talk, Will, Appreciate your perspective."

Putnam had no idea what the conversation meant in the scheme of things, but his assessment of Sydowski stayed high.

Putnam had told Aisha about his lapses in memory, and to divert her concerns, he began talking about aging in general rather than his own afflictions.

"Aisha, I have come to believe that as you get older, you need to understand the difference between elegies and legacies. If you mostly look backward, you can get so wrapped up in elegies to the past, to the supposed wonders of what once happened, that you forget to ask yourself about your legacies for the future."

Aisha smiled and asked him, "What's your legacy, Will?"

He was quiet for a long time, and she decided he wasn't going to answer her. He sat, swirling the ice cubes in his fruit juice, looking at the rock on his desk and his map of the world.

Then he said, "I asked hard questions and I taught a few kids how to ask hard questions. Maybe they're still asking them—I don't know. But I never pretended to have the answers—I worked hard as hell on getting the questions right." He paused. "They're still the right questions."

Then he decided to return to a subject they had talked about before, but inconclusively. He thought he knew her feelings and was afraid to raise it again. But he needed her answer.

"You won't come with me, will you?" And as he heard the echo across the decades, he felt a faint sting of Thuy's pain.

She spoke, trying to ease his distress. "Will, you Americans sometimes think you need exotic women to be complete, when it's really that you're always searching for the familiar when you're out of your element."

"Am I out of my element?"

"Oh yes, my New England pilgrim. You are. You have learned and understood more of our ways than most Americans—but you are who you are and always will be. You will return to your woods and books and music. And small towns with tall, white steeples. And you will be at home."

He knew she was right, and yet he felt the coming loss of what he had tried so hard to comprehend at its essence—a country, a culture—and Aisha herself. For he knew the other part of what she was saying when she told him that he would be at home in America, which was that she never could be.

As he returned to his office, he received a text message from Steven Jefferson telling him that he had arrived in Thailand. Putnam usually took 21st century communications technology for granted, but every now and then he stopped to marvel at the fact that a few moments ago his son had sent him a message from the other side of the world which had arrived on a small piece of equipment he carried in his pocket. Of course, his son never thought about it as unusual, while Putnam and others born in the 1940s were suitably in awe of what had become routine.

He sometimes resented the immediacy of it all, while appreciating how much it came with a pervasive power to connect. *Only connect,* he thought, and then recalled with a tug at his heart an earlier, more emotional use of that phrase. With Steven, at least, he had connected.

Putnam had steered as clear as he could of the advance men who had come in with Beemer. Many of them were gone, having signed on for only 12-month tours, and others had left when Beemer left. But there were still a few of them around, and it was inevitable that sooner or later he would run into one.

The collision came at a meeting where Putnam was trying to wrap up his recommendations on civilian agencies. He'd worked hard on it, paying special attention to the agencies serving kids—civilian NGOs, USAID, and military.

He made his presentation, *sans* PowerPoints as usual, with a handed-out 1-page executive summary covering a much longer memo. He was wrapping up when a self-important twenty-something interrupted him and asked, "Ambassador, I don't understand why you're recommending that we assign an inspector general to all these agencies that serve kids. Can't we just let the Iraqis do that? We're trying to build up their government, not second-guess it."

Putnam paused, making sure that the shallowness of the assistant to the assistant's remark sank in for the group. Then he slowly answered. "First, we're not going to let the Iraqis have final oversight on what our own agencies are doing. Second, the Iraqis get as much say in this issue as they put money into it, and so far it's almost entirely ours. And finally, the idea of an inspector-general function is unfortunately one of the things our wise constitution builders left out of the wonderful new Iraqi constitution. The level of corruption in this government we're 'trying to build up' is still on the Al Capone level, which I'd be glad to document if you'd like. I wouldn't trust their agencies with anything that might affect the life of a kid who lives here."

The assistant mumbled "I see. Thank you."

Putnam tried not to feel good about shooting the fish in the barrel, but he justified his self-satisfaction by noting that he could tell Aisha that he mentioned US corruption as well as the Iraqis' and that the bottom line was about kids.

Petrosian came to Putnam at the end of the day, clearly upset. "Sir, you asked me to look into the visa policy for our translators. And you mentioned that young guy you met in Afghanistan who was trying to get out. It worked out for him because it turns out he was born in the US. But sir, hundreds of our staff are already asking for visas, in Afghanistan and Iraq, and yet we're processing them as though it was a dressmaker in Paris asking to come sew in New York. It's a total mess, and no one seems to be in charge here or back in State."

Putnam had flashes of the notorious pictures of the embassy roof in Saigon and the helicopter lifting off. He was furious.

"Dammit! We leave people behind, which is even worse than what we did to them when we were here. We disgrace ourselves by failing to protect those who helped us."

So Putnam continued to press for specifics on the exit planning for the local staff, and the embassy visa staff continued to blame Washington for slow processing. Twice he sent emails back to State pressing hard on the issue, but was told both times that the delays were due to the several layers of screening that the other agencies were insisting on to ensure that no terrorists came in with the local staff.

It was a vicious circle, with everyone and no one to blame, and he sensed the makings of a sizable, but mostly invisible tragedy.

Putnam got a call from an NGO official that he had met with several weeks before. The official seemed very nervous and asked for a meeting with Putnam. When they met, he haltingly said he had come to Putnam because he had tried going through other embassy and military channels, but, as he told Putnam, "They pretty much told me to drop it."

He went on to explain that his agency had been working with the Human Services Ministry for three years and had been routinely asked to give the ministry an "oversight fee" to cover the expenses of the Ministry's supposed support for the agency's contract to operate food and shelter programs for children in three provinces. The problem was that there was no support and no oversight—it was just a bribe to allow the NGO to stay open.

Then the NGO staffer said they had met with the head of the Human Services Ministry, who had told them, in so many words, that they were all rich Americans and they needed to pay the Iraqis to allow them to continue operating, threatening to close them down completely if they didn't pay. He added that effective immediately the payment would be doubled "because of the trouble you're causing by objecting to our methods." The NGO official explained that the size of the new payment would mean that more than a thousand children would have to be cut from the program.

Putnam said he'd look into it, and asked the official not to discuss it, promising to get back to him in two days. He made some calls to the auditing unit in the embassy, where he had been careful to make some friends, and he verified that on unrelated USAID contracts that went through the same ministry, there had been what the deputy in the audit unit carefully called "discrepant payments without verifiable recipients."

When Putnam asked "You mean bribes," the audit staffer said "Sir, we've been told never to use that word."

Putnam sat in his room, thinking about what he had learned, and then about a long-ago meeting with a church official. Later that night, he was with Aisha and he explained it to her, asking her not to disclose any of it.

Aisha said little while he told her what he had learned. When he stopped, she asked him, "What are you going to do, Will?"

He said, looking at the picture of himself with the little girl, Amira, at the orphanage, "Once, long ago, I backed off on a scandal where kids were getting hurt. I felt dirty for years. It was a lousy feeling. So I'll go all the way on this one if I have to."

The Ambassador called Putnam in after getting a short memo from him asking for a meeting on "the problems in the Human Services Ministry." Will had been careful with the memo, describing the diversions in general terms and naming no names. But it was clear what and who he was talking about.

The Ambassador was not happy. "We've been asked to back off on this one, Will."

"You can back off, Roger. I can't do that. I won't do that."

His voice got quieter, and he held the Ambassador's gaze without looking away. Slowly he said, "There is no way I am going to let this guy off. I will go to the Secretary and I will go to the media, and I will resign. But that bastard has stolen his last dollar from these kids. It is over, and if I have to go down on this, I'm going to do it."

The Ambassador sighed and said, "It's not about you or me, Will. It's not a fight we need to have with these guys, not right now."

"There's always a reason to back off, Roger. But not on this one. Not this time." He hadn't taken his eyes off the Ambassador.

And finally, the Ambassador said, "All right, Will. I can't say I disagree. I'll tell Washington we have no wiggle room on this one. I hope there are no repercussions you can't handle."

"Roger, I'm really not worried about that," said Putnam.

After that, it was just about the endgame. A very strong message was privately delivered to the premier, and specific shipments of weapons were put on hold. The minister was re-assigned to the economics ministry, and a legislator from the Premier's party was given the human services ministry. The premier gave a speech about Iraqi sovereignty, mentioning no specifics but charging the US with "constant, inappropriate pressures on Iraqi agencies."

For once, the State Department spokesman acquired a spine and said, tersely, "We reject the Premier's charges, and we hope he continues to place the best possible people in his ministries so that they can serve the people of his nation."

But there was a price. Putnam got a formal message from Sheila Zakarian that the Secretary appreciated his forthrightness but hoped Putnam would be able to work through channels as normal procedures dictated. Translated, the message was *stop breaking china over there or you're of no value to us.*

Aisha called on the private line Will had given her. She was frantic.

"I need your help, Will, and it's urgent. I can't talk about it on the phone. Can you meet me in an hour where we had our last meal together?"

That had been at her apartment, and he quickly said, "Yes. On my way."

When he got there, Will could see that she was frightened.

"Will, do you remember the little girl we met at the orphanage? Amira? The one who came up to me and asked you for books in English?"

Her voice was strained, and her hands were moving quickly up and down in an insistent gesture, trying to get Will to act without making clear what she wanted him to do.

"Yes, of course. I had USAID people send the orphanage and the school a box of books—we got her name and addressed it to her."

"She's been kidnapped." As she continued to speak, Will opened his phone and called embassy security, asking for the head to meet with him as soon as he could get back to the embassy. They hurried to the car that Petrosian had waiting for them in a nearby garage, and Aisha kept talking as they drive back to the embassy. "Someone in the village must have decided the orphanage and the school were getting too close to the Americans. They kidnapped her."

Will had never seen her so upset. "Will, they're going to kill her as a lesson to the rest of the village. We've got to do something."

They arrived at the central office of the embassy security detail, who had called in a two-star whom Putnam knew had a special operations command role. He was only slightly surprised to see Sydowski in the group as well.

Aisha described a call she had just gotten from the head of the orphanage. The general, Cy Larson, shook his head as she finished.

"Ambassador, we go after her and they'll keep taking more kids just to set up ambushes. This happened three months ago in Anbar. They took two of our translators. We got some intel on where they were holding them and went in. The place was booby-trapped and we lost two of our team with three more badly wounded."

Sydowski spoke up. "We just can't do it, Will. We'll lose more guys."

"What happened to the translators?"

Larson looked away. "They found them on a road way out in the province. They'd been beheaded, and a crude American flag was carved into their chests."

Putnam said, "Somebody knows where that little girl is. I know we can't pay ransom. But we've been giving out so-called honor payments. Can't we set it up so we can do something like that?"

Sydowski said, "Will, the odds are not great on this one. They're going to try to use her to take some of our guys down. That's what they do. It's not about how or how much we pay them. They're going to want to show they're a threat any time they want to be, and that requires killing or capturing someone who matters."

"Then I'll drive out there by myself and try to negotiate with them."

"That's pure suicide, Will. They'll take you hostage and then we'll have an incident that will make headlines all over the world. And you'll end up dead. We don't need any more martyrs out here, Will."

Larson spoke up. "If we know where she is we have a shot at getting in and getting out without a problem. But we need to be sure she's there." Then he turned to Aisha. He had obviously done some background research on her. "Can your contacts find her?"

She nodded, saying "I've already begun trying to get in touch with them. What is likely to happen, General, is that my contacts are going to want some payment in recognition for their help."

Larson said "I assumed so. We could do that." He glanced at Sydowski who nodded.

Later that night, Aisha contacted her cousin. After some back and forth he agreed to try to locate the girl in return for a sizable payment. The team working on her rescue decided to tell themselves that it wasn't ransom done that way because it wasn't going to the kidnappers.

Back in his room preparing to go to the rendezvous point, Putnam made a few keystrokes on his desktop and pulled up the picture Aisha had taken when they visited the orphanage. He left it open, and sat staring at it.

Petrosian came in and asked him, "What weapon you want, sir? Doesn't make any sense to go unarmed."

"I carried a .45 in Vietnam. I could probably remember how the safety and the trigger work."

They arrived at a warehouse in a nondescript village twenty kilometers from the orphanage. The team surrounded it as unobtrusively as they could with a company of soldiers. A small truck was opened, and a robot rolled out and slowly entered the front door of the warehouse. The team leaders gathered around a monitor that showed them the inside.

The colonel in charge of the detail said, "Looks like it's empty..."

And just then an explosion blew out most of the front of the warehouse. The explosion knocked two members of the detail down, but the rest of the group had taken cover when the robot had gone inside.

The colonel said "God help us if she was inside."

Then they heard a cry, and a house three doors away from the warehouse opened. A small child was pushed outside, and the door slammed. She looked back over her shoulder, and started running toward the team.

Putnam began walking rapidly toward her, hearing the colonel shouting "Putnam, no, there might be—"

But he kept walking, and the little girl kept running, and then they met, and he swept her up and grasped her tightly, turning so that his back was to the house she had come from, shielding her from whatever might still be there. Amira was crying, but he heard her say "I knew you would come, Mr. Ambassador. Thank you so much for the books. Thank you."

In seconds, the security team surrounded them and quickly lifted all three of them, Putnam, Aisha, and Amira, into a Humvee, all three crowded together in the second seat, the safest place in the vehicle.

A day later, Aisha and Putnam were replaying the rescue in her apartment. Amira had been relocated to another orphanage in the city, and Aisha had spent most of the first day with her, getting her settled in. Aisha had begun talking about adopting her. It had been a difficult conversation, and she decided to change the subject to something lighter.

"Will, I need to talk to you about something." She smiled, adding, "This is only half-serious. I have been thinking about our conversations. I'm not sure that making foreign policy by *movies* makes much sense. We've talked about all these movies—*The Music Man, The Way We Were, Lawrence.* If the problem with American foreign policy is that it is over-simplified, how are movies helpful when it's an art form that has to simplify to be understood?"

Putnam picked up on the playful part of her question and went along with her mood. "But these movies reveal some of who we are. And you brought up *The Way We Were,* not me. At their best, movies are as much an art—a popular art, I grant you—as the ruins out here or the kids learning to draw verses of the Quran in those schools."

They continued talking, with no conclusions about either movies or adoption, but an easy relief at being together after the tension of the rescue. Putnam left to return to the embassy.

His next set of meetings were draining, He had suggested to the Ambassador that Easton's replacement should be asked to press the Pentagon for more data on collateral deaths to civilians, but the Ambassador had balked. He clearly had little appetite for a confrontation with the military in his first months in Baghdad. Putnam's prognosis was not good.

He was tired, and his thoughts turned to Aisha. After spending so much time together, she had the ability to re-center him, helping him to move past exhaustion to a calm that cleared his thoughts. He asked Petrosian to pick her up at the university where she was giving a workshop to a group of women who had worked with her when she was in the government.

While he was waiting, Putnam made some notes on his last meeting with the Executive Council. As he wrote, he heard two explosions, far enough away that he felt no urgency about seeking cover. Explosions had become a sad routine in Baghdad, and his mind wandered back to the nights when the occasional errant 105 dropping into Saigon marked another bizarre routine in his life.

The bomb that killed Petrosian and Aisha had been planted at an intersection more than four kilometers from the entrance of the Green Zone, so it did not appear to have been aimed at them specifically. Eight pedestrians had been killed or wounded, and several other cars were badly damaged. Petrosian had been driving her to meet with Putnam and took a route that was not a normal route for embassy traffic, which usually meant that it was safer.

An investigation by the security team reported to Putnam that the bomb was "a random occurrence."

Putnam was numb, able only to move through the days after the bombing by going through the bare minimum, sleeping, waking, eating little, dressing and undressing. In an instinctive effort to make some physical acknowledgment of his losses, he stopped shaving. He soon seemed to his colleagues to have aged a decade.

He had attended a memorial service for Petrosian held in the embassy, but after long minutes standing in front of the group, attempting to say something about Petrosian through his silent weeping, he finally sat down without being able to utter a word.

The two people who had made his time in Iraq tolerable were gone, and nothing he could say could express what their absence meant to him. Their death extinguished the possibility of brightness in the place where they had helped him cling to hope.

His "church" of sacred music failed him as well. Sitting in his room, he played some of the requiem masses he had collected over the years. But he found they only deepened his grief, taking none of it away.

He didn't interact much with his colleagues, and they gave him a lot of space for mourning. But when he did, he realized that his memory lapses had gotten worse, and it became more difficult for co-workers, especially those who didn't know him well, not to act surprised when he couldn't find the word for what he was trying to say or the memory he was trying to pull out of his brain. The loss of his two closest friends had given his brain another shock, and at his most lucid, he began to realize how deep the damage had been.

In despair, he returned to contemplation of his earlier days in Vietnam. He spent time re-reading Ward Just, whom he regarded as the best of a fine group of chroniclers of the American sojourn in Asia, dipping back into his marvelous phrases. *We were startled by the beauty of the country and surprised by its size.* He remembered being shocked when he learned how much longer Vietnam was than his own California—hundreds of miles longer, north to south, and larger than Germany.

He looked around, wanting to share this factoid with Petrosian…and then slammed the book shut, plunged back into his sorrow.

He remembered an unfinished piece of business, and arranged for one of Aisha's co-workers to take Amira into her home, leaving her with enough money for Amira's education. But he decided, reluctantly, not to go visit her because he knew that the child gain nothing from seeing an elderly American crying uncontrollably.

Finally, he realized he was going to have to resign. He notified Beemer's replacement, a career State Department official, and a few others, and was mildly surprised when the Ambassador told him they wanted to have a farewell ceremony for him. He knew he would have to go through with it, however difficult, as a means of trying to show that he hadn't completely collapsed. He was financially secure, but he hoped somehow that he would still be able to make some kind of contribution as a consultant or with a firm. He knew that if word went out that he was a shattered wreck, it would hurt his chances for any continuing role.

So he prepared himself for the valedictory, and when the day came, he felt ready for the small gathering of the senior diplomats and military personnel he had worked with, as well as a few of the lower-level security and embassy staff he had gotten to know best in his work.

The appropriate send-off speeches were made by the appropriate speakers, and it came time for Putnam to "say a few words," as the Ambassador put it, in phrasing that Putnam knew meant *as few as possible, please.*

He began slowly, but with growing firmness and warmth in his voice. "Thanks to all of you. I've perhaps pressed too hard at times, and I want to say I'm sorry if I seemed too insistent. You are a stalwart band of brothers and sisters, and I have been privileged to work with you for the past few years."

He paused, almost so long that the Ambassador took a step toward him, thinking he had either faltered or was finished. But Putnam raised his hand with a slight wave-off motion, and then continued.

"I doubt that those who send us here really appreciate, as I have come to, what they ask of us. And I know they do not understand what they ask of those of you and your troops who are out on the front lines. I'm not talking about the danger—though there's plenty of that, as we've all learned to our eternal sorrow." He kept on, mentally turning away from the faces of Aisha and Petrosian. "I'm talking about what those around the tables in DC expect us to do in imposing our will on a place we still understand too little.

"'The people are the prize.' It says that in 3-24, it's been true since Alexander and the Greeks came through here, and it's common sense.

"And there are wonderful people who live here, who will be here after we leave. They are from a culture millennia older than ours, more civilized in some ways, and surely more brutal in others."

He looked at them, hoping that at least some would understand. He knew some would dismiss what he was saying as the tired reminiscing of an old diplomat, but he also knew that some of them understood because they had lived through it without reverting to slogans or surrendering to the deep frustration that marked them all at the low times.

"This is a campaign, really, in both the military and the political senses of that word. I tried campaigning once, long ago, and I was not very good at it. It requires a clear message and a good messenger, and I fell short on both counts." He paused. "In our work here, we may have some of the same challenges that I once had.

"Our messages about democracy and human rights and security have gotten muddled sometimes, and too often our messenger has been caricatured. We are seen only as soldiers bearing arms or civilians bearing cash, rather than a nation back home trying to make a better world for the children who live here.

"You see, I've come to realize that *the people* are not the prize. The *children* are. I know I've said that—or tried to say that—in a lot of meetings with some of you. But I believe it. I've come to believe that that's really the only metric that matters. That's what it's all about—or should be. If we paid more attention to that—just a little bit more attention—perhaps we could leave here with our heads held as high as when we came in."

He sat down, to more applause than he would have expected. Then the Ambassador rose, and told the group, "I am pleased to announce today that three four-year scholarships to US universities will be awarded to outstanding students from Iraq for the next twenty years. One is in your name, Will, one is named for Michael Petrosian, and one is named for Aisha Araden."

And then he finally let the tears fall, touched by the act of personal recognition, reminded that these colleagues, like the nation they represented, were capable at times, at their best, of acts of uncommon decency and justice.

PART THREE

After, in Eastern Connecticut

The journalist had come to interview Putnam for a book he was writing about the two wars. Ten years ago, Sam Leonard had won a Pulitzer covering a lengthy demonstration in Mexico and California focused on immigration issues. He had approached Putnam through Ernie Scott, who had known Leonard for many years.

Putnam had retired to a small town in eastern Connecticut, back to his New England roots. As Sam Leonard entered his home, Putnam showed him around. The house was totally solar, with windows facing east into the sunrise. His yard extended to rows of tall pines on two sides, with the road in front and a garden in back.

The spacious living room had floor to ceiling bookshelves on two walls, with pictures from his various posts on the third wall. The fourth opened into a small dining room and onto a tidy kitchen.

Putnam offered Sam coffee and a cigar, and Sam accepted both. They sat down in comfortable arm chairs next to a sizable fireplace.

"Thanks for seeing me, Ambassador. You've had an extraordinary career, and I appreciate the chance to talk with you about it. Ernie has been urging me to talk to you for some time."

"Call me Will. Ernie told me to look you up after Saigon—glad we finally connected."

"All right." He paused, looking at Putnam's pictures on the wall behind his chair. There were pictures of children from Vietnam, Iraq, and other places, along with pictures of embassies where he had served. A small rock was mounted in a picture box in the middle of the wall. A set of dog tags hung off the edge of the box.

Leonard said quietly, "A tale of two embassies."

"And a few other places along the way."

"I'm told you came to disagree with the mission in Iraq, sir."

Putnam was silent for a long time, and Leonard wondered if he was refusing to respond to his frontal tactics.

"I appreciate your getting right to the point, although I hope we talk about the rest of my career." Seeing Sam's nod, he went on. "I disagreed because of how much we had forgotten about the first one."

Sam was quiet for a while, and then said. "Will, I have some questions about how you see the history in both places. You have a unique perspective, and I'd like to talk about that. That's part of what my book is about. But I also hope we can talk about what happens next. From what you've said so far and what people have told me about you, you seem to have a longer view of the two wars than a lot of other people I've talked to. And so the question that comes up for me, with that perspective, is whether we will ever try to do this again. Will we ever again try to do what we tried to do in those two corners of Asia?"

Putnam answered, slowly. "We can talk about that, although my crystal ball is no clearer than anybody else's." He was quiet, looking out his front window at the rural countryside. "I think the short answer is no. As much as we've forgotten, that terrible wall is still there at the end of the Mall. That's one of the best things our government ever did, as a memorial to one of the worst things we ever did."

He stopped and shook his head. "Nobody who's ever seen that wall or even a picture of it can ever claim that we can put boots on the ground—as the phrase goes these days—and expect quick results. It took a long time for us to understand that. From Pearl Harbor to VJ Day, World War II lasted three years and nine months. And so we got fooled into thinking that was the kind of timetable we were facing. Not the twenty years from the French defeat in 1954 to our withdrawal in 1975, or the decades in Iraq and Afghanistan.

"I worked in Vietnam for a guy named Zimball. Years later he was interviewed by a history professor who did dozens of interviews of US and

Vietnamese about the war." He reached over and pulled a piece of paper from a large book, the title of which, Sam saw, was *Patriots*. Putnam read from the paper: "'We lost the war on the ground, that's all. The idea that the press lost the war is bunk. We didn't appreciate the determination of the North. I think maybe with the right involvement and investment we might have won it on the ground, but what did that mean? A million American soldiers? Another billion dollars of aid? I don't know. I don't know if we had the commitment to stick with it.'

"Then he went on to tell the professor that his own, Zimball's, recommendation at the end was to tell the South Vietnamese that we were getting out unless they could get their act together. At the end, he had no regard for the Southern leadership. None.

"And that's what it comes down to, Sam. We will never go into a place where the insurgents have the determination on their side and we have the *gonifs*—that great Yiddish word meaning so much more than thieves—on our side." He paused and added, "It's the LOTTE factor."

"Lotte? Like Lotte Lenya?"

"Spelled the same, but no: L-O-T-T-E. Stands for Lesser of the Two Evils. We continually find ourselves in the position of choosing between the lesser of two evils when we launch on these foreign adventures. And no one with half a brain or half a heart can justify why Americans kids should die or get maimed for life to serve the lesser of two evils."

Sam asked "What about presidents who lead the charge?"

"From my vantage point, we had some presidents who never understood any of that. They had forgotten the difference between World War II and long-term insurgencies.

"But now, it's hard for me to imagine a president coming along who could ignore that history. He—or she—might want to go in with troops and an uncertain timetable, but it's hard to imagine how either Congress or the media would let them pile up years and years of casualties the way we did in Vietnam and the Middle East.

"Sam, there's this old story that I never get tired of telling, because it says so much. Sometimes it's attributed to one of the leaders of the North in Vietnam and sometimes to a prisoner we were interrogating. Whoever said it, it's dead right. 'The Americans have clocks, but we have time.'"

He paused, letting the words sink in. "They have time. And we have a national attention span that is getting briefer and briefer, even though we've always been an impatient people. We will never go into a ten-year war again, or a war that might drag on that long. Never. That would be my prediction, through my cloudy crystal ball.

"The other side of that, Sam, is that people in other countries read history, too. And every time that some countries' insurgents prove that all they have to do is out-wait the US—that we have no real staying power—then the next group of insurgents—or some second-rate dictator—gets a message that you don't have to worry about the US over the long haul."

"Will any other country fill the gap?"

"I doubt it. The French have poked around in Africa lately, but not in any sustained way. The Chinese? They've got fifteen nations surrounding them that they've invaded at some point in their history"—he laughed—"and we've only got two. They don't need to go looking for insurgencies anywhere else; they've got a few close by. The Russians—maybe, if they sober up and find ten or twenty million young people they seem to be missing. The UN? Maybe in small scale stuff, but they're never going to field a real army that would go on the offensive."

Sam frowned and said, "I understand what you're saying, but doesn't that leave the field to the insurgents—to the Al Qaedas?"

"If the regional powers don't understand that the Al Qaedas will come for them in time, then how can we stop them by ourselves? Russia and China are already learning that the Al Qaedas are in their backyards—not ours. There are a hell of a lot more extremists on the borders of Russia and China than on ours right now.

"In Vietnam, they hated China. In Iraq, they hated each other—and us, of course, for getting rid of the dictator who kept them from killing each other and left them too weak to get rid of him on their own. It was not just Vietnam and Iraq—it was their neighbors. Both countries had the terrible misfortune to be sitting at the crossroads of other larger and more ruthless nations. China, Iran, Turkey, the Saudis—tough neighbors."

He added, "And the Israelis. Small country, very tough people. They've needed to be. And now they're learning what occupation costs, just as we had to."

He went on. "If only we had read the history. Not only our own, but the British and Russian adventures in Iraq. In the 1870's, after disastrous retreats through the Khyber Pass, the British decided to stop using their own troops and began buying off warlords. It's what we tried, belatedly, in Anbar province and in other areas."

Leonard smiled. "Our thugs versus their thugs. Rent-a-thug, somebody called it."

"Yes. Something like that." He went on. "George Kennan, who knew almost nothing about American politics, was a genius about American diplomacy. I once heard him lecture at Princeton, and even as a lowly graduate student visiting for a conference, I knew he was talking nonsense about political realities in the US. But this is the same man who wrote," he reached for a notebook on the desk behind him, 'Anyone who has ever studied the history of American diplomacy, especially military diplomacy, knows that you might start in a war with certain things on your mind as a purpose of what you are doing, but in the end, you found yourself fighting for entirely different things that you had never thought of before…war has a momentum of its own.'"

"'A momentum of its own.' Damn straight. And so you start out after the Al Qaedas, and you end up in a very different place, caught in a Sunni-Shia cross-fire. You try to prevent the spread of Asian communism, and you give it great power by occupying a country that could wait us out for decades longer than we were going to stick around. And in neither place were the so-called leaders of our so-called allies worth a damn, as Zimball and so many others told us at the time.

"And then there was the colonial, imperial part of the mission. We nearly convinced ourselves, from Wilson on, that we were anti-colonial. But it was a lot harder to convince our businessmen that we're anti-imperialist, once they figured out that the Coca-Cola brand of imperialism was more profitable than the European versions of the *mission civilisatrice*. You know, we are still replaying some of that. There are still churches that are trying to adopt kids from all over the world so they can come live in America as good little saved Christians. Spend fifty grand to adopt a kid but never spend fifty bucks to help her parents keep her fed instead of sending her to a fake 'orphanage' because she gets fed there. Thank God, the smart churches have figured out that getting the kids into good families in their own country beats ripping them away from their own culture."

He realized that he had gotten agitated, and smiled. "I get worked up about this sometimes."

Leonard said, "You do, and it seems to come when you talk about the kids. You've worked on children's programs throughout your career, yet you have no children of your own. Can you talk about that?"

Again Putnam was silent for a long time, frowning. He started talking, more hesitantly than before. "That's not something I can talk about right now. I wish I had been able to raise children of my own. I've tried to be an active uncle to my remarkable nieces and nephews, which has brought me great satisfaction. They are remarkable young men and women, making big contributions of their own, in their own ways. And I've tried to support outstanding young people, some close to me, some I met along the way."

He looked over at the pictures of children on his wall. "The career part? I saw early on that war is sometimes even more destructive of the lives of children than of the warriors, and I tried to do what I could to reduce that harm."

He paused. "But that's not always a priority in wartime, and part of my…my disagreements with those in charge of our mission came when I tried to press that point of view.

"Early in my career I learned that the counterinsurgency crowd had this saying, 'The people are the prize.' Sounds right—but you have to be clear about *which* people. It seemed to me, talking to local people who understood their own country far better than I ever would, that *the people* meant those in the villages and towns where the insurgency was strongest. And then I realized, talking with our media and a few politicians who came through the country and seemed to realize what was happening, that the other group of people who were the prize were those back home who were paying for it and deciding whether or not to re-elect those who had gotten us into the mess we were in.

"And it gradually became clear, doing some of the work I did with NGOs and religious groups, that there was another way to see 'the people.' If the people in the villages here are the prize, their kids are the long-term award. And so the real metric, I decided, should be kids going to safe schools where there are decent teachers. And as I pressed that point, I saw that almost no one in the higher levels of the embassy and the military understood that or agreed with it. So I pressed harder, and eventually got marginalized."

Leonard stopped making notes and said, "I can see how that would be hard to get across."

"Yes. It was. Three year-olds don't have much of a lobby in Congress, they can't vote, and they don't make many campaign contributions. And if they're on the other side of the world—good luck getting their priority recognized by anyone who matters."

He leaned back and glanced over at some of the pictures on the wall. "The children thing goes way back, I guess. My father was a high school teacher and a football coach and my mother taught kindergarten." He smiled, remembering. "At high school reunions, people in my class would come up and tell me stories I'd never heard before about how my dad had taken them aside after some screw-up of theirs and said something to them that turned them around, made them see things differently. And in her final days, which I had the great blessing to spend with her, my mother was fading in and out of consciousness. At one point, she was carefully telling the little ones in her long-ago class how to put their coats on so they wouldn't get wet in the rain."

He stopped, blinking, Sam could tell, to keep the tears from spilling over. "They cared about their kids, and they tried to help other kids. A lot of them.

"My sisters were pretty good with that stuff, too. They were a lot kinder to us younger ones than a lot of older kids sometimes can be. So the kids stuff was always there. Whatever you did, you were supposed to do something for kids. And if you're in a war zone and you have your eyes open, you can't help but see some of what's happening to the kids. And if you see it, you have to do something about it, somehow, at whatever cost." He paused. "For me, the cost was drifting out to the edge of irrelevance. Becoming too shrill, too critical, too 'half-empty,' some called it."

His anger was coming back, and he went on, fists now clenched. "Half-empty? Hell, that cup was almost totally dry. So I said so, often and loudly enough to piss a lot of people off. So be it."

He went on. "I knew when to be quiet, I wasn't just a self-righteous loudmouth. I worked inside the system, stayed quiet until there was a chance to get someone else out front or find the money to make a difference. But toward the end, I got tired of pussyfooting around. My brakes were failing, I guess, and I shot my mouth off more often. It was just so damned obvious, I thought, so why not say it. Say that kids were getting hurt on our side and the little kids as well."

He paused, wanting to be clear. "These days I think of anyone between 18 and 30 or so as 'kids,' so when I say 'our kids,' I mean our troops.

"Some of those in the meetings listened. But what pissed me off most was when the damned generals dismissed it when I'd try to say we were putting our kids at risk without needing to."

Imitating a blustering voice, he said, 'No one needs to tell me how marines should take cover. We go first where the action is worst.' Bastards. Somebody missed them when they shot at them in Vietnam and now they get to send our guys out into a firestorm of hurt caused by stupid tactics and our chicken-shit allies. And kids from little towns all over America go home without arms and legs. Or don't go home at all."

He was quiet for a moment, and then his fist came crashing down on his chair. "For what? For *what*?! So they could prove they could follow orders? That's nothing but the Nuremburg defense, and our kids deserve better.

"You know, Sam, the novelists of both wars did as good a job as the journalists. Maybe better. This new guy Klay has a story in his book *Redeployment* on aid projects in Iraq that was almost too painful to read. About how they added up points for projects and tried to pick the ones that were safest. Painful.

"Art has a long way to go to capture war. But if you can watch the after-battle scenes of *Platoon* through the chords of Barber's *Adagio*, and not ask "*Why?*" over and over, you have never thought seriously about American history. What right have powerful, old men sitting at long, polished tables to send young men out to such misconceived tasks? Fucking *dominoes*? Fucking *weapons of mass destruction*? We could perform atonement for the rest of this country's existence and not make up for mistakes like that."

His voice had risen as he became more and more animated, and he knew he needed a break. He looked at Leonard and said, "I need to stretch my legs or they tighten up. You want to go for a walk? You can keep that thing on," gesturing to the recorder.

"Sounds great."

Putnam's house backed on a regional park, and they walked toward its nearest trees. After a few hundred yards, they came to a clearing where a picnic table and a firepit were tucked in against some large rocks. Some canvas chairs sat next to the table. Putnam brushed some pine needles off the chairs, sat down and gestured to Sam to sit in the other chair.

"You've never remarried, Will. May I ask why?"

"Ah. The career explained by the personality." He looked at Leonard, silent for a while. "I don't want to talk about my marriage. But I will talk about women. Cultures are how people build and sustain relationships, with families and across deep ethnic and religious chasms. In my experience, women *get* relationships—even the women who have been hardened by their climbs up past the thorniest rungs of the ladder and the places where there were no rungs at all.

"Early on I learned that listening to women had a huge payoff, as well as often providing much more enjoyable scenery. My mother was worth listening to, and I had the good luck to meet other women who were both good company and wise about their cultures." He laughed. "And now I suppose we are moving into the personality part. I never remarried, I guess, because I enjoyed women too much. I'm told I tend to be a naturally reticent person, and women draw me out, help me—force me, sometimes—to engage more with the world than I might do, left to my own devices. Some women are also stronger than men, I've found. They go through childbirth, they have the strength it takes to nurture, and they put up with our predatory wanderings.

"One of the many things I learned from a remarkable woman I spent time with in Iraq…" he paused, closed his eyes for a moment, and then continued, "was how much our history tells us when we hear it in replay. She would tell me things about our history that I just didn't know—and I was pretty good in history, and I read the stuff.

"She could go on about the Indians—our Indians—and what it meant for insurgency. She talked about the tragedy of the Indians, like many insurgents, never being able to band together well enough to keep the colonials and the bloody settlers from running them out. Except for the Wabanaki Confederacy and Tecumseh, she said, our Indians never combined their forces. And so we fought them tribe by tribe, sending tribes we had bought against the tribes we fought. It sounds like Anbar all over again. But she really knew who we were. Better than many of us, I fear."

He was silent for a long time, and then moved his hand across his face, as if to wipe the memory away. "God, I miss her." Then he smiled. "I had the great fortune, in both places, to find out how to do a kind of hands-on anthropology through personal intimacy." He sighed. "They taught me so much."

"How is your health, Will, if I may ask?"

"Not that great, but far better than the alternative, as the saying goes." He leaned forward and rubbed his forehead. "I've had some memory loss, as we all do. Seeing its early effects was part of what led me to retire."

Then his face brightened. "I'm now part of some exotic experiments that Yale and the UConn Med Center are doing, with new meds and therapies. They tell me some pieces of my memory have actually gotten stronger.

"It's fascinating, really. The meds are interesting, and they're learning more all the time about what biochemical mixtures keep memory functioning. The market is there, obviously—we can't have millions of geezers wandering around not knowing where they live. They might end up in the malls, blocking serious shoppers."

He laughed, and then got serious. "But what I'm most struck by is that some instincts I had about memory are proving to be on target. Sam, they found that music is a huge storehouse of memory. Music does something physical to the synapses and the neurons, actually helps them regrow connections. We can all recall lyrics and melodies we haven't heard for fifty years. So they use music as part of the therapy, and I get to walk around humming rock and roll songs from the fifties."

He laughed. "Turns out Shakespeare was off a bit. Music—not sleep— is what knits up the raveled sleeve of care."

He showed Sam his latest generation smartphone, saying "My memory is in here—appointments, things to buy, all voice recognition, all in here. And then when I get a random memory of playing football or kissing a girl in high school—I talk about that too, and then that's in the memory. Then I say 'sort by year,' and it makes it all flow in time."

Sam asked with a smile, "How could we get one of those for a country?"

Putnam laughed and said, "Now that would be a big step forward." Then he looked serious. "But you know, Sam, a country can't remember or forget. There are 320 million of us and each of us has a memory—a good one or a bad one. But a country doesn't have a memory. It relies on its leaders and its media to explain what happened, and then we process it into our ideas about history and who did what to whom, and then we vote. And that builds the nation's next set of memories, if we elect people who can remember the past, or we elect those who are condemned to repeat its worst mistakes."

"Will, you're one of the few American diplomats who was involved in both these wars. How are they different—and I guess I should ask, how are they the same?"

"Great question. I suppose part of the final chapter of my professional life was trying to answer that question. It's different only if we choose to make it different. Only if we emerge out of the amnesia and remember, or elect people who remember, what happened and why, how to prevent it and how this is a different place and time."

He went on. "It's funny, I guess, that my own memory problems and our country's seem to run side by side. I've thought a lot about memory lately, as they run these experiments on me. You think a lot about what's really gone, what's not there in the neurons any more. It may be just as hard for a country to hold on to its memories as it is for someone aging into his later times."

Then he laughed. "Amnesia is not all bad. I always thought that when I ran out of money to buy books I would just start rereading them. Now the bonus is that, by then, I'll have forgotten what they say anyway." He gestured back to the house. "All those bookshelves—that's my brand new library!

"But your question was how are they different, and how are they the same. I once made lists of those factors, have them filed away somewhere. Let's see what I can remember." He recited, as if from a lecture he'd given many times.

"What was the same? In both wars, we came into a place where we had no roots, where we were the outsiders, trying to impose a new order on an old culture. We eventually understood that the people were the prize, but we had little clue about how to win the prize, and we fell back on our enormous firepower instead of our brains or the best of our own culture.

"You know, people come to the US from all over the world to get smarter, to get to our universities and our research institutions. But what we were offering was to go there—to other countries—and kill off their oppressors—or who we thought were their oppressors, and then leave. We built schools, and hospitals, and trained people to work in them. But we wiped out those gains every time we fired on a wedding that we thought was a terrorist gathering or wiped out an 'enemy village' that was just a bunch of people afraid of the insurgents and unable to trust their own government.

"What was different? Well, we killed a lot fewer of the wrong people— the so-called collateral damage was much less. The drones and the C-130 fire control and the satellites all helped us do much less damage. But it was still way too much to be welcomed as liberators. A claim that we only killed thousands of civilians instead of millions isn't going to look that good to history. By putting our troops down in the middle of a cross-fire between different gangs of thugs and thousand-year religious vendettas, we ran the risk of wiping out a lot of people. And when we did, predictably, their survivors and clan members started shooting at our guys. So what was different was the tools we used to try to kill fewer innocents, and what was the same was that we still killed too many of them.

"Another big difference, obviously, was between the draft and the volunteer army. We lost some of those kids in Vietnam because they were just so badly trained they had no idea how to keep out of trouble. But My Lai and Abu Ghraib were both horrible mistakes, the first by draftees and the second by volunteers. Terrible leadership explains each of them, in my view, and the voluntary status had little to do with guys just losing it and going berserk. Guys lose it when their buddies go down, and that's about war, not the draft.

"But there was a big difference in the quality of the average war fighter in the Iraq war, which was vastly superior to that in Vietnam. Some combat troops in Vietnam went on to do great things—John Kerry, John McCain, Chuck Hagel. But the leadership in our troops in Iraq was infinitely better. And so were the troops, usually. That made it an even greater tragedy when we asked troops that good to try to do something that impossible."

He frowned. "The rock-bottom loyalty of those troops to the mission is undeniable. But the hardest question I can ever think of asking is when does that loyalty run into Nuremberg?"

"'I was just following orders.'"

"Right. And the outrage is how dare we ask kids and officers that good to follow orders so doomed to failure—so unlikely to be sustained, given who we are and who the Iraqis are."

He went on. "If you look back, Sam, in some ways the critical moment was when Petraeus reverses McChrystal's orders to try to reduce civilian casualties. That is when we went morally bankrupt, in my view. You never avoid civilian casualties as an absolute—you have to protect our troops. But McChrystal, to his great credit, drew the line in a different place, and demanded that our troops take greater risks to increase civilian safety. Petraeus just wanted to win and go on up the ladder, and didn't care how. McChrystal, like Shinseki, had an honesty problem. Not really Petraeus' issue, we found.

"More differences: The scale of private contractors is very different. They were there in Vietnam, doing construction projects, but they are multibillion dollar multinationals now. And some of them have more firepower than one of our regiments. The chain of command runs back to Washington—even Beemer complained that they didn't really report to him. Some of them specialize in the wet stuff, dirty stuff. But the locals tar all of us with the same brush, and some of those firms cost us much more than what we paid them.

"Another thing that was different, I think, is that somehow in Vietnam we managed to retain a better relationship with the people than in Iraq. He laughed, "I read in the *Times* the other day that the hot new place for Americans to retire is—wait for it—the south coast of Vietnam. Cheap cost of living, food some Americans learned to like, and natives that really, really like us, as Sally Field would say. Go figure. We kill two to three million of them, and then we go retire there. John McCain and John Kerry deserve some credit for going to Hanoi when they did, but there is something in the Vietnamese people that recognizes that vengeance is usually useless.

"What have we become—what is different? More cautious—fewer boots on the ground. More aware of other cultures—having failed to understand several. More tempted to buy our way out of trouble:

contractors, rent-a-thug tactics. We're more likely to send money than troops now. Perhaps from now on we'll only send them our money and our food—not our young men and women. We rely now on money and technology: drones and clones, privacy invasions instead of amphibious ones. DNA is where the next war or the one after that may be fought, biowar, cyberwar—where our money and our science give us advantages the insurgents don't have—yet."

He paused and looked back into the forest behind them. "Bottom line on the miltary differences? We are just not going to risk having our kids killed or maimed for life just to keep savages from savaging innocents, if no one on the ground will protect their own innocents. The hawks will scream, but they are never going to convince people that wading into someone else's fight works out for us."

He went on. "Behind all those things that are different about the two wars is the obvious fact that we're a different country now. Polarized politics matters. Think about it—LBJ got attacked by people in both parties, but there was nothing like what happened with both Bush and Obama. If Obama came out and said the sun just rose today, the wingnuts would say it was midnight just to disagree with him. The media is totally different, too. Walter Cronkite told us we were losing—and tectonic plates started to move in our politics. There is no Walter Cronkite today.

"Forty years ago gets you from the Civil War to the 20th century, from the end of WWI to rock and roll. The 60s and 70s are a foreign country compared to who we are today. And that's a huge difference."

Sam smiled and said "Your Iraqi friend may have known a lot of American history, but you seem to have a pretty good grasp of it yourself."

"Thanks—I think."

"Will, you were very close to the media in both places. Can you talk about that? How did you handle things that were classified when they asked you about our policy?"

"Tough question, Sam. I'll answer part of it. I never crossed the line in giving out information that was legally protected. Today there are so many things on hard drives and thumb drives that the idea that secrets will always stay secret is ludicrous. Somebody is going to throw these secrets out on the internet and they will be out there flashing around for centuries, in whatever form the internet takes in the future. In my time, I made suggestions to smart reporters, and they did the rest. I told them which direction to look in, I never told them where things were. And I never did anything that risked harm to anyone. I wanted light shone into corners where we were careless, where we were at risk of hurting people caught in a needless crossfire."

Sam said, "I want to come back to what you were saying about our future policy. What we've learned—or may have learned. I want to make sure I understand what you're saying about these lessons of the two wars you saw up close."

Putnam nodded. "All right. Let's see if I can say it as clearly as possible." He was silent, and then said, "I think the so-called Vietnam syndrome never went away, and the syndrome we are going to get out of this latest round is going to deepen skepticism about counterinsurgency. There is still a deep isolationist strain in our politics, and this has fed it. That is not altogether a good thing. It is very bad for the prospects of humanitarian missions in the future. But it will mean that theories about dominoes and theories about how easy it will be to find and remove weapons of mass destruction will have a very uphill road to travel. We also learned that you can burn up a trillion dollars in no time at all. And obviously we can use that money in lots of better ways, both at home and around the world.

"I've been doing a lot of reading lately on Vietnam and the Middle East, trying to sort out what we screwed up—and the places where we did it right, which are fewer but also worth understanding. The debate about counterinsurgency—the COIN stuff—has gotten fierce, with advocates on both sides trying to re-fight insurgency wars all the way back to Malaya in the 50's—even further, looking at Ireland in the '20s and Palestine in the '40's. One of the academics calls the advocates 'COIN-dinistas.' The Brits were supposed to be the all-time COIN masters. But it was on their watch that Basra went to hell in southern Iraq."

He laughed. "Funny thing about all those books—none of them talk about what it costs. The guys who wrote those books needed an auditor, or a budget guy, or, hell, someone who could just *count*. Because none of them even tries to estimate what COIN costs!

"One of the things I hope we learned in Iraq is that the resources it takes to penetrate or infiltrate a culture are a hell of a lot less than what it takes to crush one. Dollar for dollar, scholarships are cheaper than battleships. And their effects may last a lot longer. We can't afford COIN if you take it seriously, because it requires either a great local army to replace our troops or a long-term occupation by our troops. Neither comes cheap."

He paused, knowing what he was going to say next would seem even more idealistic. But he thought of Petrosian, to whom the future could have belonged. And Steve Jefferson, to whom it still did. And he went on.

"With what we spent in the Middle East since 2003 we could have gone to Mars or totally wiped out poverty in the US. Maybe both, if you factor in the long-term disabilities our kids took home with them.

"The costs are critical. All those businessmen, from McNamara to a president with an MBA—and they never added up the costs. It makes sense to try to build civic good will and security up from the village and neighborhood level. The problem is that it takes so many troops and so much money and is so dangerous that we will probably never again try to do it over that period of time with that much treasure—blood and money. Never. Maybe with extraordinary local leadership. But if you had that kind of leadership, you probably wouldn't need our troops."

He paused, and went on. "Americans don't like headlines that seem to show we're losing, and we don't have the staying power to win over the length of time it takes. COIN got discredited long before the Dutchman got itchy pants.

"You know, I've read a lot of the biographies and autobiographies from both wars. Hendrickson on McNamara, Gates, the books on Petraeus and the other COIN advocates, Bernstein on Clinton, the Ricks book on the generals no one had the guts to fire. The leaders all seem to have regrets, and sometimes they talk about what they owed to the individual soldiers they led. But none of them ever seemed to ask themselves the real question—why was that kid in that Humvee driving down that street? Why was that kid patrolling that tree line where the ambush was set up?

"The answer they couldn't face up to was not just that they had sent that kid there. The answer was that our kids were there because it wasn't safe for the locals, and we had to provide security. And it wasn't safe because the locals didn't have a government or police force or militia or anything else that could make it safe against other people who wanted to run the place. And that's not our fault. It becomes our fault when there are so many of us that our guys become the target.

"A very smart guy I worked with in Iraq once summed it all up with a set of six premises. He said, if I can remember it, that there were six premises that got us into the two wars. And only one of them was right. That's a lousy batting average for the so-called best and the brightest.

"The best argument for both wars is that we bought them time. Not that we held off communism, or dictatorships, or even that we made the world safe for capitalism that moved millions out of total poverty. But that we belonged there to give people in the villages a shot at a better life."

He shook his head, frowning. "There's two big problems with that argument, though. First, you can use it to justify invading dozens of countries, and second, it was after we left that the Vietnamese economy took off—and not because we trained good little capitalists, but because they learned, like China, to make stuff that we'd go to Walmart and Target and buy. Our occupation had little to do with that, as China made clear."

Sam asked, "So what is the answer, Will? If COIN doesn't work and Americans can't ever understand other cultures enough to change them so that they're not a threat to us, what's the answer?"

Putnam stood up. "Let's head back to the house, I'm getting chilly." As they walked, he returned to Sam's question

"I'm not sure what the answer is. I've learned enough to know it's the right question, but I don't know the answer." He paused, drew on his cigar, and looked out at the edge of his land, at the tall trees that marked his property lines.

They walked into the house and Putnam lit a fire. They sat down again, enjoying the warmth.

"So, what about COIN and the 9/11 rationale? I know this, Sam. Insurgents ye will always have with you. Both because there are lousy regimes around the world that deserve to have insurgents, and because there are evil thugs, drug cartels, and others who will take advantage of weak states and ancient rivalries to gain power. And also because hungry people have nothing to lose. The visibility of our inequality will continue to feed small wars, as long as you can see on a TV screen or a phone anywhere in the world how much the best off have compared to the worst off.

"And the fact is that some of those insurgents will come after us, or will go after people and governments that we can and should protect. So we aren't going out of the anti-insurgency business any time soon. But counterinsurgency the way we've been doing it, with armies of a hundred thousand or more—that's over. We will insert special operations troops in other countries for short-term protection missions and, in special circumstances, for very short-term humanitarian operations when ethnic or religious groups are threatened. But we will never leave those troops or regular troops on the ground in places where the local thugs can't be controlled by our remote assets or their own governments. I think the lesson we have finally learned is that counterinsurgency that turns into occupation of hostile territory asks too much of our troops. And we will never ask for that sacrifice again, unless there is a direct, verifiable threat to us. The terrible truth is that there was no such threat in Vietnam, nor in the Middle East. And the sixty thousand-plus lives we gave up in those two debacles were a price far too great for what we got out of it.

"So to boil it all down, we shouldn't be there because it costs us more time and blood and money than we have or want to give. And we shouldn't be there because pacification becomes occupation which makes our troops the targets. You want bumper stickers for the semi-literate voter? *COIN costs too much. Pacification turns into occupation.*

"I've always thought that if a benighted bunch of troglodytes wanted to live in the 7th century, they should be allowed to, if they could do it without contaminating anyone else with their godforsaken ideas. Let the rest of the world watch how that works out."

He paused, anger showing on his face. "Same here at home. I've wondered why Ron Paul and Rand Paul don't refuse all federal aid for their districts and their state and call for an end to Social Security and Medicare for all their constituents. We may need an educational project in this country where people could see what looney, right-wing ideas really look like on the ground."

Sam smiled and said, "Isn't that what Texas and Alabama are for?"

They had arrived back at the house and Will brought Sam a cup of coffee.

"Graham Greene, one of my all-time favorite writers, once nailed the whole counter-insurgency thing in a paragraph." He went over to one of the bookshelves and pulled out a small, ancient-looking paperback and opened it to a page that had its corner turned down. "The American says they—the Vietnamese in this case—'don't want communism.' The British reporter says *They want enough rice. They don't want to be shot at. They want one day to be much the same as another. They don't want our white skins around telling them what they want.*"

Leonard said, "Ok. That's clear. But I've still got to ask—doesn't that just leave the biggest bullies in charge of the schoolyard?"

"If there are a lot of kids who are letting a few bullies take charge, and the teachers or whoever is in charge of that schoolyard—to stay with your metaphor—are letting it happen—why should our kids end up in Arlington or broken in half for the rest of their life?"

He leaned forward, wanting Leonard to understand it. "The irony of our incompetence in understanding other cultures is that we are sometimes—*sometimes*—most effective when we don't try, when we just say well, that's your culture and we're staying out until you make your culture work better for your people."

"Sounds pretty cold-blooded."

"Yeah. And presidents who take that route will get beat up for being passive. But it's a better charge than being aggressive and wasting lives and money."

"But it seems at odds with your saying the metric should be kids in other countries who are safer."

"Yeah. But it seems to me that there are a lot of new ways to keep the spotlight on what happens to their kids without risking our kids. George Clooney has that satellite up there watching the Sudan, other people are using technology for human rights monitoring. We can shut down your bank account from across the world if we want to, find out where you're putting your money and freeze it cold. The Treasury guys can do stuff now with cyberfinance that wakes bankers up screaming in the middle of the night. Drones that drop food and medicine instead of bombs. Phones that let kids report abusers and traffickers and geocode where they're living, or report when teachers aren't showing up in schools or doctors in clinics we paid for. New non-military tools for the good guys—you journalists should be writing more about all that."

Putnam paused and looked at Leonard, trying again to get his point across. "There may no longer be any hard and fast rules for making war. But there may be criteria that we can use to think more clearly about it. My criteria would be simple. What are we asking of our kids and what we are we likely to do to theirs?"

He smiled. "They brought me in for a policy session on Syria a few months ago—some kind of Wise Old Men exercise the Secretary had dreamed up. They wanted us to tell them to do something, since they were essentially doing nothing at that point. And so I laid out a scenario.

"What can we do in a mess like Syria? We could never ask our kids to step into the middle of that many crossfires—crossfires between Assad and the rebels, crossfires among the rebels, crossfires among the backers of all sides. If we went in, our troops would fire on anyone who fired on them—and eventually everyone would be firing on them. It would be stupid to go in on the ground in that kind of bloodbath. Not one American soldier's life would be worth it.

"Their kids? Over a million kids have been thrown out of their homes, thousands of them killed, the rest dislocated for decades, probably. I would try to shame the kleptocrats and plutocrats of the Middle East into paying for those kids' schools and food, and then I would vote for us making up the rest. Why? Because we can—and because that looks like a better use of American power to me.

"And then comes the hardest question—what do you do if you can't get the food to those kids, in Syria, Somalia, anywhere? Is that where the doctrine of responsibility to protect comes in? Is it worth an American soldier's life to get a Syrian kid a meal?"

He smiled. "I've been thinking a lot about this, even talked to some of the defense contractors a while ago. And I think there is an incremental way around that one. You use drones to do air drops of food. Then they shoot down your drones. Then you take out their air defense—but only the site that was used to shoot down your drone--and you stop. You announce we are going to feed the people you won't. And if you try to stop us from doing that, we will take out your means of denying food to your people.

We make it clear: we will destroy with overwhelming firepower any air defense site that fires on a plane or drone bringing food.

"We make clear that for now, this is about hungry people, not taking on your troops, or taking sides among all the lunatic rebel groups. It is fundamental—it is about food. And our country will not let people starve any longer just because a dictator has decided they are expendable."

He was quiet, thinking about what he had said. Then Sam asked, "How did they react when you proposed that?"

"A few of them liked it, because it meant we were doing something. But the majority got very worried because it's fairly clear that Russian troops are manning at least some of the air defense installations in Syria. My reaction to that is we quietly tell Vladimir and his kleptothugs that we're going to fire on any air defenses that shoot at our food drops and he'd better get his guys out of the way.

"If I had a son, or a grandson, and he and his country somehow made decisions that put him in combat, I sure as hell wouldn't want him to risk getting killed so one group of theocratic thugs in the Middle East could dominate another group of theocratic thugs."

He frowned and was silent. Then he said, "But if he were part of a mission to get food to a group of kids starving to death in Syria or Somalia—maybe I'd feel differently if I got word he'd been killed or wounded. Maybe."

He was quiet, and then added, "At least it would pass the Matthew 25:40 test."

Sam's Franciscan past brought the verse to his lips as a reflex. "Unto the least of these."

"Yeah."

Putnam got up and poured himself and Sam some more coffee. He sat back down.

"The other part of it is that we've never solved the problem of civilian casualties. I spent a lot of time in Iraq trying to get our military and the civilians to recognize that just doing less collateral damage than we did in Vietnam wasn't necessarily doing good.

"Let me state the case for collateral damage, for risking harm to civilians, as ruthlessly as it can be stated. When you are fighting an enemy whose cowardice or strategy results in his hiding in the midst of innocent people, you cannot kill him without risking killing some of them and their children."

His voice raised and became more intense, as he began jabbing his finger in the air. "An enemy or insurgent who hides behind children is morally without any human value, and should be eliminated. If innocent children are harmed, it is regrettable, but that man will not harm any more innocent children. Stripped of its weasel words, that's the case for firing away at schools.

"The counter argument, of course, is that the innocent people in whose midst he is hiding should kill him. It is the argument of *The Magnificent Seven*, in which the villagers finally rose up and killed the bandits, once they had been helped by the mercenaries. Just a movie, though a classic— one we borrowed from the Japanese. But Kennedy's statement about Vietnam—'It's their country'—was much more than a movie. It was almost a policy. Almost, but never carried out.

"Pacification becomes occupation, and when you are the occupier, you become the target, not the bad guys. You mobilize the insurgents when you harm the civilians. And if the civilians are just waiting to see when you will leave—you have no business being there in the first place.

"COIN doctrine says the people are the prize. Therefore winning their hearts and minds becomes the goal for COIN tactics. But it is profoundly illogical to say you can do this by firing into buildings or places where people are hiding among the innocent. And you lose all hope of any moral position when you risk harming the innocent. The 3-24 doctrine says little about this dilemma, other than to vaguely warn against it. That's part of its moral bankruptcy."

He laughed. "There is an Israeli military historian, Martin van Creveld, who says you should throw out most of the COIN literature since it was written by the losers in COIN warfare. You see, this debate goes back to the Greeks, to the Napoleonic wars in Spain, and dozens of other so-called small wars. Large armies and insurgencies have been in conflict for thousands of years, and all FM 3-24 does it to update some of it in army-talk. The Air Force guys are mad because it leaves out most of the potential uses of airpower.

"And if you get out of the country where our guys are getting shot at, and rely on our overhead or offshore assets and blow up anything that looks like a training camp, you're back in the collateral damage swamp again. And I guarantee you that we are going to see drones coming at targets in the US all too soon.

"So I try to add all this up, and I conclude that collateral damage, civilian casualties, invalidate any strategy that risks such harm. Their cost is nearly always greater than any return."

"But, Will, that means you don't go after Osama Bin Laden because there were kids there."

"No, it doesn't. You don't bomb him when you find his safe house. But you do risk the lives of troops who can try to keep civilians safer than any bomb, no matter how smart that bomb is. And that's exactly what we did."

He took a sip of his coffee. "But there's two more things that go beyond counterinsurgency. We have to look up from the small wars to the bigger picture, to pull the lens back further. And I don't think we do enough of that these days."

He stopped, and Sam wondered whether he was getting tired. Then he continued. "First, our relationship with Canada and Mexico will be the most important connections we have in the next century. Those connections will affect our energy, our domestic crime problems, and the safety of our borders. The economic stability of those two nations, who are part of the Pacific boundary that has protected us for so long, will be of enormous importance to our military and economic stability.

"Second, we have to deal with the paranoia of the Chinese. Thanks to their recent history at the hands of the British, the Japanese, and ourselves, they are paranoid in ways that are very hard for us to understand. Surrounded by fifteen nations that have invaded them or been invaded by them, they fear their neighbors—for good reason. Their demographics are terrible, and their minorities are as threatening as anyone we've encountered in the Middle East. We have no Muslim nations on our borders—they have several. They know what we did to the Soviet Union in Afghanistan. And that scares them, and makes them paranoid in a way we haven't ever been, even after 9/11. And maybe we've learned that you have to be very careful dealing with paranoids, because they can see anything you do as hostile."

He was quiet for a moment, and so was Sam, making some notes. Then Putnam spoke out. "You know, part of this is about immigration."

"Immigration?"

"Yes. We found room for many, not all of the Vietnamese who needed to come here because they were on our side. Two million people. There are entire Somali settlements here now. Some of our churches are quietly doing this great work of resettlement for people who have to leave their home countries. We are screwing it up in the Middle East, however. We are leaving thousands behind who worked for us, and some of them are not going to survive because of our immoral neglect of their claims on us."

He looked over at a large map of the US on the wall where his pictures were hanging. A map of the U.S. and a map of the world were hanging side by side. "One of the great advantages of growing up in California and working in the East when you don't have much money is that you end up doing a lot of driving across this vast country of ours. I've done it maybe twenty times. And when you do that, you figure out just how much empty space there is out there. Millions and millions of acres. Dry, lots of it, but we are only a few technological twists away from getting desalinization to work well enough to join the Israelis in making deserts bloom. Lots of sun and wind out there, too, so that takes care of the power. Then the question is who gets to live here. No reason we couldn't have 400-450 million people here—many of whom will work a lot harder than some of our lower middle class wants to these days. In return for their hard work, they get to live in a place where the only shooting is done by an occasional crazed gun owner, not whole armies and militias tearing through your village every week or so."

He smiled at Sam and said, "You nailed it in your coverage of the march into California from Mexico ten years ago. That was about immigration, and who gets to live here."

He went on. "So who gets to live here? The old white guys who want to turn the clock back have this serious demographic handicap—they keep dying. That will take care of itself in time. So when we find children being harmed, we don't always have to go kill evildoers. Sometimes we just can help people escape them. It's a big world. And for every kid who needs to come here, there are ten who could be kept safer in their own country."

He said, "I may sound like a broken record on this. But again, for me, the final metric is kids going to good schools safely. We will have lived up to the full American potential when we finally add a new metric to our foreign policy: how many kids are safe tonight?"

He smiled and said, "On one of my farewell journeys coming back home from Iraq, I stopped off in Venice. I'd never really spent time there. Lovely city, maybe with a lot to teach coastal cities these days about how not to drown when the water comes in. Anyway, I wandered around the museums. Peggy Guggenheim has this wonderful museum of modern art right on the Grand Canal, and I spent some time there. It has a remarkable sculpture garden. And in it I found this little bench, made out of marble or something, with this quotation written on it. It says "Go where the people are sleeping and see if they are safe."

He paused, shaking his head. "See if they are safe. Better than dozens of volumes of counter-insurgency strategy. Maybe that's where our foreign policy is heading."

Sam said, "You have a remarkably optimistic frame of mind, for someone who thinks a lot about what we screwed up."

"Yes, I guess I do. It takes a sizable measure of optimism to be able to confront the god-awful mistakes we've made. But that's the whole point of all of this, Sam. How can we learn from our mistakes, once we've finally understood them and admitted them? How can we remember what we may have forgotten about losing our way and then finding it again? I believe we can understand the past and use it to make better calls in the future. You've got to hold up the mistakes and look at them—look at them hard, not bury them. You've got to help people understand why they were mistakes, and how to avoid making them all over again. It's the most important work remaining, for me.

"And one final thing. It's what worries me about the idea that we will never sign on again to a ten-year war. It's about accountability."

He smiled. "It's something we can learn from theology. Dietrich Bonhoeffer has this phrase in his work—'cheap grace.' He contrasts it with 'costly discipleship'—what it really takes to be a Christian, or to be faithful to any religion that values human life. Cheap grace is convincing yourself that going through the motions is enough. It's how I think about most of the people back home who have no clue about this war, because they've become so insulated from it. They think their only role is putting plastic ribbons on their cars and watching military homecoming videos on Facebook. Then back to the mall. No increase in taxes to pay for the war, lousy follow-through from the VA until there's a scandal, and looking the other way when drones kill civilians. Cheap grace—it's how 99% of us fight wars now."

Sam asked, "Maybe too harsh on the families of the vets? They pay a price, right?"

"Of course they do—you're right, Sam. So drop the 99% down to 97%. Still means most Americans are blissfully unaware of what we are ask these young men and women to do out there, day after day, night after night.

"I'm not in politics. But I wish there were one politician—just one—who had the guts to say 'You put them there. Not just the policy makers at the long, polished tables. You, the damned voters. You put the troops there. You put our kids in those Humvees driving on roads mined with IEDs. You're responsible.'"

Sam was quiet. Then he asked, knowing it was his last question, "Will, the one difference you haven't talked about is the difference in you, between who you were in Saigon and who you were in Iraq."

Putnam smiled. "With my memory fading a bit, even with the medical treatment I've been getting, I've spent a lot of time writing and reading about both wars. I want to get down what I can think clearly about while I can still remember things." He paused. "But I find it's the little things that stick. A little blind girl in Saigon, the sound of a 105 dropping into the next block, music in my room in Baghdad, another little girl in a village in Iraq. Some kids from Fresno in a Guard unit out in the boonies.

"I'm different, sure. I take more chances, although I guess the older you get the safer you're supposed to play it. I don't see it that way. Why play it safe in the ninth inning if you're not winning? When I was in Saigon, I played it safe—I didn't know how to take chances then. I wasn't sure I could make a difference." He laughed. "There's still good odds that I can't, but I can sure as hell try, Sam."

After Leonard had left, Putnam sat down at his desk and returned to the writing he had been doing before Leonard arrived. He worked for an hour, trying to get down his thoughts on the dialogue with Leonard.

As he rose to fix his dinner the phone rang. It was Steven Jefferson, who was home on leave, calling to ask if he could come see Putnam in two days. With great pleasure, Putnam told him to come whenever he could.

Putnam knew that Steven was one of his legacies. Thuy had given him, without his knowing it, one of the greatest gifts of his life. And Aisha had left a great hole in his life, the deepest personal tragedy he had ever lived through. But he had lived through it.

As he prepared to see his son again, he knew that Steven faced many of the same challenges he had faced. The struggle would go on, trying to understand Americans' role in the world while trying at the same time to get the rest of the world to protect children. Steven's generation had their work cut out for them, and Putnam wanted to do what he could to ease their way, drawing on what he thought he had learned, what he could still retrieve from the further corners of his memory.

The End

AFTERWORD

Some of this happened. Some of it should have, perhaps. My time in Vietnam corresponds to some of Will's, but significant amounts of the story have been changed to protect numerous people—and myself. I leave it to the reader to guess which parts are real. I was drafted, I was an enlisted member of the US Army assigned to the JUSPAO section of the Embassy in Saigon working with US and Vietnamese media. Later, I ran for office and was, briefly, luckier than Will. There was no Thuy. And obviously, I didn't serve in Iraq.

But Dale Shirley was real, and so were the other Americans, more than 65,000 of them, and thousands more Vietnamese, Iraqis, and Afghanis who lost their lives in these wars. In their memories, this effort is made to recall and understand some of what happened.

Two other sets of loyalties led to this book. The first is to the men and women, in my war and the more recent ones, who served and came home. I work professionally with veterans' organizations, and I am certain that while today's veterans got a better greeting when they returned, neither my generation of veterans nor theirs is getting what they need and deserve from the nation they served. And the second set of loyalties, as I hope the book makes clear, is to children all over the world who are also at risk as a result of war, too often innocently caught in high-trauma cross-fires, suffering losses they never deserved. For the sad truth is that the story of the abuse of children in orphanages is based on very reliable sources.

I have moved some timelines around for the sake of fictional clarity, shrinking the time frames of our roles in Iraq and Afghanistan. The quote from George Kennan is from Fernando Gentilini's book *Afghan Lessons*, and is drawn from Ahmed Rashid's book *Descent into Chaos*. Some of the details about life in the Green Zone are drawn from the extraordinary book, *Imperial Life in the Green Zone*, by the former Baghdad bureau chief of the Washington Post, Rajiv Chandrassekaran.

None of those mentioned in this afterword or thinly disguised in this novel is responsible for my interpretations of what happened and what didn't happen in Vietnam and the Middle East.

Lots of debts to acknowledge, but first and foremost to Dick Leone, who kept the series of letters I sent him and a group of friends from Vietnam and handed them back to me many decades ago. Having those letters around, together with a journal I kept, prodded me to write something about that time. Recent events have sharpened the prod, and this is the result.

George Belcher, a great friend from Vietnam USAID days, has helped jog my own fading memory with great skill and understanding. The literature on counter-insurgency grows by the day; I should credit US Navy Lt. David Gardner, my nephew, with some very helpful clues about how to find my way through some of it. Another nephew, Matthew Wilson, served with the Air Force in Iraq and Afghanistan and has tried to help me understand that part of the picture based on his excellent published writing about his own experiences. Helen Gardner, who was there, too, helped me remember. Nancy Young, Larisa Owen, Bob and Karen Gardner, and Ira Chasnoff have provided me with precious time and great places to write. Many thanks to all.

I suppose I should also add, since I have cited and noted my great admiration for Ward Just, that his recent novel about an ambassador (though not to the Middle East) who served earlier in Vietnam was published after I had conceived and written most of this novel.

Another disclosure and disavowal seems necessary. I went to Vietnam without ever fundamentally questioning our mission there. And, as my wife is quite willing to note when it slips my mind, I originally felt that our action in Iraq was justified. So this is far from a "told you so" work, but more in the nature of the rethinking needed when we look back—which is all the more important when we try to look ahead.

A final quote, borrowed from Katherine Lee Bates and a few of my other books:

> *America, America,*
> *God mend thine every flaw*
> *Confirm thy soul in self-control*
> *Thy liberty in law.*

July 4, 2015